ALIEN
MADE

Jozeph Picasso's Alien Trilogy
(Act One)
Filmmaking Adventures

A Sci-Fi Noir

ALIEN MADE

Jozeph Picasso - Alien Trilogy
(Act One)
Filmmaking Adventure

Karl J. Niemiec

LapTopPublishing.com

Carmel, Indiana 46033

ALIEN MADE

ISBN EAN-13 978-0-9833663-0-0

Disclaimer:

Though much of this trilogy is based on real events in the author's life, this is a work of fiction. Names, characters, businesses, places, events, and incidents are either the products of the author's imagination or used in a fictitious manner. Any resemblance to actual persons, living or dead, or actual events is purely coincidental.

Alien or otherwise.

For
Erin, Vaughn, Kolton, Hudson and Paisley

Twisted inside these science fiction adventures
is the truth of how our family began

I love you always, Dad

In sweet remembrance of the unconditional love from Bubba Dog

Jozeph Picasso

PROLOGUE

There are two things in life I really can't stand, being shot pointblank by angry women and blindfolds. Both tend to put me in a real screwed up mental space. And right now I'm about to implode.

After three superficial wounds were attended to, whatever these people are, put the shackles back on and blindfolded me. I don't know why because I couldn't have said where I was if I wanted. I thought I was downtown LA at the Men's Central Jail on Bauchet Street. But that proved to be a naive assumption.

I know I'm not in the same putrid smelling vehicle that brought me to where I was gunned down by a pissed off woman using an advanced laser weapon. She claimed to be a human working in the DA's Office. I'm now in the backseat of something futuristic. From its faint high pitched whirling drive train, gaining intensity with acceleration, it's like I'm unwittingly the fall guy in a violent science fiction action flick, and no longer the hero of my peaceful mundane life. From the odd sanitized smell of what feels like high grade leather, I'm not in a cop car either. And whatever's driving this thing won't answer my questions.

After about forty-five minutes, we hang a sharp left and the road gets bumpy. I figure we're on some slum valley backstreet in need of repaving, but then we hit gravel. The vehicle doesn't bother to slow down. Since I'm not in a seatbelt, I start bouncing around in the backseat completely unable to protect myself. Until it almost seems deliberate before we come to a complete stop. The front door opens. The vehicle is left silently running. The driver gets out, moving to the backdoor and opens it. I ask what is happening and still get no answer. I ask where we are and get the same reply. Something strong pulls me out of the car. My wrists pinch from the shackles. It pushes me into a fast hobble for about twenty feet. I get kicked from behind, which makes me plop to my knees in the sand.

The silence of the moment is so intense I can feel and smell the parchedness of the night air on my face to the point where my lungs ache for forgiveness. Oh, crud. This is it. Left dead in the sand, with my eyes blindfolded. One pop to the head. Isn't that how it went? A family thing? A flat pull of the trigger? How ironic I should die in the same manner as the four tenants I'm being framed of murdering.

A slight updraft and I get a sudden dank breath across my knuckle hairs, as though before me gapes my deep open grave. I don't want it to be true. So I wait without asking, wondering who will look after my dog if I don't dig my way out again?

The heavy footsteps from the driver fade away. Why? I don't know. It may just be my mind drifting, but suddenly I get an empty feeling that I'm alone in some desolate landscape. The vehicle door shuts. The car backs away and speeds off. Should I move? Should I get up? If I speak, will someone else or thing push me into my grave?

I'm not a big joiner in fun group activities. I'm just a single guy sea legged through childhood by my fisherman father. No mother, no cousins or grandparents to speak of. I'm basically a loner at my core personality. My two best childhood friends have already passed away. I never had that great American big warm family life. The holidays and birthdays are mostly spent alone or with a passing through girlfriend. My life has always been on the move, thinking I am on my way to somewhere better. Somehow in the vision of my life, I never saw this moment as my final destination.

It's as though I've somehow been confronted by multiple kinds of mindboggling aliens. And I'm interacting with foreign customs that just don't seem to fit here on Earth. Ridiculous to think, I know. But these murders and these strange violent people popping in and dissipating out of wherever I am are really happening.

That cocker spaniel left in my building, now that I know I saw do very unearthly things. Only I still don't know who's human or not. I have no idea how to explain this to anyone else on any human terms.

2

Who are these strange people, these beings? Why am I involved? Normally, I'm not some inexperienced twit who needs to look beyond the reality of the here and now for reasons as to why I exist. But I am asking this, why am I here right now experiencing this end to my seemingly unfulfilled life? True, I allowed my temper to get the best of me. With all this killing and double dealing about blue stones, causing so much damage to my apartment building and car, just because unscrupulous factions of alien mobs want them. Yes, I found the stones in my building. And yes, I still have all three hidden until I figure out whom to give them to.

Is it too late? Is it almost over? Can I say I'm sorry for raising my voice, using foul language, and demanding to be reimbursed for the damages to my life and belongings? Is this my true showbiz destiny, to die in the ultimate bad Hollywood ending? A missing never was because I have a big mouth and a sense for social justice?

All I know is, if I live, if I don't end up an invalid trapped in a bed or rolling chair, a stone's throw from a coma. I promise on my ashes that from this moment on I'm living a richer more confident creative life. Somehow, somewhere inside of me there's a better, stronger filmmaker trying to get out. With a higher purpose than what I've put on screen thus far. From now on I'll write what I know. I'll feel with all my natural given senses. I'll reflect the beauty and the ugliness of my soul. And attempt to capture some kind of meaning, some kind of everlasting good upon film in an honest gesture to help my fellow man. From this moment forward. On my oath. May my hard drives crash.

Karl J. Niemiec

1

THREE DAYS EARLIER

Living in Los Angles, I was beginning to understand how Moses could spend forty years traversing the same desert. When, three years ago, at the ripe old age of twenty-seven, I finally sold my first screenplay. It will probably never get made unless I direct it myself. Which I prefer to do, but nobody is offering. So, just before the taxes were due, I bought spooky Mystery Towers in Sherman Oaks, California. Suddenly, I was no longer drifting through sand, a nomad pitching my tent on endless land. I had roots, responsibility, and what might turn out to be the longest running nightmare in modern real estate.

My name is Jozeph Picasso, six foot even, not counting my genius bump, resting at one-eighty-five after two months of nonsmoking and counting. Please, no applause, just throw food.

After running out of money and basically getting kicked out of UCLA Film School because of it, I've bounced around LA the past six years trying to make a living as a beloved filmmaker. So far, it hasn't quite worked out. It's fair to say I live a financially induced reclusive life while directing a string of unheralded short films.

My backup plan, Mystery Towers, is rumored to be the first building in the Sherman Oaks area. It was built by an eccentric German oil baron in the late 1800s and early 1900s for his American mistress, who for some reason never lived in it. The original legal title, blueprints and photos for the building have been lost, so I'm speculating by what I found in the LA Times archives. When asking real estate agents about Mystery Towers, most of their replies were,

"Are you nuts?" I guess so, but the place seemed to call out to me. I stopped telling people that, because when looking at the spooky place, people get the wrong idea.

Sometime in the early twenties it was turned into Mystery Towers Inn by one of the previous owners. It sat vacant for nearly thirty years while surviving family members fought over it after lightning took down an old clock tower above the double front steps. This left just the two towers on the corners of the front street units. The south tower I turned into my apartment and office.

After a lot of money the building is a working twenty-four-unit apartment building. There are eight on each floor above ground, and one garden studio out back by the pool.

Forget about the outside. Sitting at the corner of Graystone and Mystery, it was an overgrown, tangled mess when I bought it. But once I cleared brush and sandblasted off the road soot, it proved to be a three-story grayish sandstone structure hidden from the street by massive pines. Without the clock tower, it gives me the sense that it's meant to be the corner of something bigger. Maybe only a small part of the original design was built. Or the rest of it is hidden in another dimension and we just can't see it. Another topic I don't bring up to prospective tenants, unless I don't want to rent to them.

It has very large rooms inside that were once just guest bedroom suites. Some people think the building's stone stairwells appear spooky because the sconces are too dark, but I think they're energy efficient, despite the frequent spider webs.

Luckily enough, the building began to fill up after almost two years of new permits and renovations. Six months after I moved in, my actress girlfriend came off a successful Equity Theater tour and moved into my apartment with her white poodle, Bubba. Six months later she moved out to go back on the road. Leaving Bubba and a pile of dirty clothing. Eight months after she left us with me pushing twenty-nine, I finally started writing a script called *Crazy Kind Of Love*. Now that I'm pushing thirty I've finally found time to finish the first draft and I can't wait to print it out and sit down with a nice six pack of cold Rolling Rock, and read it nonstop. Fade In to Fade Out, with pencil in hand, my favorite time of year.

Alien Made

I'm technically broke with zilch to sell this town but rental space. The script I sold to buy into this nightmare, *Violent Behavior*, is stuck in development at Paramount Pictures. The agent who sold it for me got busted smoking pot in the backseat of a taxi in the Bahamas with two Goth lesbians and a monkey and left the biz. She was nice, but like many people in this crazy town, she had personal issues. Hers was an obsession with human death. Thus, I've gotten zero new writing assignments out of my first studio deal because nobody with the marketing power is clamoring to eat from my creative efforts. And that's the basic food chain in this town. You eat if you help feed the bigger fish above you.

Unfortunately, none of that past life really matters anymore because presently I have a real life threatening annoyance that started in my building three nights ago. It's a very unhappy and unnerving dog. But every time I drag out of bed to get close to the terrifying howling, it stops. I'm not crazy. Bubba and all my tenants hear it as well. None of us can tell where it's coming from. Then some nitwit visitor started a vicious rumor that it's probably coming from within the walls themselves. She claims she saw a rabid cocker spaniel with monstrous eyes pass through the wall of the first floor hall. So, we're all on edge. And it's been an unbearable, mind numbing howling, echoing through the already spooky stone hallways and stairwells for three nights running.

Don't get me wrong, I like dogs. I'm still looking after my ex-girlfriend's white poodle, Bubba. I love this dog. He's the best friend I never had growing up. I loved my ex as well, but Bubba turned out to be better apartment trained. So we encouraged her to go back on the road where her messy lifestyle belongs to stagehands. She quickly fell in love with a lighting technician. So we haven't gotten a card or phone call from her since. Not that I mind all that much. But leaving Bubba without a word because she was upset with us is wrong. She's gone, and we're getting along just fine without her. I keep telling us.

Honestly though, now that I own property, I righteously believe some people shouldn't own dogs. And I will avoid renting to someone who has just befriended a canine or feline if I can without being sued. But what good does that rule do me now? Absolutely none until I find this damn howling dog.

2

So once again, I drag my tired bottom out of Mystery Towers, after walking Bubba, letting him do his doody dance, wash my hands and head to a coffee shop in Studio City.

It's an addiction, coffee and the news ink. But not today. I can't concentrate on the paper. Murderous thoughts keep filling my head. Fifteen minutes go by. I'm vegetating, pissed, groggy, and forcing my nose over a black cup of hot Joe to make the thoughts stop. I must look like a dangerous lunatic because people are scrutinizing me with pinch nosed expressions of wishing I was not there. I suddenly realize the mass murdering chant filling my head is actually my nails drumming on the wood table beside my cushioned chair.

Okay, I'm insanely grouchy. I kicked out a tenant, Mr. Essinola, who owed me three months rent. Money I was desperately counting on to pay for work on the central air. He had two kids and a wife living in apartment 101. But he was down in Chile trying to raise cash. I actually never met him prior to his family moving in. With twenty-three vacancies in a very different looking building staring me square in the bank account, I took who I could get, planning to weed out the losers later. This town is full of drifters and grifters posing as successful happy families on the move. But if you look long enough, you'll find they're often just a shell game on the run.

When Mr. Essinola finally showed up, he wore suits costing more than my1966 red and black ragtop Corvair Corsa, brand new. Another month goes by without a dime from them. So I give them the two more weeks they ask for. Nothing. What am I supposed to do? I admit I tried to befriend them. But I didn't care for the little kid who was always playing in the hall with his handprints everywhere.

Another apartment manager from one of the previous owners' vouched for them. More like dumped them on me. The wife proved to be a liar and an undomesticated pig. The teenage daughter, I'm sure, was doing her boyfriends and leaving used condoms all over the empty apartments. And the young kid was constantly playing with lighters and matches.

The day I finally served them, I caught the kid with a lighter up on the rooftop lighting one of my seven front pine trees on fire. Honest, I wish I were making this up. He was on the roof, leaning over my terrace, trying to catch the dried pine needles on fire. I nearly had a fit. But that's not the end of it, by far. Mr. Essinola gets into it with me about me trying to keep his family from singlehandedly destroying my lifetime investment.

Anyway, I served them after he yelled at me, and they took off the very next day. Now I have no way of getting my money back from them unless I take them to court. So, I'll have to serve them a small claims summons. My guess is they moved back in with the wife's sister, in the same building they lived in before. Only, they didn't move everything. And legally I can't go into their apartment to see what damage has been done until they have everything out, or thirty days if it appears they have abandoned the apartment...unless of course, it's an emergency.

Waiting is making me crazed. I don't know what's gotten into me this morning. My mind keeps visualizing them all blindfolded and shackled hand to foot, and shot in the heads out in the desert, left for the wildlife to pick over their useless bones. I try to push this vision away. But it's as if I'm standing over their bodies holding my gun at this very moment. I can smell the death and I'm actually enjoying the insanely horrid justifiable visions of them plopping into the desert sand one at time, plop-plop-plop-plop. I shake it from my thoughts again. This is truly insane. The negative energy is so unhealthy it's tearing at me. I could never do such a callus thing. Knowing that, somehow actually frustrates the still sane parts of me all the more.

It's this howling dog pushing me to this. I want this dog found, gagged and feasted upon. Not really, I'm sure I'd find it a bit gamey.

3

I look into my empty cup. No fortune told there. I'm done with my coffee, but don't want to go home. I haven't started my systematic reading of the LA Times. And I'm just sitting here hoping something pretty will buzz me. But the only buzz I get is from cup of Joe number three. I'm in a horrible funk because these horrid visions have left me with this bad feeling. Like something is wrong. Or something astronomically awful is about to happen to me. Maybe I should get in my car and keep driving to the beach and skip heading home right away. But no, I can't. I've got responsibilities now, tenants to deal with, and one family in particular, the piggy Essinolas who dwelled in apartment 101. So I trudge to my car and drive home.

It's been three days since I've served them. I can't stand it any longer. The monkey on my back is festering into a true emergency. The evaporation of my sanity. I don't want to know mentally as much as I need to know physically and fiscally what they've done to apartment 101. So I go up and get the keys and come back down to case the joint.

I go in. Son of a bitch! I'm beyond shocked, I'm sickly appalled. The apartment is so dirty, it's hard to describe. The carpet's color, good carpet, two thousand dollars' worth, is barely recognizable. The kitchen is so disgusting only cockroaches could love it.

And believe me, they do. I'm talking thousands, crawling everywhere, and scurrying back and forth, playing ping-pong, shooting pool, dancing. I'm telling you, this is the ultimate cockroach motel. These bugs love it here.

How anybody could live like this is beyond my comprehension. How this many bugs stayed in one apartment and didn't spread out over the entire building is also beyond me. Unless they've had as much as they could eat right here, and from the looks of the grime, heck yes, it is buffets of slime!

My investment is ruined. There's no way their deposit will cover what I'll have to spend in order to put the place back in rent shape.

Ah, damn, the screens are torn and filthy. I couldn't tell from out front, but they are pushed in at the bottom. And the original stained glass in the dining room is cracked. The window shades are missing several slats, and what's left of the terrace door's shades is bent.

Then I see it. Or smell it, I'm not sure which sense came first, the smell or the sight, but it's poop. At first I think human, but my mind stops short of visiting there because frankly I just can't allow it.

There's more. The further I go into the apartment the more I find. And urine stains are everywhere. These pigs turned apartment 101 into a dog kennel. Then it hits me. Dog! That barking dog!

I follow the trail across the dining room into the living room and to the den. 101 is my apartment but smaller, due to a service hall behind the master bedroom. I see no sign of food or water, just urine and poop. The windows are all closed and the terrace door is locked.

I go into the spare bedroom. And there he is. The cutest cocker spaniel you'll ever want to meet. But then he looks me square in the eyes and curls back his lips to show his teeth and I'm telling you that dog transforms into something that I don't think it was meant to be in nature. I stop in my tracks. There's no way I'll approach this dog. He could be rabid or starving. I simply retreat back into the walkthrough kitchen to find a pan and fill it with water. But when looking for something clean enough to put food on, I glance up at a Blip sound to find the dog standing in the dining room watching me.

Note, I didn't say he walks into the dining room, I said he was just all of a sudden there, watching me with those eyes. I'm not sure but I think he's hunting me. Perhaps he's that hungry or maybe he heard my bubbling stew comment about eating him and didn't find it funny. I look down wanting something to protect myself with and back up at another Blipping sound and he's gone. Blip comes from behind me, so I turn around, even more freaked, and there he is sitting by the door. I'm trapped. This is way too weird for me. Perhaps the visitor who claimed to see a cocker spaniel walk through walls wasn't such a miserable prick after all, because there's definitely something unnatural happening in here.

Under a pile of junk on the mildew stained granite counter I find an open can of soft dog food. If I feed it, he might not attack me. So I scrape off the top into the garbage disposal, which doesn't work, and put some of it on a teacup size Statue of Liberty ornamented dish, ruined by a small chip. Perfect, because these slobs have just taken my right of happiness away. The ironic nature of the dish I'm sure I'll appreciate in some other life. But in the here and now I take both the water and food out to the terrace and quickly back off.

Blip! Immediately the dog appears at the water dish out of thin air. No lie. I'm actually stunned by what I just witnessed, even though I already saw it happening moments ago. Is he a ghost? A demon? Am I nuts? Just in case, I go through the rest of the apartment very quickly while I have the dog distracted. Something in me needs to know if there's anything else creepy, or if hopefully someone is playing a TV hoax on me. But no, there are three bathrooms, each more disgusting than the last. The toilets are so filthy that evidently the dog chose to shrivel up rather than drink bacteria out of them. Why didn't he just Blip out of here? Wait, he has been. That's why we couldn't tell where it was coming from. Has he been sneaking in to other apartments and eating their pets' food? I shake my head. I can't be thinking this now.

Great, the master bedroom is still full of junk furniture. It isn't clear by the broken Ikea trash in the living room and the yard sale junk in the master bedroom if they'll come back. So I head for the door as quickly as my feet will carry me, keeping a watchful eye on the balcony door to make sure the dog was still there and wasn't planning to trap me inside this disgusting place to kill me. When I get there, the door opens and the mother of the pig family enters. Lying Leticia Essinola, followed by the daughter, teen slut Sonya. They somehow don't see me at first as I steady my heart, even though I'm standing right there in front of them, trying not to pass out from the sudden unexpected opening of the door.

4

Until I say, forgetting about the dog, "You people are pigs."

They go into a mild glazed-eyed daze, suddenly focusing on me. I'm almost an aberration, because I'm the one pissed off person they're trying to avoid—yet here I am seething in front of them while all those horrid thoughts climb out and over me, baking me as though these dry thoughts of murder are my own. I know what I have to do to get even with these people. The desert isn't far. I want to drive them there in the trunk of their car so badly I can smell the open air and feel the hot desiccated sand beneath my tingling toes.

It is then something else possesses me to open one of the double electric ovens. As if I need more evidence to support my pig family allegations, only to find it completely ebonized by overcooked grease. I mean, I couldn't even try to get a stove this black. There is a frying pan in there so coated with burnt grease I can't see metal, top or bottom, inside or out, and the handle is unrecognizable burnt wood.

"How could you people live like this?" I'm reacting involuntarily at this point. If telekinetic powers ever ran in my family tree it will spontaneously mutate right now and roast this pig clan on a stick!

"It was like this when we moved in," Sonya says.

I'm speechless...but I recover fast, pointing instead of grabbing. "Hello, I own this building, I remodeled it. I spent my life savings trying to make a decent, affordable place for you creeps to live in!" I can't believe...no...wait, I can, because these people are pig liars. They wouldn't admit to breathing unless I could see bubbles. And even then they'd blame it on gravity crushing their chests.

I'm a millisecond from losing all involuntary control of my mind, body and soul. I'm a true portrait of a crazy man. The things I want to say are so twisted up in my diminishing vocabulary that my eyes begin a rotating iguana protrude forcing my temple hair follicles to sweat. It actually hurts. Something very unnatural is happening to me. I feeling so much inner anger that I'm about to turn inside out.

The rest of my life spent in a padded cell for double homicide is enacting itself inside the stove, flashing before me like nitrate film, when Mr. Essinola shows up with a large canvas bag and a stick. He has the nerve to demand to know why I'm in his apartment. I can't believe this? I'm visually insane, standing before him, a complete possessed nutcase plotting against my own freewill to take his wife and child out to the desert and kill them. And he wants to know why scary me is in his destroyed apartment before he has everything out.

I'm still somewhat inarticulate because of wanting to say so many things at once, but only for a flash, before my hostility surges out of me like a swelling volcano, ruefully zitting out, and I yell. I get up in his dark skinned face and I allow spit to free flow with my words. I tell him point blank, loud enough for anyone to hear, that he and his disgusting pig family are about to be taken out to the desert and shot in the head for what they've done in this apartment.

I fight with all my might not to do these things. What's happening to me? I feel as possessed as that Blipping dog. Is that dog controlling me? I stick my hands in my pockets to keep them off his neck. And wait by the door while they get what they need. That dog! The prick husband goes straight to it on the balcony with the canvas bag, fearing it enough to approach it from behind. In one quick practiced swoop of his arms he's got it inside the bag and he is on his way out, taking the bagged dog and his pig family with him.

I follow them outside, down the north steps, through the pines to the street. "What is with this dog? Hey, I'm talking to you. It's done something to me, hasn't it. What's with the dog appearing and disappearing? Why did you leave it to dump in my building? Don't think you're getting away with what you've done here. Hey, you prick! Come back here and give me your forwarding address."

Of course pig-king Essinola doesn't even bother to reply. Why give me the satisfaction? He unambiguously throws my building keys into the sewer and departs to lands unknown. The creeps.

But I don't care what it takes. I will make these people pay. This is not racial, and screw political correctness. These dishonest people, the Essinolas, they lack respect for rental property. It's some kind of common genetic evolutionary caveman dysfunctional dirt floor behaviorism that draws a line between living and surviving, owning and renting. They are—the whole family—a brood of disrespectful sullen pigs wallowing in the subhuman filth. Contaminating their environment, with no regard to the consequences of anyone or thing that becomes mired in their droppings. Eat and defecate. And they've got one spooked up dog!

This isn't just about rent. I'm not above helping out a family in need. Who hasn't been down on their luck? It's about how they treated my property and the disregard for who would live there next.

That astronomically awful thing I dreaded happening has altered my vision of life. I stand thinking that the La Brea Tar Pits have somehow become an unwitting metaphor for my life in LA. The LA on the flipside to all those suns over palms postcards. What tourists see when they come here to sip the waters are thin glossy picturesque photos of a fertile, imaginary quenching oasis. But once they step foot to live in this pungent, endlessly growing city, they see how we're all really stuck, slowly being sucked down into an uncivilized quagmire of overpopulation, falling victim to a ruthless predator's next meal. And the only way out of it is hard cash to beat away the inevitable end for as long as possible, certain death.

A wave of anxiety washes over me with these dour thoughts and suddenly my life is nothing more than a handwritten lie on the backside of a discarded California postcard, lost along a crowded highway. Because right now, everything isn't good, life isn't grand and I don't wish you were here. The fact is, even though I solved the mystery of the barking dog, I'm pretty sure I just witnessed something entirely lacking earthly explanation. And it somehow has a hold of me, controlling my emotions. Now instead of having a sense of achievement, I'm left with the unsettling feeling in the pit of my stomach that somehow that spooky cocker spaniel will come back to alter my mundane life forever.

5

Okay, so last night, thanks to lack of barking from that weird dog, I let all my pent up, violently weird thoughts go, and got some satisfying sleep. I don't know what all that bad energy was all about or where it came from, but it's gone, and I'm feeling okay. I actually had a wet dream that escapes conscious memory. So, with randy hopes, I point my '66 ragtop down Ventura Boulevard to drink coffee and invade the newspaper around ten o'clock, as usual.

Within an hour I finish the comics, which I consider my treat for reading the entire paper, put my coffee cup and plate on the counter, and take my entertainment section home. I don't feel as wonderful as when I woke up this morning, because now I'm not looking forward to having to drag all the Ikea junk out of apartment 101. And I have no intentions of picking up after that dog. I'll pay the cleaners extra for that doody.

I've got a working actor, probably a few years older than me, living down in a studio garden apartment next to the laundry room in the garage. I let him live there for free in exchange for fixing up the studio and keeping the laundry room clean. I also hire him to do odd jobs for me or watch the building while I'm out longer than a day. So far J.J. has merely managed to fill the studio with movie set debris. Why, I haven't a clue. But he likes the stuff so I don't complain.

I'm planning on asking him to help me clean out 101, but when I pull into the drive to let myself in downstairs, I notice two plain dicks slouching around my front stoop. I mean it. They look like a couple of dicks, watching me with through the trees. They also seem to know who I am and are waiting to give me a hard time. Great.

I don't bother driving down into the dungeon thinking I'll just quickly get rid of them and continue on with my life. But as I get out of my car the demeanor on their faces isn't friendly or otherwise, just a bored recognition that they have spotted the person they are waiting for. So, I put my emergency brake on, and close the door, leaving it running at the top of the cobblestones.

"Can I help, you guys?"

"Yeah, you Jozeph Picasso?" the taller of the two asks, his high forehead glistening in the near noon sun peaking through the pines. His brown polyester blend sport coat is one of those that tasteless men never throw out. They wear out.

"Yes." I'm starting to not like the shape of this. I have the feeling as though they expect me to make a run for it. If only these pines were the beginning of some great big forest. But I haven't done anything wrong as far as I know, so I move over and up the south side steps that are divided by a ten foot blue spruce. I use it to check the stellar morning sun. These cops must be comfortable standing in this solar glare. They must also know a better deodorant than I, because even though it is only mid June, it is a stinking hot morning. Global Warming or not, the overcast we often get out here in early June had started in mid-May and had already stopped coming around. I look up at the sky. It will be another hot rainless summer.

The shorter, fatter one in black shows me his badge as he looks up to see what I'm looking at. I'm Detective Mike Tucker. This is Sergeant Leonard MacAroy from Homicide."

"Good morning, officers. Is there a problem?"

"It's about four of your tenants," Detective Tucker says.

The small hairs on the back of my neck stand up. "Which four?" Like I didn't already know. That Essinola crud called the cops on me because I made threats. I can't believe this.

"The Essinolas," Sergeant MacAroy says.

"Look, I can explain. Those people ruined one of my apartments."

"Apartment 101," Tucker says.

"Yeah, you want to see it?"

"Sure," MacAroy says.

I guide them through the heavy stained glass front doors, which are to my annoyance once again held open by two chunks of my building's river rock foundation. I lead them the fifty feet to 101's door. "I'll need to...." I stop because the double front doors aren't closed. "They must've come back. Wait until you guys see this place."

"We saw it," MacAroy says.

"You...." Damn, they've been snooping. "Then you understand." I escort them into the foyer of the apartment and into the disgusting kitchen, like an underpaid tour guide to the museum of filth. "Is this a pig sty, or what?"

"Filthy, but we got kids. So we're immune," MacAroy says.

"Look at this. They left a dog locked up in here. No water or food. It barked for three scary nights. I was so pissed I could've eaten it if I weren't so afraid of it eating me. Well, you know, figuratively."

"Where's this weird dog now?" Tucker asks.

"I'm assuming it's with them. By the way, there is something odd about that dog. I'm not exaggerating. It's all they came back for."

"You've seen the dog do weird things?"MacAroy asks.

"Yeah, I did. And I'm telling you, there is something not right taking place in this room."

"Not right, how?"

"That dog disappeared and reappeared in different places, with a Blipping sound. When it looked at me, there was something very evil inside it. And moments later I started feeling, you know, evil myself."

"Evil? You mean possessed?"

"I don't know. It ignored me after I gave it water and food. But when they came for it, Essinola put it in a canvas bag and had to sneak up on it from behind. It was all I could do to contain my anger."

"Why?" Tucker asks.

"Look at this place. This cost money to fix. Anyway, they're probably all staying back with a sister, I think. If you're looking for them. I don't know the address off hand, but not far from here in Van Nuys. I'm sure I have the info upstairs in their app file."

"We didn't find the dog. Nor the sister or her kid."

"Wait a minute. Is this about my yelling at these people?"

"You wanted to take them out to the desert."

"Okay, I said that. But look at this place. Look at the oven. The daughter claimed it was like this when they moved in. I remodeled two years ago. Wouldn't you want to take them out to the desert?"

"Did you?" Tucker asked.

"Excuse me?"

"Did you take the Essinolas out to the desert and kill them?"

"Come on. The desert in my air cooled Corvair? Be serious?"

"We're dead serious," MacAroy says.

I can't help it. I smile. "They're dead? All of them, the little kid with the lighter, too?"

"All four of them," Tucker says.

I start laughing. I can't stop myself. This is too much. I suddenly feel that there is some form of cosmic justice in this insane world. Like some sort of big karma scenario that can't be seen up close, casting a retro verdict upon those who are truly undeserving of this Earth. Someone had actually taken these pigs and…. "Wait. You guys don't sincerely think I went through with this desert murder thing. It was merely a suggestion out of frustration. Come on."

"You felt evil," Tucker says.

"Only while the dog was here. I felt good after it left the building."

"Where were you last night?" MacAroy asks.

"I proofed and printed out a script until eleven thirty, watched an unsatisfying dirty cable movie until around two, and went to bed."

"So, no Facebook postings, texting or e-mails that would place you in front of your computer?" MacAroy asks.

"No."

"You got a cell phone?" Tucker asks.

"Yes, in my car. But I didn't use it last night."

"So you were alone?"

"Just me and my left hand."

"That's too bad," Tucker says.

"Not really, I slept like a rock, had wet dreams and woke up with a smile on my face."

"Anyone see you writing?" MacAroy asks.

"It's not an audience participation sport."

Tucker talks as he writes. "No writing partner. Okay, you make any phone calls on this landline? Anything else that would put you here in the building around, say…10:30 pm?"

"No. I walked Bubba…"

"Bubba...? Who's he?" MacAroy asks.

"The boyfriend maybe?" Tucker asks giving MacAroy a look.

"My ex-girlfriend's poodle. I walked him before I went to bed. You know, I made my rounds to make sure all the lights were on and stuff. This place is spooky enough when all the lights work."

"Yeah. Anybody from the building see you, maybe you didn't see them that we should ask?" MacAroy asks.

"I doubt it. Come on, you don't actually think I shot these pigs?"

"Who said anything about shooting?" MacAroy asks.

"Who drives out to the desert to beat people to death these days?"

"People do," Tucker says.

"Well, I didn't beat them or shoot them."

"You're sure? They were blindfolded and shackled hands to feet."

"Left in the desert sand to feed the wild life," Tucker says.

"I'm positive."

"Then you won't mind us heading up to your place and checking?"

"Do you have a warrant?"

"We do if we need one," MacAroy says.

"No. I've got nothing to hide."

"Great. You own a gun?" Tucker asks.

"Yeah. A nine-millimeter."

"Have you fired it lately?"

"I go to the firing range. I write some action stuff so I like to get the real feel. It actually feels good to have one around this place."

I lead them from the apartment to the elevator and push the button. It doesn't light. The elevator moves anyway, pushing a paranoid chill up my spine from within the shaft...I'm leading myself to the slaughter.

"Where do you keep your gun?"MacAroy asks.

"In a holster on the back of my desk chair."

"Is it loaded?"

"Yes."

"You mind turning around?"

"What for?"

"Precautionary," Tucker says, taking out his handcuffs.

MacAroy nudges me through the opening doors.

6

"What is this? Wait a minute. I've changed my mind. You'll need a warrant to get into my apartment."

MacAroy spins me around and Tucker cuffs me. "Take a look at this while we ride up." MacAroy holds a signed warrant to search the entire building. Tucker presses three several more times as though it'll make us move faster. When it finally stops, Tucker nudges me out of the elevator towards my door. "The keys."

"They're down in the car running in the drive."

Tucker pushes my face up against the numbers 308 on my door and MacAroy goes back down grumbling something about me being a pain in the ass already.

They have no idea. "Bring my cell phone up, too. It's in between the front seats."

"Shut up," MacAroy says.

I wait there with Tucker, listening to Bubba bark, causing the two Pomeranians to start in across the hall.

"You got a real mutt farm growin' here."

I just rest my forehead against the door thinking about the Essinola family prone in the desert sand. Bugs eating at them as their bodies bloat in the sun, their digestive juices staining their ill gotten clothing, since they dressed so well while owing me so much. It makes me smile, until MacAroy gets back. "I didn't see a cell phone," he tells me as he unlocks the door and they crowd me into my apartment. Bubba is there with a squeaky white toy bear in his mouth. He drops it and starts barking again when he sees I have two unfriendly strange companions.

"It's okay, Bubba." He keeps barking. "Bubba, stop, go on, and get in there. You guys mind taking off your shoes?" I slip out of my topsiders.

"We got a smart guy here," MacAroy says.

"I'm serious. I've got a foppish thing about clean carpet."

"Get over it. Where's the gun?" Tucker asks.

"Across the living room, in the tower. On the back of the chair, like I told you."

"Show us."Tucker pilots me further into my apartment, across the living room and up the five stone steps that lead into my stone floor tower office, with a deliberately nonworking gas fireplace.

Bubba goes back for his teddy bear, thrashing it about on the carpet, as we make our way into my office.

Looking around, "Nice, it's a real tower," Tucker says.

I'm feeling Rapunzelish, in need of saving from these cads.

"This it?" MacAroy asks, moving to my desk chair.

"You see any other guns?"

"When was the last time you fired this?" MacAroy asks.

"Five, six months ago, I think. Just before Christmas."

"You think?"

"I don't know the exact date. It was sometime last winter."

Detective Mike Tucker takes out his hanky and uses it to take the gun out of my holster hanging on my desk chair. He smells it, and hands the nine millimeter over to Sergeant Leonard MacAroy. He smells it, too. I don't like his reaction any more than I liked Tucker's. He crinkles his nose and holds the gun out to me and lets me take a whiff. Like I'm on their side on deciding that I'm guilty of mass murder. It smells heavily with the scent of spent gunpowder. Much too heavy for my liking.

Apparently, Tucker and MacAroy feel differently and see a day's work coming to a close. They've got their filmmaker. Nothing left but the editing of the paperwork to put me in the can.

MacAroy opens the magazine. There's four shells missing. He smiles nicely to me. "Not too bright, are ya, Picasso?"

Tucker begins, "You have the right to remain silent...."

I don't bother to listen to the rest. I've written it so many times in my stories I have it memorized. What I can't understand is why my gun smells like it has just fired four rounds. I cleaned it the last time I used it. I'm not that stupid. I grew up with shotguns and twenty-twos and hunting and stuff. Use a gun, you clean it. When Tucker finishes, I give freedom another try. "Come on, guys, do I look so stupid that I'd kill four of my tenants with my own gun, after threatening them, and leave it dirty, with four shells missing, right here so you two crack officers can find it?"

"Is pretty stupid," MacAroy agrees.

"If I killed someone, one of my tenants who owed me money, wouldn't I arrange for an alibi other than my poodle?"

"We've seen it all before," Tucker answers.

"You got someone to take care of your dog?" MacAroy asks.

"Yeah, I've got someone."

"Call that someone from lockup. Let's go." Tucker is all heart.

"Wait. Am I under arrest?"

"Let's see. You're in handcuffs, and I just read you your rights. Yeah, I'd say so."

"For allegedly killing the Essinola family in the desert? With blindfolds, shackles and four shots to the head?"

"Looks that way." MacAroy pulls out a plastic bag and puts my gun in it.

I can't help it. I start laughing again. The two cops look at me like I've lost my mind. So does Bubba. But I can't help it. It's too ridiculous to be true. In my bed last night, I kept thinking about how angry I had gotten, how evil it made me feel. How it tore at my soul, knowing how wrong it was to wish I could shoot them. I actually wanted to take them out to the desert and kill them. It's scary to think the dog had something to do with it making me kill the humans controlling it. Maybe I wished too hard. Maybe I haven't woken up yet and this is just the funny but tragic part of the dream where I get caught. But if it isn't, I'm in a load of trouble for something I hope I didn't do. Bubba follows us over to the door.

"It's okay, Bubba. I'll be back as soon as I call our lawyer."

"Don't count on it, Bubba."

"Come on, guys, he doesn't understand sarcasm." They shut the door in Bubba's face and lock it with my keys.

"Take his shoes, Mac."

"Come on, I'm barefoot."

"Just want to scrape and test for desert sand," Tucker says.

As we go down the stairs, I can't help but wonder when someone had gotten into my apartment. And if they did, why didn't Bubba bark? Maybe he did and I didn't hear it. Or maybe they came when I had Bubba outside for his late night walk and brought the gun back when I either took him on his morning doody dance or while I was out having coffee.

I didn't go back into my office area after I stopped writing. Wait, yes I did, to shut off the printer. But I don't recall noticing my gun gone. It could be a day or two before they run ballistics and test my shoes, unless my lawyer makes a fuss. But since my lawyer is into property law I don't expect to be out quickly— without having to post a sizable bond.

So, I just sit back against the cop car seat and enjoy my smelly ride downtown to the Men's Central Jail.

"You two ever think about not urinating back here?"

"Shuddup, you wouldn't be the first dumbass to wet his pants back there," MacAroy says.

I should be more nauseated about heading to jail. And I am, though I'm more concerned about what will happen to Bubba if I stay there. The thing that has me most confused is that damned cocker spaniel. I'm not the least bit psychic that I know of. Nor do I believe in ghosts. But I knew that dog would come back to haunt me. And here it is. I'm riding in the backseat of an unmarked cop cruiser that needs an intro to a good junkyard. Just why are these two lug nuts looking for the dog? And what kind of dog is it really and where is it from? I mean, is it some kind of government experiment gone wrong on the run, or stolen from a lab? An alien creature maybe? A blipping biological disaster induced mega powered warfare dog? What made it disappear and reappear at will? How did it affect me so much? Why is it in my building? And last but most important, how did I get so damn lucky to be included?

7

If one never experiences sitting on a wet smelly floor of a prison's holding cell, filled with alleged thieves, rapists, murderers, carjackers and drunk drivers, then one will never feel the self pity I'm suffering right now. Of all the lowdown things that have infested my near thirty years to date, joining this cast of wasted humanity in a morbid docudrama is by far my most humbling experience.

The young guys all seemed glad to see me, knowing I'll get passed around first. And if anyone thinks I'm exaggerating, then come sit beside me and listen to the punctuated topic of conversation amongst the delightful young men. We are all doomed for a trip around the world.

But I'm not about to respond to them even though they know my name. Honestly, I haven't managed the courage to mumble a single syllable to anyone, or make eye contact; I sit in the middle of the floor and feign nonentity, gazing blankly at the bars before me.

Thank goodness for a few acting classes and having somewhat of a demented writer's mind. Only, my pal Mooky squatting next to me, because of not wanting to get stains on his jeans doesn't seem to get my non responsiveness as a sign to leave me alone.

Mooky, a young black man from Watts, allegedly, if not proudly, in for stealing six and a half pickups all in one day, is beyond strange. He smells neither drugged, nor of alcohol, and judging from the light in his yellow-green eyes, he's far from stupid. Just out there beyond the realm of reality, in touch with his personal universe. And, as he promises, about to be let free due to his ingenious, villainous mental faculty, and the lack of evidence. Plus he has power over commoner human minds like mine and has the capacity to telepathically free himself from any human sector. I don't care. If he starts Blipping in and out of here, maybe he'll take me with him.

Until that happens, I don't give a damn what he claims on his criminal resume, as long as he doesn't touch me. However, I've always felt that if one really desires to control the human mind. One should start with their own. But Mooky is intellectually way beyond all of that.

Oddly enough, besides the speck of moonlight, the adjacent cell is empty. Though here we are packed thirty to a crate. The truth of which is that I am still breathing on my own...and somehow that thought makes me okay with the less than four star accommodations.

The cops want the spooky dog. They know about its weirdness. Why? If they want the dog, so does someone else. It could possibly be the person who borrowed my gun and set me up by fulfilling my darkest dreams. But how did they know about the blindfolding and shackles hand and foot? Was I thinking aloud at the coffee shop? Did someone read my torrid mind? Did I talk in my sleep? What have I gotten myself into?

Mooky looms in front of my face, smiling ear to ear, as though he can hear my every thought. He stares me in the eyes, willing me to see the truth. He nods his head in agreement because I suspect him. He's so weird that he almost seems inhuman. My eyes water trying not to focus on his face. I've got to get out of here.

8

"Picasso! Get your ass up and over here," a familiar voice rings out.

I'd been sitting here reasoning for so long I don't know if I'm hearing or thinking this but if I'm thinking "over here" aren't I already there, so I look up and it's my good buddies Detective Mike Tucker and Sergeant Leonard MacAroy, the Hansel and Gretel of the LAPD.

"Come here, you dumb ass. Get off the floor. Jesus, do you know how dirty this place is?" Tucker says.

Those are the most decent and profound words I may ever hear. Plus Mooky Dog was visibly disappointed, proving they were meant for me. Maybe he made it happen. Maybe Mooky loves me after all.

My brain signals to my lower body to rise above the floor to float and go forth upon this earth and take me to the voice. Yet my body has sentiments of its own. And merely tilts forward over my lotus situation. Both legs are deader asleep than Lincoln. The sleep has grown all the way up past my knees to halfway up my thighs. I can't stand, so I rise on my hands.

My fellow inmates part the murky waters before me, the bars nearing, a foreboding shoreline, as I slither towards them, hoping I won't get gang kicked to death in the process. But hey, if I don't show all my cards who knows what game I'm playing. So if crawling is what my body can muster, then crabbing is what I'm doing.

I get to the bars and one leg has almost come back to life. I pull myself up onto that leg, my left leg. My right leg is dangling loose, a dead sycamore. The fact that I am only feeling the agony afflicted upon me by myself, makes me happy. I am saved. I put my face through the bars.

"Get me out of here," are my first words in what felt like three years. I have no watch on. By the speck of moonlight I can guess it's about 9:30 p.m.

I swing out with the door, only to be grabbed from behind and put on my foot. "My foot's asleep."

"Grab his arm, Mike." MacAroy grabs my other arm. They pull me off the door. "Get the door, Liberty."

A hulking guard slams it in Mooky's disappointed face. They drag me down the corridor, with all twenty-nine sets of inmate eyes watching me, rebellious to the end, making these two-bit cops drag my crazy act away.

Mooky squats there at the door, watching me go. I try not to look at him, but Mooky lets his voice trail after me. "I'll look you up, Picasso. Don't worry. Ain't no grave deep enough to keep me from finding you." Great, I can't wait for that moment.

Tucker and MacAroy continue dragging me to the end of the hall, and then push me through three sets of locked doors, down another long corridor and into what feels and smells like a three hundred degree armpit of a room. They set me down in a dirty wood chair, making me stare into a stereotypical brilliant incandescent light bulb and handcuff me to a metal desk. This is not a funny situation, but somehow looking at these two sadsack dicks, I can't help thinking I'm stuck inside a rehashed Twilight Zone.

"You've got nothin' to be smilin' about," MacAroy informs me.

"Believe me," I tell them.

"We haven't found the dog," Tucker says.

"I'm sorry. It seemed like such a nice weird pooch, too."

"We don't want to hear your hallucinations," MacAroy adds.

"If there's nothing special about this dog, then why do you two retreads want it so bad?"

"Unless you want to go back in there, stop gettin' wise." Tucker is not having a good time. He keeps checking his watch. Maybe his shift is over.

"The dog's at a kennel for a flea bath. Can I go now?"

"No. Ballistic reports show that the Essinola family was killed by your gun. No other fingerprints, just yours," MacAroy said.

"You checked that already?"

"When it's important," Tucker answers.

"What's the good news?"

"We're not so sure you done it. So you got one call," he adds.

"Wait a minute. You don't think it's me?"

"No, we're not convinced. Your shoes were clean."

"Who cares? I have other shoes and boots. I'm a perfect fall guy. Nice work, your job is done stuff."

"None of the footprints we found matched your feet. But that don't mean you weren't there. So you're still a suspect. You want that call or no?" Tucker seems pained over my pending freedom.

"I want that call and I also want to know who you think killed those people and set me up. So I can watch my backside when I walk out these doors."

"We don't know who. We just know it has something to do with the dog," Tucker says.

"We called every groomer in the city." MacAroy lights up a cig.

"Maybe this groomer isn't licensed," I suggest, not wanting to enjoying MacAroy's secondhand brume.

"You think?" Tucker asks.

"It could be anywhere. This family improvise. They used my apartment as a dog kennel, didn't they?" I'm not getting much love here. They just watch me. "What time is it?" I ask.

"Time to make that call. You got two minutes," Tucker says.

They get up and leave me there handcuffed to the leg of the metal table...both hands. The prods. So I slide my chair back and get my tingling right leg between it and the chair and give the table a toppling to free my hands. I go over to the phone on a file cabinet and dial the only number other than my own I can remember. Naturally, I get a machine. "Erin. It's Jozeph. Pick up the phone if you're home." I wait. One break. Just one break isn't much to ask of this world.

9

I'm standing in front of my life savings. Twenty-four units of gray cut stone. It's a weird place, but it's my home. Behind me are Tucker and MacAroy. I know they're looking at me, but I don't want to look back. Screw 'em, and the stinky car they gave me a ride home in. I haven't been in jail before this and I don't want to go back. I'm out but by no means able to walk the path of a free man.

"Hey, Picasso. You're still our number one suspect. Don't go no place."

"You know where to find me. Right here with this twenty-four unit anchor around my neck"

"And do us a favor. Keep your mouth shut about this to the neighbors."

"What for?"

"Just do."

"What about my gun?"

"You can have it back when we jail the person who used it."

"In the meantime how do I defend myself?"

"Get a lawyer." MacAroy seems to think his partner is funny. He chuckles all the way back behind the wheel. I, on the other hand, find no solace in their humor. Armed with my keys, I go in to take a shower and throw my clothing away.

My apartment seems empty without me. My poodle shoots out the door so fast he doesn't give me a choice. He'd been holding it since I left. "Holy dung beetle, Dogman! To the poodle bush!"

Outside, Bubba takes the longest leak in the history of domesticated dogs. Afterwards he does his doody dance then drags his bottom along the sidewalk while I analyze a gray four-door late nineties Mercedes parked across the street. One of those lung-tumor-causing diesel daisy killers that I'd like to pull a drive-by on every time I get behind one in my ragtop.

I watch them because sitting in the back passenger seat looks to me like Mr. Essinola. Then again, I hadn't looked closely at Mr. Essinola except in a blur of yelling at him face to face. Being somewhat farsighted, perhaps this man is just the same type of guy who wears the same type of expensive suits. But I got a hunch there's more to it than that. Maybe this guy has access to Essinola's wardrobe because maybe he killed him.

This scenario calculates in my head as I bend to pick up Bubba's mess, "Bubba, stop that." Bubba looks up at me with his sheepish poodle eyes as to say, "Hey, my butt itches, you got a better idea, Dogman?"

At the sound of a Blip, I check the Mercedes. There is solely one person in the car, the driver. The back passenger is gone. Damn, bad people move fast. I notice Bubba's expression changes to "oh-oh" just as a gun is put to my lower spine.

"Pick up the dog," the passenger says.

"What?"

"You heard me. Pick up the dog."

"Come here, Bubba." Bubba comes to me, his tail wagging. Some watchdog. "He won't hurt you. He's harmless." I drop the plastic bag with Bubba's trick in it into the gutter, with full intentions of picking it back up when this guy is done hassling us.

"Shut up. Bring him over to the car," he says.

"Why? He's harmless."

"Look, dummy, move to the car with the dog, right now."

"Okay, okay." This is not Essinola's voice, it's deeper and meaner and I'm certain a lot more dangerous than the prick I'm suspected of murdering. I look around to see if anyone is watching. Damn. Where is the rest of Los Angeles when you need them? He leads me to the back door of the Mercedes and opens it for Bubba and me to get in.

"Not you."

"What?"

"Are you deaf or just completely dumb?"

"No, confused." I still haven't gotten a good look at either one of these guys.

"Put the dog inside. Stay facing that way."

"What is this? He's just a poodle."

"If you want to see your poodle alive again, you'll find my dog."

"Your dog?"

"You know damn well what I'm talking about. Find my dog."

"And if I do, how will I find you?"

"We'll know."

"Who are you guys?"

"Close the door and walk away."

"Come on...."

10

Son of a.... When I wake up, a black Ford Explorer is idling over top
of me, blaring its horn. Apparently, the woman living in the condo
across the street is having her kid picked up by a friend's mother.
Living in the front of a building they find it unnecessary to master
the technique of using an intercom or cell phone. In more civilized
neighborhoods I hear they still do.

A young budding redhead, about thirteen, bounds out of the front
door. She gives me barely a glance as I pick myself out of the gutter.
The woman driving the Ford and her kid only want me out of their
way. No, "Are you all right?" No, "Sorry, I almost ran you over." No
recognition that I have blood running down the back of my head. To
them I'm a dead palm frown mucking up the gutter.

I wobble up to my feet taking note that my body must've blocked
the runoff from someone's overzealous sprinkler, so I'm half wet. "Did
you see a gray Mercedes parked here?" I put my hands on the Ford's
hood to steady myself.

"Call the police, Mom. He's obviously some homeless freak!"

"Tammy, please." The mother hangs her head out the window.
"Just move out of our way, mister."

Don't these people recognize me as the man taking care of the
building across the street? Is their life so important that they can't
tell I'm bleeding from a blow to the head and I'm dressed...okay, I'm
dirty, and look like I've been in jail overnight, but hey, am I not still a
neighbor?

"Just get out of our way. We got front row Justin Beiber tickets!"

Well, that about explains everything. Who am I to stand in the
way of teen fantasies? I step out of the SUV's way and they zoom on

to the corner as I stand there wondering what is happening to me. I'm feeling woozy. Where is everybody?

I look down to find tire tracks running out from the wet gutter that had gone around me. Around me! I could've been dead. Did anyone take notice that I'm not just some bag of garbage left out in the gutter? Jesus! Someone help me. Someone stole my poodle.

No one comes running, no one opens their windows, and no one takes notice or even turns on their lights. Have we gotten to the point in our civilization that a man bleeding in the street is meaningless unless it's us? Isn't anyone mad as hell and not taking it anymore?! Then I realize it's still dark and I'm just thinking loudly. I stumble back across to my property. Home. I pick up Bubba's trick in a baggy, nearly falling on my face from leaning forward on wobbly legs. I could've been somebody. I feel as though I've been violated. And I have. I've been poodle-jacked!

11

Upstairs, I stand in the shower for close to an hour.

A waste of water, because no matter how long I stand here, I still feel unclean. Someone took Bubba. They didn't even tell me not to call the police. And I don't want to. I've had my quota of dirty cops for the day. This has become personal. Whoever these people are, they have clearly tried to set me up for murder. If they thought it would stick, they didn't seem too disappointed by finding me back here.

But taking my dog, okay, he's not my dog, but he is my friend. What makes these people think I would have any idea where their dog is? And I'm assuming they mean the cocker spaniel that used my apartment building as a live dog kennel horror show for three days and nights. True, I could've been one of the last people to see the dog alive. But, so what?

There is no reason to believe this dog is dead, because the way it looked at me I'm not so sure this dog didn't kill the Essinola. And those cops could be just lying about my gun being the murder weapon. However, seeing Mr. Essinola had crossed the border lately and was attempting to make some kind of business deal to cover his debts - though he seemingly failed - maybe the dog is some kind of special trained dog. Okay, this isn't making a lot of sense. How do you train a dog to appear at will? Was he attempting to take that dog out of the US or had he brought the dog into the US? I'm assuming it's not that easy to bring an animal into the US without papers.

Maybe something is in its stomach. Or implanted under its coat and it's causing this weird behavior and it's that object they snuck across the border. That's just out there enough to not be the obvious answer. Somewhat high concept, kind of above what is realistic, but why not. The old false lining of the jacket gag. Or maybe I have no idea what I'm talking about and I'm merely standing here wishing this is all an implausible story plot so I won't have to unwittingly live it. I get out of the shower to stand somewhere else.

12

While standing in my kitchen staring into my refrigerator, but not really looking for something to eat, I hear pounding at my door. It's Erin who lives with a female coworker in apartment 104. We've been hanging out and drinking wine since they moved into Mystery Towers and my ex moved out. Both are on the lamb from either a boyfriend or husband and have teamed up to take the Mystery Towers Magical Tour. Janet left her husband for a married lawyer boyfriend, and is very noisy about it. But Erin is dangerously single.

Erin stands alone at my door with a pitying look on her face.

"What happened? I've been calling your cell all day."

I give her my customary "Enter please. Sorry, I can't find my phone. I think someone took it out of my car."

She takes off her shoes, while sitting in a green theater chair I have at the door for such purposes. My few friends know of my fetish for clean carpet, no shoes allowed. I direct her to my living room and we plop down on my oxblood leather couch for our close up scene. She sits beside me waiting, drama mounting. Her soulful dark green eyes look upon me with concern and sadness. She brushes back her long brunet hair. Frankly, I'm not sure what has happened, so I'm not sure how much I should tell her. And I was told by the LA Ice Follies' Frick and Frack to skate over the issue. So I lie. I tell her how I had yelled at the tenants from 101 and that they had me arrested for threatening them. And that's why I called her from jail.

She just looks at me blankly, like she was waiting for me to get to the punch line. But that was it, that's all the punch I'm planning on telling her. So she continues with the blank look.

"What?"

"You're lying."

"About what?"

"About all of this."

"Am not."

"Are too, those people are dead."

"Oh, yeah, there's that, too. You want a snack?"

"No. Where's Bubba?"

"My ex came by."

"Fine. I'll see you later."

"What's the matter?"

"Nothing. If we're not close enough friends to tell each other the truth when we're in trouble then, fine, I'll talk to you later. Janet and I are leaving for drinks. Bye." She leaves.

Great. One of the few friends I have, and now she's pissed. This has been one crazy messed up twenty four hours. I lock the one hundred year old double doors behind her and turn on my sixty inch Hitachi surround sound, scanning the news reports. No blurbs on desert shootings, or crazy, murdering landlords, and no reports about poodles held hostage. It's late, and I try to work for a while polishing my script, *Crazy Kind of Love*. I've got as far as pencil in hand, but my mind keeps drifting to hurting Erin's feelings. So I vacuum the halls and sweep the stairs as my penance until tenants start sticking their heads out their doors, asking why I'm making such a racket at this hour. I only stop when I see someone has put four cigarettes out in the north staircase leading to Graystone. Maybe I shot the wrong tenants. Or just not enough. I go back to the TV and pass out in the middle of Late Night with Jimmy Fallon. Nothing personal, Jimmy, it's just the crazy day catching up with me and dragging me into very strange dreams.

13

When I wake up again, it's 3:00 a.m., and I'm all sweaty. The TV is still on, and I'm still alone. He's not just a dog, he's Bubba. He's my pal, my wagging tail, and snorts of hello when I come home. He's my kisses when I rub him. He's my morning full of joy when I wake up. He's my dog, my poodle...and I'll do anything to get him back. Well, almost. I am in deviant Hollywood. Okay, Sherman Oaks.

Even though it's late or early, depending on how you feel about 3:00 a.m., I seriously need air. So, I go to make sure all my timers are working and to check the new plants that I have planted along Graystone on the north side of the building. I got a good deal on five Australian ferns but they are not taking to the dog saturated soil and all the pine tree shade very well. I'll be lucky if one of them survives.

I go into the stone arched passage toward the stairs that lead to Graystone. At first I think someone is smoking in my staircase. And I think I'll finally bust the person responsible for the cigarette butts I keep finding. So I follow the smoke down the dark stone staircase to the four inch thick arched oak door which I find propped open by a heavy river rock that I recognize again as part of my building's foundation.

On the slate three-step stoop, between two surviving original lion statues, is a young tenant who lives in apartment 106 with her mother and fourteen-year-old brother, Idean. Long dark hair, just wow, but sixteen, and sitting there at 3:00 a.m., smoking a cigarette. Serina looks bored enough, so I let the subject of the cig butts drop and even ignore the propped open door.

The area is barely lit by a single rusty cast iron lamppost that, like the sconces inside the stairwells, was gas at one time. But it has since been redone to hold a flame like 50 watt bulb. It has four weird emblems stamped in the cement mooring. I have no idea what they mean but they look German. So, I plan to find out one of these days. A ten foot iron gate separates the grounds from the cracked sidewalk; throwing flashing shadows back across the building and under the trees as headlights pass by. Needless to say, it's dark, spooky and somewhat mysterious. So I tap lightly before I exit Mystery.

"Oh, my god!" Serina says.

"It's just me, don't have a hearty."

"I just watched *Scream*. I almost died again."

"You died once?"

"Yeah, like my heart stopped pounding twice during the movie."

"So, what's the problem?"

"Nothing. It's like, you know, it's summer and all this heat."

"At this time in the morning, something is always a problem."

"I just couldn't sleep. My mom's not home, so I like, came out."

"Maybe you should've, like, put on some clothes first."

"I got this on." She fingers a flimsy white men's wife beater shirt, barely covering her overly full breasts slammed into an overgrown black bra, and sits in nearly see through boy's plaid boxers.

"That's what I mean. It's not safe out here dressed like that."

"I'm okay. The gate's locked."

"Why don't you go sit out by the pool?"

"The witchy lady that lives out there, like complains to my mom. She's threatening to put a spell on me, or something."

"Debbie, in 105?"

"She says like, the smoke you know, goes into her room. Duh, it's smoke. Like close your window, witch."

"Okay, stay here. I'll join you."

"You just get home?"

"No. I just woke up. Things on my mind."

"The Essinolas? What a reality flash."

"Yeah."

"I didn't know the girl much, but my brother played with Robbie."

"Yeah. Don't I know. What did you hear about them?"

"They were like, you know, from Chile or someplace down there. The girl was in my grade, but she had this way like rep you know. A whore, from what I hear. I mean I'm not baggin' on her 'cause she's historic and all. I'm just sayin', you know, like that's why I didn't run with her or nothin'. Not that I'm pretending to be some virgin queen."

"I had my suspicions... about her, I mean.

"Yeah, you got eyes for me too, Mr. Manager Man?"

"What? Sure, but you're way too good for a hack writer like me. Besides you're off limits, you're a tenant."

"I see you hanging with my neighbors, Erin and that other one."

"Janet."

"I see how you are. You two making romantic movies together?"

"What?"

"Come on, up on your balcony, drinking wine at night. Laughing all the time. You like Erin. I know she likes you."

"You've got to stop hanging around outside my apartment."

"Like anything around here's a big secret. She'd be good for you, though. Man up, bust a move."

"Yeah, okay, so what do you know about the Essinolas?"

"I know the daughter used to take her boyfriends into the empty rooms and like do it right there on the carpet. I heard these guys baggin' on her. She was, like a nasty. A real rep case."

"Why didn't you tell me?"

"It's not a subject, I feel like comfortable bringing up. Like how's the filmmaking, Mr. Manager, heard any good sex lately? Only she's dead now, so it really doesn't matter anymore."

"Have any of the boyfriends been around?"

"Today? I don't know. What for?"

"Just asking. How long you been smoking?"

"About an hour. You want one?"

"No, thanks. I meant, when did you start?"

"Oh, like a couple of years ago. I know they're like not good for me. In case you're about to lecture."

"I'm not."

"If you ask me, it's adults telling us not to smoke that makes it so cool. I mean, if they got together to ban teenage nose picking in public, you'd find kids on every street corner thumbing their nose at society."

"That's very funny. You think that up?"

"Yeah, like just now."

"Well, that's very insightful. Mind if I use it?"

"Pick all you want."

"Thanks." We sit a moment, she smoking, me dying to take a hit.

"I've been thinking of smoking those cool cigars, like Eastwood."

I just look at her, trying not to lay it on too thick.

"You might as well say it, Mr. Manager. You gotta sometimes."

"Smoking one of those cigars is like smoking seventy cigarettes."

"No. Get out of here."

"I wish."

"What about people dying and stuff? Who cares about them?"

"You and me, I guess."

"Nah, I'm a kid. I'm not ready to care about other people yet. My life maxes me out enough as it is. You want one?"

"Like, yes. But no. When the Essinolas left here, they went to stay at the mother's sister's place, right?"

"I guess. I know they were talking about leaving back to Chile."

"You know anything about their dog?"

"They had a dog?"

"No, the sister had a dog."

"Oh yeah, like, a cocker spaniel or something. Wasn't he cute?"

"Darling. You have any idea where it might be?"

"At the sister's, I guess."

"No. Not there."

"Maybe at the sister's store. The clothing store downtown."

"She had a store downtown?"

"In the garment district."

"That explains why they always had new clothes."

"Is the dog lost or something?"

"I don't know. Maybe."

"Jozeph? You didn't Norman Bates them or anything, did you?"

"Who said I did?"

"We were in the garage when you were yelling at them, you know. Telling them how you wanted to shoot them in the heads and all, like you know, bang bang in the desert. And well, like it happened just like that. You didn't, did you, shoot them?"

"No. Did I mention anything about shackles or blindfolds during my ranting and raving?"

She thinks a moment. "No, I don't think so. I'd still dig you if you did kill them. But I don't know if I'd feel comfortable talkin' to you, you know. Like maybe you'd off me or something if I set you off. You want one?" She lit up again.

"No. You should go to bed."

"After this."

"How's the modeling career?"

"Ah, you know. A mystery. Yours?"

"A travesty."

"Is that bad?"

"Only if you're me."

"So you're what, thirty-five, forty?"

"Feels like it, thanks. Twenty-nine for another month, but I'm immature for my age." We sit there for a while, she smoking, me thinking. I don't want her sitting out here all by herself. It isn't safe. Of course, coming from a suspected mass murderer freshly released from jail, those are big thoughts. I get up to examine my plants. So, according to Serina, I made no threats of blindfolds or shackles to the Essinola's. But I know I did think of them over a cup of Joe, and dreamed in great detail about them later that night. I'm starting to think that Mooky-freak from the holding cell knows more about me than he should. And that Frick and Frack of the LAPD must be in on it. Are they working together or against each other? And how did I get stuck in the middle and become the *usable* suspect? I get the sordid feeling that maybe I'm murder bait. A rush of paranoia hits me hard. I look around to see if anyone is watching.

Serina looks up at my sudden kneejerk realization, as she flicks her cigarette butt through the gate. "Good night, Mr. Manager."

"Good night, Serina."

"How's Bubba?" She moves inside the door.

"Just fine." I hope. I watch her walk up the stairs, as the door closes behind her. Man, someday, somewhere, some lucky guy will have that to come home to, find his place a pigsty, and sigh a give and take.

14

While cutting out my articles, wondering who took my cell phone out of my car, and being somewhat of a civilized, unemployed filmmaker, halfway through my second cup of Joe, I realize I do not want to trek downtown in search of someone else's crazy dog. I want to go home and sit on my veranda, pencil in hand, cold beer on table, and read over the first draft of *Crazy Kind of Love*, while petting my loveable poodle. I must anyway. Like it or not, and a deep depression hits me straight between the eyes. What are my chances of finding a trick dog that may or may not already be taco meat? My consolation is that if I find this dog and manage to get it back to whoever clobbered me, I could possibly see Bubba again. I use this mantra to steer me downtown to Olympic and Ninth, where I finally outfox someone for a parking spot.

My '66 ragtop sticks out in this din of traffic like a red nose on a white faced clown. Most people, and hopefully young naive car thieves, have no needs for Corvair parts. So chances of anyone actually stealing my collectable red and black, 140 horsepower, four carburetor, non-turbocharged, convertible Corsa is slim. But I always put my steering wheel club on just in case of joyriding, or some burrito stand robber, needing a getaway car.

But at the here and now store, I really have no idea what I'm looking for. So, before heading downtown I stopped by the property manager's office in Van Nuys who rents to the sister of Mrs. Essinola, aka pig family mother. Berry Leibowitz didn't have an exact address to the shop. He did have a name. Booty Rest. What that means to the buying public, I haven't a clue. He likes to talk about the old days in Hollywood. Normally, I like to listen, but I got him focused long enough to find a piece of paper that said the sister-in-law's shop was on Ninth just south of Olympic, in the middle of all the fabric stores.

I asked if he'd heard from my two cop friends, Mike Tucker and Leonard MacAroy, and he said he hadn't. Though a babe of a woman in pumps with bright blond hair, claiming to work with the DA's office, stopped by to ask a few questions. She was with two men in suits who waited out in the car until she waved them in. He showed me her card. Mary Devonshire. She told him about my ex-tenants' bodies being found out in the desert. And had him sign a statement allowing his tenants' apartment to be searched. He hadn't heard from his tenants in a few days. But he had told her about the Booty Rest downtown. My guess is that the two Spanish men in suits were the two men who had taken Bubba and clubbed me in the street. But I didn't tell him how close he had come to biting the big one.

Berry also told me that the Booty Rest was an import/export of children's new and used clothing that he claimed hid the fact they were knocking off designer labels and shipping them across the border. Not that he cared as long as they kept up with the rent. Before I left, he casually asked me if I had killed them. He smiled when I told him no. Said he didn't think I had, but wouldn't blame me if I did.

Booty Rest? It wasn't hard to find. The place is locked up though. With enough flyers stuck in its security gates to indicate it's been locked up for days. All around, the streets are teeming with pimpish rainbows of gaudy fabric, and the mixed smell of bus fumes, steaming sewers, and nearby food stands.

There is a leasing agent's number on the wall next to the locked gate of Booty Rest in both English and Spanish. Apparently, the buildings to the right and left of this one are owned by the same people. Even though all the stores are fully occupied at the moment, the number remains out front. I write down the number, planning on calling it when I find my cell phone or get back home. I'll ask the store owner, or at least the employees of the fabric place next store, if they saw anyone other than me lurking around Booty Rest.

Once inside, I stand at the counter waiting for what looks like the brighter of the two younger clerks to take notice of me. She comes over and stands in front of me, a ring in her nose, hair purple on one side, jet black on the other, and shaved halfway up to the temple. Probably attractive to another life form. But she surprises me with her harsh English accent.

"What?" She asks.

"I'm involved in a delicate matter that includes the tenants from next door, the Booty Rest, and I was wondering...."

"Wonder somewhere else," she says.

"Why not wonder here?"

"Because I'm not the free wonderland bureau."

"Perhaps you heard a dog barking the past couple of days. Maybe see it appear out of nowhere?"

"You want to buy something? Otherwise, you disappear."

"This is important."

"What's important is my Beamer payment. So unless you donate to my bail from this dump, beat it," she tells me.

So I ring the service bell again. Only louder. At this point, a young man, who I judge to be the less intelligent of the two, makes his way over behind the counter. I can see in his eyes and matching nose ring that this could possibly be the boyfriend or fellow band member. He looks at me like I'm a horsefly speck. "Maybe you didn't hear the lady, faggot," he says in his harsh English accent.

"Hear the lady? I haven't even seen the lady."

"Bugger-off, faggot," he says.

"Thank you, no." I ring the bell even louder.

By this time I have everyone's attention in the store. A woman, with bleached out hair in a faded gray sweater and painfully stretched green and yellow plaid pants, comes over and poses casually behind the counter to protect the cash drawer. She has neither tattoo nor a ring in her nose so I have hopes she might be a little more cooperative than the other two. She's enjoying the show, which makes me like her right away.

"What'd they do now?" She asks.

"Forgot their manners."

"Sorry, mister, I'm Mom. My kids were raised by their father. Apologize," Mom tells them.

"Why, this faggot insulted us first," the male one tells Mom.

"I see. Never mind them. What can I do you for?" Mom says.

"I'm interested in the shop next door. Booty Rest."

"Yes. I'm in the process of evicting them. Are you interested in the space?" Mom asks.

"Not exactly, I'm interested in finding a dog they own."

"Their dog?" She asks.

"It's a long story. The life of my dog might depend on it."

I expect to receive the strangest look from this woman, but instead Mom reaches under the counter and takes out a card. "Two men came by yesterday, one angry Hispanic and the other maybe Jewish, in suits, looking for a cocker spaniel. The angry prick gave me this and a warning to keep my mouth shut. One of them hit these two. Not that I blame him, but we're still a bit edgy."

I take the card. North American Construction. A Van Nuys address. Hector Estrada, President. "They give any indication why they want the dog?"

"No." Mom pulls out a great big Colt 45. "Why do they?"

"I don't know. But they took my poodle in exchange for their cocker spaniel."

"I have a poodle." Mom puts the gun away.

"Flea bag," the female says.

Mom hits her.

"Ouch!"

"You do?"

"Yes, Fife. They took your poodle?"

"Bubba. I was hoping to maybe find clues inside Booty Rest."

"Poodle, I told you this faggot is full of...."

I cut him off by slamming the service bell. "Your kids could use a beating."

"You wouldn't by any chance be offering, would you?" Mom asks.

"Could I?"

"Unless they choose to shut up, take you over to the store, and show you around."

"What do you say, kids? How about showing Uncle Picasso around the building?"

"Screw off, you...."

"Maybe you could show me?"

"No, Glass will show you. Or I will shorten her lunch hour. In fact, she's on lunch now, aren't you, Glass."

"No."

"Glass and Ash's father, Bent Gnarly, was rather sick, and looked just like them. Only worse."

"And if he hadn't OD'd we'd be on tour with him now, bitch."

"I've had them for three months. Had to take blood and fingerprints to make sure they were even mine," Mom says.

"Charming, kids."

"It's been boring. They were abducted by alien vampires."

"We were," Glass says.

"They probed us," Ash adds.

"I picked them off the streets of Liverpool living off Daddy's royalties," Mom says.

Ash and Glass move around the counter. It's then I realize that they're spoiled rotten, twin punker brats.

"Which one of you two butt probes wants to join me next door?"

"Look, you want to take a look, take a look, but I ain't spendin' my lunch hour off the clock showin' your crack-ass around." Glass turns to her mother. "So both of you can piss off." She storms away in a huff of tattoos and chains.

"That leaves Ash." He opens his mouth in protest and I grab the back of his shaved head and push him away from the counter. On the back of his head is tattooed: "Lick Me". I think not.

Mother smiles. "I like you, Mr. Picasso, how would you like a job teenage sitting for me?"

"Can I?"

"Daddy took them on tour with *Pins and Needles* while I dried myself out in prison. That was sixteen years ago. This place belonged to the family so I stuck with it. Here's the keys. Don't break anything over there, unless it's an arm or a rib or something painful like that."

"Don't worry. I'll be genital. Let's go."

"I told you he was a faggot." I smack Ash on the head.

"Faggot." I smack him again, harder.

"All right, all right...you're givin' me a friggin' headache...this way, freak," he says.

That's more like it.

15

Ash leads me out the back into a cramped dirty alley of storefronts built in the early 1920s. It looks and smells of cooking grease like it hadn't been cleaned since. A white 90s Honda Accord sits with a broken passenger window and a missing front tire. The dashboard is ripped out, and someone has pried open the trunk and taken everything that might have been in it. We make a quick right up a ramp to a hollow gray metal loading door cut into the back of Booty Rest. Ash moves to unlock it and is startled to find that it isn't locked. Great, I'm not the first bozo here.

"Maybe you should wait out here."

"No kidding. You a cop or just some snoopin' a-hole?"

"Lately I haven't noticed a difference." I reach over and arm myself with an empty beer bottle from a barred window ledge and push the door open with my foot.

The lights are all off, and don't come on when I hit the switch. Maybe I should call the cops first, Tucker and MacAroy in particular, but I'm more interested in finding Bubba. If walking into this dark building leads to that end, then I'm game, as long as I don't become fair game of that spooky dog laying in wait.

The place hasn't been disturbed. No ransacking or pillaging from what I can see so far. Surprising, seeing that the door was left open. I make my way past the stockroom, filled with incoming boxes addressed from probably five or six different knock off rag shops, all empty, none of which have "Chile" written on them. A flat bare wall divides the stockroom from a boxed in counter space with a cash register and a high-back chair. The place is nearly empty of sellable merchandise. It looks like this is the end of the business line for the

Booty Rest. In contrast to how these people lived, everything is in near systematic perfection, which strikes me as odd as anything else at this moment. But before I get halfway into the showroom, I can smell it. Death. "Holy Shroud, Dogman, hit the gag reflex!"

"Man, what is that?"

"I told you, stay outside."

"Smells like dead rats."

"It's rats all right, but not the four-legged ones."

"You mean like dead people rat smell?"

"Exactly like that. Unless what's hanging over there on that rack is a mannequin."

"That's her. Look at all the blood."

It's Leticia's sister. "She's the lady who owns this place, right?"

"Yeah. And that's the other one who works here."

I turn to find a younger Hispanic girl crouched in the corner. Her neck is twisted unnaturally. She's most likely a counter person and the one responsible for keeping things in order. She looks to be about in her mid-twenties, no rings on her fingers. Besides a broken neck...she has two bullet holes in her chest.

Death is never pretty, and after a few days, smells even worse. At least this time they couldn't pin the murder weapon on me.

It dawns on me that this is the young girl who'd pull a white Honda Accord and honk for Leticia Essinola's sister, the one hanging in the rack over there, to come out of my building. That would be her Honda outback. It didn't take long for some locals to start stripping. Certainly obnoxious honking isn't a motive for murder. But with my luck, I'm not about to bring up my little spats with her to the fancied motive twins, Tucker and MacAroy.

"Maybe we should call the cops."Ash reaches for the counter phone and I stop him.

"Let's use your phone. Prints."

"Yeah, good idea, I'm wanted in Ireland and Scotland anyway. Can we go now?"

"Sure, it's about time for your lunch, isn't it?"

"Not anymore."

16

By the time Tucker and MacAroy are done with me, I'm sitting out front of my place, my top's up, I'm not getting fried, but I'm bonding to my vinyl seats, thinking: Tucker and MacAroy never once asked about Leticia's sister's kid. In fact, considering that I found the bodies, I was ushered out of the way as fast as they could process me. No one asked about the North American Construction business card I was given, so I didn't offer it up to the cops. What are they hiding, and why am I pushed back on the street if my gun is indeed a murder weapon? Listen, I'm not complaining, but is my life in danger, is my dog a goner? Poor Bubba, what am I supposed to do? I don't have a clue to where their weird dog is, and I don't even know how long I have to find it.

I get tired of thinking unanswerable thoughts, so I back away and drive to Van Nuys where I pull to a stop out front of the Victory Boulevard address for North American Construction, just blocks from the county court house. I get out of my car and walk up the block, looking for access to the alley. I figure, if the guys who clobbered me are in their office they wouldn't want to see me unless I had their dog. I make my way back around to what I think is the rear of North American Construction. The alley windows are all painted white. No gray Mercedes lies lurking about. I try the glass door, it's locked. I put my ear to it. It's hot from the sun, and smarts, so I don't try it a second time.

Instead, I do the one thing I know Bubba can't resist. I knock. And believe it or not, my poodle bell is working. I can't just stand here and wait to see if anyone answers, so I hightail it back behind a dumpster and wait. No one rushes out blue faced with guns looking for me. It's just Bubba barking behind the door. After a moment he stops and I go back to the door and knock again. And again I run to the dumpster. And again nothing happens but the poodle bell. As cruel a trick as it might seem to Bubba, I have to make sure he is alone. And if not, I'm not sure what I'll do. I'm winging it here.

Okay, so Bubba is alive, and alone. He's also locked in this storefront office, and knowing Bubba, he's trying his best to hold it until someone comes to walk him. And if someone does come to walk him, that would be my chance to get inside and look around.

So I go back to the front of the building and look into the windows. Bubba sees me and goes crazy, his tail wagging and a big smile on his goatee face. He looks happy enough, if not confused as to why he's in there and I'm outside this glass door and not opening it so he can come out and lick me. But hey, he's alive. At this point, it's all that matters.

I tell Bubba to go lay down, which he does. He's so good. I make my way back to my car, thinking that it was really stupid to leave a card behind before murdering people at Booty Rest. Or was it? Did they want me to find Bubba? This could be a trap. I look around in panic. There's a ghetto bird not far away silently floating above the court house. Are they watching me from way up there? I step back out of sight. I hate being so paranoid. But I love living even more.

I can't leave my car here and expect to lie low watching the building. So I stay close to the buildings and slip out to the street under the palms. I get in and move my car about a block and a half into the residential area so I won't have to pay for parking. I pull under a lone magnolia tree in full bloom in front of the only house that bothered to water its grass. The helicopter is still up there. Why can't I hear it? I listen. All I can hear is the bustling Victory Boulevard noise and the faraway construction clamor along the 405 and the maddening ringing in my ears from a growing case of tinnitus. I look up at the over flowing date palms and the wind is blowing towards the helicopter. Is that why, the wind is blowing the sound away?

I realize there is nowhere to hide except behind the smelly dumpster. My only other choice would be to climb up on the roof. This doesn't appeal to me because of the heat and the distant helicopter.

I'm hungry, so I decide to disguise myself as someone foraging for food. I open the front trunk, where I keep an old T-shirt I use for wiping down my seats. It's filthy, and just what I need. I pull it on and take out a pair of tan work pants that I use to work on my car. Tucked in the corner behind the headlight cavity is a secret compartment that's not really secret. I keep an old Tigers hat filled with castoff nuts and screws, bulbs, and washers. There's also a set of keys to everything in a sliding tin magnetic box. I keep it stuck in a cutaway inside an old parts list book. The hat is disgusting and perfect. I take some wet dirt from the gutter, grease from inside my engine compartment, a thick mixture of Valley grit and motor oil, and apply it gingerly to my hands and nails, making sure not too much goes on my face. My shoes are much too clean so I pull on a pair of rain boots I keep in the trunk for when the dungeon floods in heavy rains. I head back, shuffling my feet, hunching my back, playing the homeless guy all the way back to my home, in the alley, no longer caring what sees me. I see my reflection as I pass a darkened window and not even Bubba would recognize me like this until he smelled me up close.

By the time I get there, it's around 4:00 p.m. and even hotter. The only available shade is beside the dumpster, so I cop a squat and wait for someone to come walk Bubba. If they use the front door, I'm screwed. The sun beats down on my head until about 6:30, when it dips behind the date palms at the end of the alley. Cars and trucks come and go and people patronize the stores around the area but no one bothers to chase me away. I am beyond hungry. I haven't had anything but coffee and my customary blueberry muffin all day. Plus, I really have to pee. I stand up and go for it behind the dumpster. What the hell, I'm a bum - when the gray diesel daisy killer pulls up and parks in the middle of the space provided.

Only, the Mercedes isn't driven by a male this time. A leggy woman, mid-thirties tops, gets out. She artfully fills an expensive light blue suit, balanced on dark peach pumps, ankles thin, calves hard, and what a bottom.

I don't make her face because I'm trying to avoid eye contact, but her hair is a fiery red that only natural redheads can organically sprout. It flares around her head as though it is a constant battle to keep it from sun spotting with strong tufts of curl.

And I, looking like a bum, relieving myself to boot - damn, make that on my boot. I keep my back towards her as she makes her way to the door. Ah, Bubba, you lucky dog.

I don't know how long it's been since Bubba had last been let free, but he bounds out the door with poodle zest and goes on the first parking curb he comes across. Like father like son. Afterwards, he wags his tail while the woman stands thinking, as if to ask "How about a doody dance, lady? Sit, bark, rollover?" Have I mentioned what a good dog Bubba is? She moves back to the lung killer and opens the door. At this point Bubba notices me and starts barking. Great. Then his tail starts wagging again and he runs up to me. Bum or no bum, I'm still his daddy, and he jumps up on me, happy as a poodle-clam.

What can I do? I bend down and pet him, like a normal occupancy challenged person. And I get the dog dirty. Calling him boy, and other generic things, not letting on that we habitually sleep together. Only Bubba doesn't understand the hoax. He wants to go home. As far as he's concerned, right now is as good a time as any.

The woman comes over with a new leash. She is also carrying a small caliber handgun just big enough to put an end to my life. She points it at me, the gun, not the leash.

"Let go of the dog. You're getting it filthy."

"Hey, I was...is that loaded?"

"Let go of the dog or you'll find out."

"Maybe you haven't noticed, but the dog's humping my leg, I'm not humping his."

"What are you doing here?"

"I was sleeping."

"Filthy bum."

"Yeah, well, I got thrown out of my place a couple... you wouldn't by any chance have work for me, would you...I've done construction."

"No. Move away from there. Come here, dog."

"Don't you know its name?"

"Just shut up. Come here, dog." Bubba wags his way over to the redhead. He isn't sure what's happening but now that I'm here this woman must seem okay. She puts the leash around his neck. I never have a collar on Bubba unless I'm taking him off the property because he minds so well. So she has to wrap the leash around his neck and snap it on like a choker. With the attitude and gun I'm almost envious. Add a blindfold and she could turn into a perfect nightmare.

"You could hurt the poor little fellow like that."

"Shut up. Come on, dog. Don't be here when we get back, bum." She chirps her car alarm and chips up the alley with Bubba at her heels, distracted just enough by dumpster diving me not to relock the backdoor. With any luck, Bubba will take his time before doing his doody dance. And if I remember correctly the only patch of grass is the first house to the right of the alley, up about half a block, where I parked my ragtop.

17

I wasn't expecting to get inside by myself. I was just hoping to find Bubba. But this may be the best opportunity I'll get to find out who these people are. When they disappear around the corner of the building I take my cue and quickly move to the unlocked door and go in. There is still plenty of reflecting sunlight so I don't need to hit any switches to case the joint. "Let's case the joint." I love that line in the old movies. I never had much use for it until now.

The need of paint place consists of one inner office with a large black and gray particleboard desk set, a smaller outer reception office with a gray metal desk atop a single file drawer, and a waiting room with adjoining economical eight foot conference table for eight. Pictures are on the wall of what were probably past jobs of corner shopping malls, and renovated food stands, and a few low scale two bedroom, one bath ranch homes. I move to the inner office and start riffling through the drawers. Nothing other than your basic office junk until I come across a locked drawer, the kind that is built into every desk sold in the last fifty years.

I move back to the first drawer, the middle one, and take out a flathead screwdriver and pry open the locked drawer. It is full of files, contracts, and blueprints of proposals on possible future construction jobs. Okay, so what? North American Construction isn't just a front and they are actually in business to build things. So why is some nasty redhead walking my dog and pointing a gun in my bum face?

By this time Bubba will be mid-doody dance, so I grab up the entire drawer full of files and head toward the backdoor just in case this is all a set up. But as I get to the inner office door, the outer door opens and Bubba comes rushing in. Damn! I duck around the door and sit down on the leather sofa.

What am I supposed to do? She has me red handed. I might as well wait comfortably for what happens next.

Bubba strides in like everything is okay, glad to see me again, and sits down next to me. "What up, Dogman? You stink." I hear water running and dog food pouring into a bowl. Then the outer door opens and closes, followed by the key in the lock turning.

She isn't here to work. She's gone and I'm locked in the office with Bubba, without even a simple goodbye. I wipe the wasted smirk off my muzzle and start thinking of what to do, how long I have to do it, and is she or anyone else coming back to kick my head in because they know I'm here snooping around?

While I think it over, I give my Bubba some lovin'. He is more than glad to see me and rolls over onto this back to give me a clear shot at his belly, so I wipe my finger tips the best I can on my pants.

"Feels good doesn't it, Bubba?"

"You betcha, Dogman."

I'm not the only one who could use a bath, and a breath mint.

I give it two minutes, listening for unwelcoming sounds, before I start to feel I'm safe enough to leave. So I get up and move to the backdoor. Do I take Bubba with me, and let them know I was here, or do I leave him, and stay undercover? In any case, I want to go through their files and figure out who these people are.

My first impression of the backdoor isn't a pleasant one by far. It's a deadbolt, the kind you need a key to open from either side. Why didn't I notice this when I came in?

Bubba doesn't care about the whys, he's ready to leave. He looks up at me, wagging his tail, "Let's go, open the door, Dogman, I'm ready." Relax, Bubba. So I make my way back to the front door and find the same thing, a deadbolt. I look around for a window to climb out of, nothing. What is this? The bathroom! I open the door to the bathroom and find that it doesn't have a window. Who makes bathrooms without windows? I start looking around the office for roof access, or skylight, nothing anywhere, just a fan vent in the bathroom. In an hour it'll be dark and in half an hour I'm gonna be starving.

Bubba gives me the look. "Let's go." Unfortunately, we can't. We're locked in. What to do? What to do? I decide to make my way back into the office with the files in hand and start looking through them. I have no idea when or who would be coming back. Or if anyone knows I'm here or not. This is just stupid enough to be a setup, but why would they? Wait a minute, I'm now their prisoner, and I walked right into it. I'll be damned. Am I stupid or what? Wait, am I imagining this and giving them too much credit? The business card, the bodies, the cops letting me go, the door left open, the silent helicopter, my dog and I locked in alone, with no way out but to break the windows. My heart is pounding so hard thinking these things that I force myself to think of something else. I pick up the phone. At least that works. I'm not sure who to call right now, so I hang it back up. If I call a locksmith dressed like this, they'll have me arrested. I've had my fill of cops. If I am their prisoner, why leave the phones working? This is killing me to no end. Do they know I'm here?

To take my mind of these thoughts, I start systematically reading through the files and find a gas station, a convenience store, an apartment building remodel, nothing unusual. I find a document with the name Victor Castro on it. I move to the far wall. Hanging there by the outer door is a certificate to operate, a business license for North American Construction, with "Victor Jorge Castro" center page. What does Victor have to do with Mr. Essinola?

I look further around the room at the pictures on the wall, and the guy who clobbered me at my place, and who I thought looked like Essinola, is all over the walls. So is the redhead with the gun. Maybe his wife, maybe his secretary, or both, or neither; from the pictures I can't tell. But every shot shows a new construction site about to be opened for business. These people have done a lot of work. 7-Elevens, party stores, taco stands, a lot of apartment buildings, and everybody seemed happy with the work. So what happened? What turned them into dog nabbing, gun pointing, head thumping creeps?

One thing I notice is that these are older pictures. From the look of their clothes and the cars the last one was taken maybe three years ago. The redhead looked good. Not that she doesn't now, minus the weight of a handgun. But she really looked happy back then.

I start reading through the files. Sure enough, North American Construction hadn't completed a job in three years. That's a long drought for any kind of business. They are only leasing this office space. So what are they into now? Why keep paying the lease on this place? And what makes them think I could find their spooky cocker spaniel if they hold my dog for ransom? Where is the young, filthy cousin kid? Why isn't he dead with the rest of the family?

All this thinking is burning what energy I have left. I'm running on empty. So I rule to lie down on the couch for a bit. I could call the police, the fire department or Erin in 104, but I decide to wait and think it through. At last resort I could bust out a window and run for it. Dressed like I am now, I'm apt to get shot by some overzealous California cowboy thinking he's saving the world from the likes of me. Bubba snuggles up with me. He'd found his food and water. I'm starving but oddly don't feel much like eating anymore. I feel like kicking ass. But most of all, I feel like lying here, thinking, fingering the sore spot just to the left of my genius bump. I've sure put it to wasted use in this mess.

Who knows, I might have a slight concussion from the blow I took in the street. Maybe I should have myself checked out and take advantage of my writer's guild insurance. Instead, I take out the card given me in the fabric store. Hector Estrada. Who is this Hector Estrada and why isn't his name on any of the contracts in these files? Is he the key to all this madness, a smoked and salted herring, or a subterfuge diverting notice from the relevant problem? Maybe the cocker spaniel is his dog. There's a thought. These tedious thoughts and less run through my mind.

And before I know it...I'm....

18

As soon as I hear it I know what it is, the paper being dropped into the mail slot. The paper? I look at my watch. I slept the entire night! Believe me, an extraordinary feat because I never sleep the whole night at home. I used to take Valium sometimes just to get an average night's sleep until the doctor found out I stopped breathing at night after Erin set me up in a sleep study at UCLA. He took my little pills away. Said I could've died. Now I just wake up at least twice a night, and from what I've been told I snore and talk in my sleep. But not last night, I slept straight through. Other than the ball of dried dribble at the corner of my mouth, still being dirty and smelly, and the tender spot on my head, I feel great. Bubba is curled up as far away from me as possible. He rolls over for his morning scrubs when I lift my head to listen, but gives me the poodle eye when he gets a fresh whiff of my stink. I get up and so does Bubba. He follows me to the front door, wagging his tail and snorting. He's got to go. So do I. I look down at the paper wondering if someone would show up to read it. I look around and no other papers are lying about. This tells me someone has been by every day and has at least taken the paper with them or thrown it out. There is no mail piled up either, so my guess is the redhead comes by more than once a day. I pick up the paper and forge around in the small kitchen area and find a stale bag of coffee and a coffee machine. Now that's civilized. I use dish soap to wash my hands and face, but I'm not getting most of it off, and my nails look sick.

Bubba isn't kidding, he has to go. I pick him up and hold him over the toilet while my coffee perks. At first Bubba just looks at me with fear in his poodle eyes, "Holy sinkhole, Dogman," until he gets the drift, or can't hold it any longer and lets go of a long satisfying pee. Then he poops something runny and I wash his bottom in the sink. After I set him down, Bubba jumps around with excitement. I just need coffee and a paper. I'll jump around later. I make my way back to the kitchen area and pour a cup of Joe, add a little non-dairy from the pint-size fridge to kill the stale taste and sit back in the office with the paper. No matter what is taking place in the world, life is okay if I have coffee and a paper. Even when I am locked in, dressed in dirty clothes, and haven't eaten since my blueberry muffin yesterday.

Now, since I think of that, I am feeling a little acidic in my stomach, so I move back to the half fridge and find two yogurts, one strawberry and another peach. The expiration dates were close enough, so I test one and despite the fluid floating on top I decide I'd live after all. I sit back down to confront the paper when Bubba starts barking, which sucks because I want to read, but is also good because it's what he'd do even if I weren't here. Then the backdoor opens.

"Come here, you little bugger. You better not have peed in here."

This is no way to talk to my poodle - my best friend - not today, not ever. She reaches in to grab Bubba and I grab a hold of her wrist and pull her through the open door, onto the floor and place a foot on her stomach. She reaches quickly for her purse and I kick it away. She grabs at my foot and tries to claw me and I seize her hand and break off two of her nails. Having interrupted my paper and Joe, then insulting my dog, I'm in no mood to be messed with.

"You son of a....?"

"Hurt, didn't it."

"....bitch!"

"I think you've hurt my dog's feelings enough today."

"Get off me."

"I don't want to." I reach into her purse and take out her gun. "This is a nice gun at close range. Why do you have it?"

"To protect myself from creeps like you."

"You don't even know who I am."

"You're the filthy bum I saw yesterday peeing in the alley."

"What are you doing with my dog?"

"This isn't your dog."

She had no idea I was in here. I think. "Yes he is. Come here, Bubba, sit down." Bubba moves to my feet and sits down. He looks up at me, wondering why I'm stepping on this nice lady who has been feeding him and walking him. "Get up. Move in there and sit down on the couch."

She gets up, and moves into the office and sits down. "What is this all about?" She examines her nails before adjusting her skirt back over her thigh, shooting me a defiant look for peaking.

"I was about to ask you that. Did you know I was in here?"

"Of course not. I would've shot you dead. I'm just taking care of this poodle for a couple of days for my friend."

"Victor Castro? Or Hector Estrada?"

"Yes. Both. How did you get in here?"

"You left the door unlocked. Bubba is my dog. Castro or Estrada took him from me yesterday. He said I had to find a cocker spaniel if I wanted Bubba back."

"What are you talking about? Victor doesn't own a dog."

"How long have you worked for North American Construction?"

"I haven't worked for anyone in years. Victor was my boss before we stupidly married. We're just friends now."

I pick up the phone to dial Erin in 104. She'll be at work at this time, but I want someone to know where I am, so I call her. "Erin? Jozeph. Yeah, I didn't make it home last night. No, I wasn't in jail again. I was locked in an office building. I'm not kidding. I can't find my cell. I told you, I think someone took it out of my car. Listen, I just want to let you know I'm okay. So you don't worry about me. Okay, in case you're worried about me. I get it, you're still mad. But listen. Yes, I'm sorry, okay. Erin, write this down. I'm at North American Construction in Van Nuys. I'm with a woman by the name of, hold on...." I go through the redhead's purse again to get her wallet. "I'm with a woman by the name of Stacey Carson. I don't know who she is yet. But in case you don't hear from me by tonight I want you to call the police and ask for Mike Tucker and Leonard MacAroy who are investigating the homicides of those four tenants. Yes, homicide. The number is on my desk. Their card is there under the monitor, yes." I look at Stacey. "My friend wants to know if you're a hooker."

"Kiss off."

"She says no. Alright, I'll call you at home by eight. Thanks, Erin. Don't worry, I'll explain later. You don't have to know everything about me. Because I like to keep some things about myself a mystery. You're welcome. See ya." I hang up. Erin is both worried and still angry. What can I do? I don't know what's happening to me. So how can I tell her anything yet?

I make Stacey get off the couch, and walk her and Bubba to the backdoor. I'm not about to wait here any longer and let someone else looking for her find me. I have to get home and shower and make this redhead tell me what we're mixed up in. So I walk Stacey to her car, make her get in behind the Mercedes' wheel, and instruct her to take me to my car. Once there, I make her park and get out. I reconnect my battery, and open the passenger door of my Corvair for both her and Bubba to get in. I don't want to leave my car around this neighborhood any longer than needed. I put her keys back into her purse and put that in the back with Bubba. Only Bubba doesn't like to ride in the backseat. He climbs into the front and gets between the headrest and my neck and watches out the window, panting. Apparently, an old trick left over from my ex-girlfriend. It's annoying but cute, for a poodle.

People wave and smile as I head out of Van Nuys and back to Sherman Oaks by heading south on Van Nuys Boulevard. Leave me alone, I'm mad! I make Stacey put her seatbelt on. I don't want her breaking my windshield should I have to stop too hastily. They're expensive. She is being quite cooperative, considering I have her own gun on her the whole time. Maybe in her world, people use these things and don't just point them. I don't know, but she isn't saying much all the way back to my place, except to assure me that I still stink. Knowing it's bothering her, I leave the windows up until Bubba sneezes snot on the back of my neck. "Thank you, Bubba."

"Don't mention it, Dogman."

19

Stacey Carson keeps her mouth shut the rest of the way back to Mystery Towers. However, the moment I park my car and she gets a full load of the dungeon parking lot, she starts yelling obscenities at me with abandon, and screaming for help. What a mouth. Bubba is completely dumbfounded, and I must admit, I'm not so sure what to do myself. So I grab a cleaning rag off the floor behind my seat and twist it into a gag. Stacey takes one look at the filth permeating the rag and stops.

"Don't you dare."

"Then, shut up."

"This is kidnapping."

"This is me trying to stay alive. Your friends already left me bleeding and unconscious in the street, and stole my dog."

"Why would they?"

"That's what I want to know. And by the way, I'm a suspect in a multiple murder case. One I didn't participate in. But my gun did. So my neighbors are already a little leery. Though, I suspect I'll be getting all the rent on time this month."

"You're the apartment manager?"

"Yes. I also happen to write, direct, and own this old place."

"Yeah, this place is creepy. Got any vacancies?"

"No offense, but I'm holding you hostage. Why would you want to rent from me?"

"Because I don't have anything to do with dead people, so your problems are yours. I have problems enough dealing with my deadbeat ex-husband. I need a place to move for a couple of months. How much is the rent?"

"It's twenty-one hundred a month. But it won't be ready until after the police are done doing whatever they do, and they give me permission to clean the place. Plus, I wouldn't rent to you if Earth depended on it."

"They didn't die in the apartment, did they?"

"No, they were shot in the desert. The whole Essinola family."

"Essinola? Manual Essinola? And Leticia?"

"Good, you knew them. Maybe you can fill in some of the blanks in my head."

"Of course I knew them. Manual was my husband's partner. He handled investors from across the border looking to build in Los Angeles. Her sister had a clothing shop downtown."

"These people wouldn't be wealthy drug lords trying to launder money through property loans, would they?"

"Look, these were good people."

"They were filthy pigs, and destroyed my apartment. Let me show you. Come on, get out."

Stacey gets out of my car without me having to keep the gun on her. We go past the garbage dumpster room and mailboxes to the elevator, taking it up from the parking garage to the first floor. I let her in apartment 101, the door being unlocked so the cops can come and go while I'm out. She stands there, as I had, shock registering on her face. Much like the shock I expressed, minus the anger, because this isn't costing her a bundle.

"My god, they lived like this?"

"Well technically, a very strange dog lived here by itself the last three days. Maybe he used the oven for dog biscuits and left it this way."

Stacey looks at the oven, then around the rest of the kitchen. She lets out a scream and I put my hand over her mouth. She sails out of the room, nearly taking my arm off, and back into the hallway. "Bugs! Thousands of nasty, ugly bugs!" Her body recoils and shudders as if they are crawling all over her. I know the feeling. But I don't look as sexy as her doing it.

"You like them, I can tell. When do you want to move in?"

"How disgusting. How could anyone live like that?"

"Some people like pets. Cockroaches are easy to keep and don't require a deposit if they only come out at night."

"Shut up. Close the door, and get me out of here."

I close and twist the doorknob lock. Screw the cops. We move back to the elevator. I suddenly realize I no longer have Bubba with me. In a panic I push the elevator button. The door reopens and Bubba scoots in, tail between his legs. He's irked. He hates it when I forget about him and leave him behind. He gives me the poodle eye. "Jumpin' curly hair, Dogman! Take me home."

I take Bubba and Stacey up to my apartment. The phone is ringing when I open the door. I know why. It's about the air conditioner. I'm having a problem with it, and my air conditioning guy hasn't a clue. It's probably been out since about four or five yesterday afternoon when the temperature peaks and the sun beats down on the southwest corner of the building. For whatever reason, the system overloads and closes down every day about this time. It's a total pain in the rump. So I let the machine pick up. Why not, the machine's full of massages anyway and probably from a bunch of unhappy tenants. I'm screwed because I owe Harry money already, the money the Essinola's stole from me. And he's in no hurry for me to owe him more.

"Aren't you answering that?"

"No. It's not for me. It's for Harry the air guy."

"You're weird."

"And you seem so normal. It's a long story."

"Can you turn on the air, it's stifling in here?"

"Shut up."

"I have the right to feel comfortable even if I am a hostage, or whatever you plan to make me. And don't get any funny ideas about touching me. I know martial arts."

"Don't worry, but watch out for Bubba, he's the lover in the family. Oh, and kick off the pumps before you go sit on the couch."

"Why?"

"Because I said so. Look, I've got to go down and reset the air conditioning. Do I need to take you with me or are you curious to know what is happening and planning to stick around for brunch?"

"Go ahead. I'll stay put. Do you have water?"

"In the dining room there's a water cooler behind the pool table."

"Great, I might have a bladder infection."

"Spare me the personal girlie details."

I open a cupboard next to the fridge and let Stacey get a glass. She takes it over to the cooler and pours herself a deep cool one that I watch skid all the way down to her navel, while I wash off again in the kitchen sink. Actually, once you get past disliking Stacey she isn't all that bad. I fancy her hair, the natural bright red that borderlines being electrifying, and her upper body still isn't lacking in anything, other than her teeth are just crooked enough to give her a biting personality. Her face, now that I study it, has strange angles that lend her a hard, snotty, almost manlike mien, masculine might better describe her jawbone. She glances at me with Aztec brown eyes, catching me mentally painting her.

"God, you are a writer."

"I was kind. If you're hungry, make yourself at home. There's plenty of whatever you might want in the fridge."

"I'm fine."

"Great. Have a seat on the couch. Watch her, Bubba. If she goes for the door, hump her kneecap."

Stacey just looks at me as if I'm unstable and makes her way to my hard and comfortable leather oxblood couch. I also bought the matching chair. Lover boy Bubba jumps up on the couch with her as I slip on shoes to go down and bargain with the air.

20

When I get back Stacey isn't on the couch. I look at Bubba as though it's his fault she isn't where I left her. He looks at me as if I'm mad. Maybe I am. Maybe I did kill those people and have only blocked it out. I don't know. One of my three toilets gargles and my trust in humanity and poodlety flushes over me for about three Standard tank minutes. By the time Stacey comes out of the bathroom I get a knock on my door. I don't want to talk to any of the tenants for multiple reasons. For one, I look like a bum. And two, they all think I'm a mass murderer. Three, I'm starving and want to shower first. So I use the peephole to see who it is. Great, it's Tucker and MacAroy. I feign not to be at home, but it doesn't work because Bubba comes barking at my feet. I swat him on the butt for giving us away. He shoots me the poodle eye. His feelings hurt. He's just doing his job. It's what poodles do. It's who they are, four legged doorbells.

"We saw you arrive in that air sucker you call a car, Picasso, so don't play stupid," Tucker says through the door.

"Your name's Picasso?"

"Yeah, but don't get any ideas. I'm no artist. Look, these people out there are cops. Do you want to talk to them?"

"I don't know anything."

"Then keep your mouth shut. Let's see what they have to say."

Stacey makes her way back over to the couch and plops down. Bubba snuggles up, wanting his head rubbed. So I open the door to find Tucker and MacAroy's mugs glaring up and glowering down on me because I made them wait so long. Whatever happened to the good guy, bad guy game? When did it turn into two angry meatheads at your door game?

"We ain't interrupting anything are we, Picasso?" Tucker asks.

"Would it matter if you were?"

"Sure it would, we have feelin's too, you know. We're cops, not goons," he says.

"So do slugs. But we still step on them. What do you want?"

"We just stopped by to see if you were all right. You didn't answer our phone calls," MacAroy says.

"Check you're cell phone," Tucker says.

"I still can't find it. And I just got back in."

"I could've sworn we told you not to go no place, and here you're spending nights somewhere and not callin' us to let us know you haven't skipped town," MacAroy says.

"I haven't skipped town. Have a nice day." I try to push the door closed, and MacAroy stops it with a big palm of his hand.

"We want to talk to your friend," Tucker says.

"Which friend?"

"The one sitting on your couch. By the by, you got a dumpster reek about ya and favor a bum we know," MacAroy says.

"I heard all your friends were bums."

"Watch it," Tucker says.

"Have you guys been following me?"

"What makes you think you're the only one who knows about North American Construction? You want to play cute with us we can have you takin' showers with LA's scummiest for not handing over that business card yesterday. At least you'll be clean," MacAroy says.

"I don't shower with cops. They pinch and hoard the good soap."

"You want to move aside, or do we have to get heavy?"

"Who writes your dialogue, Tucker?"

"Shut up, and move over." Tucker pushes me out of the way.

"How about takin' off the shoes?"

"How about shuttin' up? Ms. Carson?"Tucker says.

"Yes."

"Would you like your rights read here? Or would you care to have them read to you while we ride downtown?

"Why? He kidnapped me. Look, he's got a gun in his pants."

Tucker and MacAroy look at me. "You got another gun?"

"It's not what you think. I took it out of her purse."

"Give us the gun," MacAroy says.

"People are trying to hurt me. Look at the back of my head. Someone, this woman's boss and ex-husband, hit me on the head and stole my poodle."

"Are you listening to yourself? The big mean man hit me and stole my poodle." MacAroy is all heart.

Just then Bubba comes around the corner.

"Isn't that your dog right there?" Tucker asks.

"Yes, that's him. I rescued him today. They want the weird dog from apartment 101."

"You don't by any chance write for Disney, do ya?" MacAroy asks.

"Look, these people took my dog and told me I could have him back when I found their cocker spaniel."

"So you found their cocker spaniel?"

"No, I found Bubba. He was being kept at North American Construction's office. And Ms. Carson here was looking after him."

"So you took her gun and brought her here?" Tucker asks.

"Yes."

"So, let's have it," he says.

I hand over the gun, reluctantly. I have a feeling I'll need it back or one just like it sooner or later, if not just to shoot myself because I can't take anymore.

"Ms. Carson, please put on your shoes. We'd like to take you downtown for questioning," MacAroy says.

"Ask me whatever you want, right here. I don't know a damn thing. Victor Castro, my ex, called me yesterday and asked that I do him a favor and look after this dog. So I did. I walked him and fed him. That's all I did. That's all I know."

"That's fine. Now, would you prefer handcuffs or would you care to come along quietly?" MacAroy asks.

Stacey looks at me. "What should I do?"

"Depends. Are you into cavity searches?"

She squints at me. MacAroy takes her arm and holds her as she manages to slide her feet back into her pumps. "Make sure she gets a lot of water, maybe some cranberry juice. She's got a possible bladder infection."

Tucker and MacAroy blush, and Stacey shoots me a nasty look. I give her a fake smile.

"It's a girlie thing."

After they leave I move over to my machine and listen to the messages. Five are about the air. Two are from Tucker and company. One is from Erin, and the last one is from the male voice I met in the street letting me know he still wants his dog. I look at Bubba. There's no way I'm taking the chance of Victor or Hector grabbing him again. I move to the cupboard and take out a can of turkey and gravy and move to the terrace and plop it onto a plate for Bubba.

Over the terrace I hear a car start up and I look over to watch Tucker and MacAroy drive away with Stacey. She looks up at me as she goes. I can't read a thing on her face. There are a lot of things I'd like to ask her. But then again, she really didn't seem to have a clue. Or she had taken expensive acting classes at playing dumb. It's the naturals that seem to make it in this town. A good secretary knows no more than what is good for her wealth. And if North American Construction is dealing with anything that isn't exactly above ground then playing dumb is very smart. When I think of the redhead who first stuck the gun in my bum face compared to the redhead who sat in my apartment, I start to wonder which one is real. The tough, get out of my face one, or is she the innocent sexy one? Regardless, what does she really know about that weird-ass cocker spaniel? When it comes to women, I'm not an expert in reading signs. Actually, I suck at it. But then again, even Hefner had to pay them to pose.

21

So I eat. But first I call my cell with no luck and then shower. By myself and hog the soap. A true luxury only the recently freed from lockup can appreciate. A tuna melt is the least time-consuming for me at this point. Once done eating, I put the dishes into the dishwasher and start the machine up. I hate the smell of dishwasher soap, so I decide to do my rounds of the building. I want see what destruction my fellow tenants have bestowed upon my investment and water the plants along the north side of the building.

Back by the dark blue tiled pool, someone has dragged the antique tables and chairs across the deck and didn't bother to put them back. I don't know if anyone really notices it, but I happen to keep the turn of the century iron chairs and tables around because they match the gothic style of this weird place. They have black floral iron casting and updated dark solid blue padded cushions, and I place them where they make the pool area look its best. I don't really care if anyone moves things around. I only wish that they'd put them back and not scrape the decking paint. But frankly, no one ever swims back here but me. So why move the damn things? I have yet to see anyone sunbathing, and they usually get moved at night. I push the thought of ghosts messing with me out of my mind and put the table and chairs back where they belong. Then turn on the hose to top off the pool.

While waiting for the water to run its course, I make my way down to the laundry room to make sure my actor friend, J.J., living in the garden apartment, is doing his job. As far as I know he has no idea what has happened to me, other than knowing the tenant has moved out. I haven't shown him the apartment because I haven't had the chance. Luckily, the laundry room is in order. The floor is mopped and the machines are wiped down. It just goes to show you can trust some people. I knock on J.J.'s door and get a "Just a minute." So I wait. I take a look at the garage. I've been gone just a day, but things look different. It's still dark and dank, but it doesn't hit me at first, so I stand there with a pondering look on my face when J.J. comes out smoking a cigarette. I used to come down and mooch, and considering I've stopped smoking for just two months now, it doesn't really bother me yet. Give it about three months until my lungs start to forget how baleful they felt while I smoked, then the pangs from nicotine-deficient lung cells will start haunting me. Obviously, I've gone through this before and know exactly what I'm up against. Maybe this time I'll make it. But at the moment I'm not putting pressure on myself. I'm just telling my lungs I'm not smoking at the moment.

"Sorry, I've been on long distance," J.J. says as he walks over to where I'm studying my underground garage. "What's the matter?"

"I don't know, things look different."

"You get a whole different perspective of life after you've been in jail."

"You heard?"

"What's it feel like to be a mass murderer?"

"I wouldn't know."

"So, you didn't do it?"

"Are you serious?"

"Inquiring neighbors want to know. I mean, you got keys to our places, man."

"What do you think?"

"Personally, I don't blame you. But if I was you, I would've paid, say me, to have it done and I wouldn't've used my own gun. So, if anyone asks me, I just tell them to make sure they pay their rent on time."

"You're a big help."

"Hey, you've been good to me."

"What's with the bleached blond hair?"

"You like?"

"Depends."

"I did a TV pilot. I played a surfer dude. Small part, but it's cool."

"I didn't know you could surf."

"I can't. I'm an actor. But chicks dig it."

"Ducks, too?"

"Fans are fans. What's with Erin?"

"What do you mean?"

"She came down six times last night wanting to know if I'd heard from you. Finally, I answered the door in my underwear and she stopped coming down."

"Smooth."

"Hey, whatever works."

"What am I missing here? What looks different?"

"Oh, you don't know?"

"No, I wasn't home all night."

"Get lucky? Or back in jail?"

"A little of both."

"In that case, you should know that someone broke into all the storage bins. And busted that light."

That's what looks different. The bins are missing locks and the light is out over them. "Anyone lose anything important?"

"I don't know. I don't think everyone knows yet. They hate coming down here at night. It gives them the creeps with the light out like this. You get calls about this?"

"Not yet."

"You will. Heard you lost your cell."

"Someone took it out of my car. How long was the air down?"

"I haven't been around. But I had to reset it this morning. Was it down again?"

"Yeah."

"You need any help in the vacancy?"

"You want to come up and see it?"

"I saw it. Cops were in there this morning, two guys. Said they knew you. But didn't know where you were."

"They lied. They take anything?"

"I don't think so. I kind of hung around the front porch until the taller one came out and asked for my driver's license, so I made myself scarce, just in case. Said his name was MacAroy."

"Let's go take a look, there are some things you might want for yourself, some Ikea junk."

"Sure, I'll drag it out."

"I need an okay from the meatheads." We make our way to the elevator. I can't wait to hear the annoying complaints about the storage bins. But I'm letting tenants use them for free and made it clear I'm doing this so that I won't be responsible for anything stolen. As far as I know the tenants in 101 didn't use one. But I may be wrong, seeing I really didn't oversee who uses what space. My only requirement is that they put their own locks on the boxes and that they don't store anything that can explode, like propane tanks, gas cans or fireworks. I had to make it clear by putting it in writing.

22

Anyway, we get to 101, and I realize I don't have the key, but the door isn't locked again. I know I locked it this time. We go in with a queer feeling that we are not alone. J.J. senses it too. I motion him to pick up a white glass vase lying in the kitchen, and I pick up the nasty frying pan out of the open oven.

We make our way to the guest bedroom where I found the dog and there on his hands and knees is the guy who clubbed me. It's the guy in all the North American Construction pictures, Victor Castro or maybe Hector Estrada, muttering to himself. I got my money on Castro. In any case, he doesn't hear us, so I walk up behind him and kick him in the ass. He goes full face into the wall, crushing the new drywall. I realize then that he'd been picking through the dog poop. He's come back to clean up the mess, or what?

"Is this Madman Maid Service?"

He looks at me, eyes burning a hole in my forehead. They shift to J.J.'s face. I almost expect him to Blip away. But he doesn't.

"You want me to hit him?" J.J. asks.

"We'll hit him later. Right now, I'd like to know why. Surely you don't miss that crazy dog that much."

"You don't know what you're involved in."

"You're right on that one. I also don't know who tried to frame me for the murder of your business partner and his piglet family."

"The best thing for you to do, you potholes, is to turn around and let me finish. Then I'll leave."

Did he really just call us potholes? "Okay, hit him."

"Now?" J.J. asks.

"Yes, now, right across the back of the head where he hit me the other day."

"Okay." It's nice to have people who owe you. J.J. draws back with the vase.

"All right, okay, let me try to explain." Castro, still in the same suit, is stalling. For what I don't know, but at this point I'm not sure whether I want to know what he knows or if I want to see this clown bleed. So I don't stop J.J., and he gleefully whacks Castro right across the back of the head, pushing the front of his head back into the wall as he dodges. Only, he doesn't pass out, or make a sound for that matter. He just pivots on his butt and pulls a gun out of his suit coat that we should've expected him to have. He points it first at J.J. then at me and back again at J.J. I kick his arm just as he pulls the trigger. The bullet zips right over J.J.'s left shoulder and pokes a ragged hole in the air conditioning vent. Damn, that'll cost me! But the gun leaps out of his hand and falls inside the open closet.

Castro starts crawling for the closet, causing his knee to flatten the waste he'd been examining. I kick him in the stomach and J.J. goes for the gun. I thought I'd hit Castro with a mighty blow but it doesn't even faze him. Where I come from, a kick like that meant a week nursing three or four cracked ribs. But he just grabs the nearest lump, springs to his feet and dives out the window. Or should I say through the antique windowpane, glass, screen, shades and all. Damn, more money!

The drop is about seven feet below the floor onto cracked concrete. But that doesn't burden this man any more than my kick to his guts. By the time I stick my head out the broken window, making sure I don't get my head guillotined by late falling glass, he is up on his feet heading for the unlocked gate. I have a broken padlock keeping the image of a security gate, so he effortlessly jackrabbits right over top, leaping into the yard next door and takes off out of sight faster than I've ever seen any man run. Is he flying high on crank or what? Maybe he thought we'd shoot after him, I don't know. But now I have a gun again, and somehow that makes me da man. I turn to J.J. and he is holding the gun, checking the clip. For now, he da man.

23

"Four shots missing. I guess the guy uses this thing."

"I'm sorry, I almost got you killed."

"It's okay. I should've hit him harder."

"Harder? The guy must have an iron head and gut. Did you see that, he wasn't even fazed by us?"

"Some people are used to pain. Maybe he's had a tough life. Or ten kids at home or something."

"Great type of guy to have pissed at us."

"Yeah. You notice what he was digging through?"

I look down at the lumps of dried waste, letting the fading kennel smell sink in. "Yes, he grabbed a lump on the way out."

"I'm no genius when it comes to human behavior. But I've got to say, I'm a little disgusted. And I used to shoot heroin in abandoned buildings with no plumbing, so I've seen a lot."

I'm not sure how much I want to tell J.J. He is vulnerable down in the garage. I really don't want to involve him any more than I have to, but at this point, he's the one with the gun. "How much of this do you want to know?"

"I'm with you one hundred percent, except the expenses are all yours. And I got union medical if you cover anything out of the norm, like dying."

"Okay, then I'll be honest with you. I don't know much about what's happening for sure. Something came over me, and I stupidly made broad accusations of them being shot in the desert when they came back for the dog. And someone did just that with my gun, blindfolded and shackled them, hand to feet."

"That doesn't even sound like you."

"I know. I didn't want to say those things, but it was as if I was compelled to say and think them, very clearly. I saw it happening in my head while drinking coffee, like I was there watching it. That night I even dreamt about it. Felt good about it. Slept like a baby. I didn't mention shackles or blindfolds to anyone as far as I know. But that's how they found them. All four, shot in the head, blindfolded and shackled, left to feed the wildlife."

"Really? Where was I when all this fun was happening?"

"Surfing. I stopped to ask Berry about the sister's store, Booty Rest. He said a Mary Devonshire from the DA's office showed up yesterday with two guys in suits who sounded very much like this guy and the other I saw in a gray Mercedes. I found the sister and her clerk dead in their shop this morning."

"Were they killed with your gun, too?"

"No, my guess it was that one." I look at my broken stain glass window and how the light is now starting to come through the hole.

"Great. What do you want to do with this?" He indicates the gun. And his finger prints on it. "Can I keep it?"

I turn from the growing light coming in the broken window and take in the perfect way it lights up the squashed lump shoved down into my once nice carpet. "Better wipe it down. It'll get you more involved in this than you'll want to be."

"Hey, the crud shot at me. I'd say I'm involved." He uses the gun's sight to scratch the side of his head. "I think I fried my scalp.

What the...?

"You okay? Picasso?"

I look up from the floor where Castro had slid in the now perfectly lit spooky dog poop. I'm not sure, but what I think I'm seeing are three blue glass specks shining back at me. I bend down and pick up a wire hanger.

"What's the matter?"

"Give me a second." I pick through and separate the three glassy objects onto the threads of the carpet.

J.J. just watches as I take the paper out of the hanger and use it to scoop up the objects and take them into the bathroom and set them into the filthy sink after stopping the drain. I let the hot water run and I poke and prod the objects with the hanger until I'm sure all the dog poop is off them. I pick all three of them up and hold them to the light. "I'll be damned."

"That some kind of gem?" J.J. asks.

"I hope not."

"Aren't they too blue to be diamonds, real ones anyway?"

"How many karats would you say these are, if they are diamonds?"

"You know, I saw a thing on the Discovery Channel about this curse on the Hope Diamond just the other night. There's supposed to be chips missing and no one knows for sure if they even exist anymore. You don't think...? They're blue, but...damn, man that must've hurt passing those things."

"Now that's a curse. As far as I can tell, six people have died trying to own them."

"Not to mention the dog."

"I don't know about the dog, but there's still a kid running around somewhere."

"A kid?"

"The one who used to visit here. Remember the greasy sandwich in hand and soda can on his shoe?"

"Nobody killed little Juan? I would've killed Juan first."

"He wasn't with the bodies of the sister and the store clerk. And the two cops never mentioned him."

"Jesus. You should take this gun. Unless of course, you know...."

"I didn't." This is all starting to make sense. My mind feels so clear about it. Even though I still don't have real answers.

"You seem so happy."

"What? Oh yeah. These stones, if they are stones, must be worth a bundle. The larger one here is from a top facet...."

"A what?"

I let the stones drop into the palm of my hand to get a better look at them. "You know anyone who could appraise these things?"

He laughs in my face. "You show up with these anywhere I know, they're gonna call the cops, rob you, or shoot you and then rob you."

"Wait a minute. We have a woman in 106, right here, who works for a jeweler in Beverly Hills. Serina's mother. She could tell me."

"Would Shoul keep her mouth shut?"

"I'll raise her rent if she doesn't. Except getting her alone now that everyone thinks I'm a mass killer may not be easy."

"If I were you, and I'm glad I'm not, though I'd love to have your sixty inch TV, I'd call the police and give them these things. There's probably a reward or bounty out for them somewhere. And these people are more than likely to come back lookin' for them."

"So, if they were here looking, they already found the dog."

"Whatever you do, don't swallow those. You feeling that weird energy in the room, though?"

"I do. I'm feeling it. Powerful. He was in here, too."

"Could be. Those were some pretty gnarly moves. And he took those blows from both of us, too."

"Yeah, after meeting that dog, I'm thinking these stones have something to do with all this?"

"Yep. Probably shouldn't touch them at all. Just in case."

"Good idea. I carry them into the kitchen looking for something to put them in. In one of the cupboards, I find a small plastic food storage bowl with a snapping lid. I feel a sudden sense of loss rushing up my arms that makes me try to pick them up again. Damn.

J.J. reaches over and stops me. "Better not."

I look at him. A weird anger towards him fills me. Is it because he stopped me from touching the stones? "I left the water on in the pool. Will you turn it off on your way down?"

There's an awkward silent moment between us.

"It's the stones, dude"

"Sure.

"What about this?" He holds out the gun. "It's a nice one. Nine millimeter auto."

"You better set it down over there. If I turn these things in, I'll turn the gun in too."

"You sure?" He wipes it down with his shirt. "I could stay up on the roof and watch the place."

I can feel him watching me. He's making sure I don't touch the stones. Or make a move on him. These stones.

"No. The best thing for me to do is have a talk with Tucker and MacAroy."

"You think they know?"

"They know, otherwise I'd be in jail for murder one."

"If you say so." J.J. reluctantly sets the gun down between us on the counter. "You kind of feel naked not holding one after you've had one in your hand, you know."

"It must be an actor's thing."

"Should I lug any of this junk out?"

"Give me some time."

"Jo-Jo."

"I won't touch them. I'll hide them."

He nods and leaves me there standing in thought.

What am I supposed to do? People are dying, grabbing up dogs, digging through dog poo, blipping and leaping fences, and now I'm holding onto what might be blue diamonds. Who knows how much these things are worth or who they really belong to? Who shoved them down the cocker spaniel's throat, or up its bottom? What did they do to him while inside of him that might have made him act the way he did? Is it irreversible? Have I harmed myself? I felt a jolt of something almost euphoric, just for the moment I touched them, and a great loss when I let go of them. Worse, I even felt rising anger when J.J. kept me from touching them. J.J. felt it, too. Did the dog pooping them make it mad at me because they were no longer inside him? Was he trying to keep me away from them? Did he?

At least I have a gun again. Not the same. Who knows what the unaccounted for nine millimeter bullets killed? Maybe they killed the kid, maybe the sister or shop keeper, or even the dog. Wouldn't that look good, my fingerprints turning up on the gun that killed any of the above after my own gun came up as the one that killed the whole Essinola family? This can't be a coincidence. I don't see Karma being paid back here either. I'm in too deep. And the only control I have is keeping these diamonds until I can clear my name.

I look at the diamonds. I like them. I want to keep them. Just knowing I control them, I feel good inside. Powerful even. I double check the safety and tuck the gun in my pants and head to the garage wondering why we don't hear of more kids shooting their balls off. That'd put a damper on gang violence. "Crime down in East LA, due to the rash of ball-less gangsters. Other stupid news when we stop laughing."

24

This is crazy. We've all read the Hobbit. But after shrewdly hiding
the stones in my car's trunk, I'm coming out of the elevator onto the
first floor feeling a growing deflation. I almost involuntarily turn
back, and go get my precious, when I hear a curdling, heart stopping
scream that originates from the middle of Mystery Avenue. I can hear
it because, as usual, someone has left the street door open. So, I
sprint through the open doors, just in time to watch the redhead
come to a complete rolling stop out in the middle of Mystery Avenue
and the diesel spewing gray Mercedes fly around the corner. I soar
down the right side front steps, not touching a single one, as Stacey
turns over revealing the gash in the center of her forehead, like a
bloody third eye. The focus in her other two bronze eyes is somewhat
elusive, and I'm not so sure she recognizes me right away, because
she lashes out at me with her unbroken nails and grabs a hold of the
meat of my calf and gives me a gnashing Jaws would have been
proud of. The next thing I know I'm down in the street, on top of her
no less, and it sure seems like we're doing the hoochy koochy right
there in the middle of broad daylight. Until she grabs my new found
gun and twists it with surprising speed out of my grip.

"Get up, you ass."

"Auntie Em?

"Shut up. What did you tell those cops?"

"Nothing. Remember, they came and got you and left me to my
lonesomeness."

"They seem to know more than I do."

"Big surprise. They're cops. They get paid for this stuff. What is
everyone looking for?"

"I have no idea. Help me up."

I help her up and she motions me back across the condo and apartment lined street, through the trees and up the front steps. I look back. Isn't there someone out there noting I'm at gun point? Anyone? No one. Not a soul on the street.

Once inside Mystery Towers I venture, "What's with the cocker spaniel? Why is it so special?"

She pushes the elevator button. "I have no idea."

We get inside and ride up. "You mind tapping the needle?"

She steps out and backs me to my apartment's unlocked door. "Thanks. See ya."

"Keep in mind I'm the one with the gun now, Picasso," she says pushing me into my apartment, and locking the doors behind us.

"It's not loaded."

"It is too. I can tell by the weight." She heads for my living room.

"They're blanks," I tell her kicking off my shoes, taking note she didn't bother.

She points at the living room wall and pulls the trigger. Blam! More money. A hole blasts right through my wall and out through my new kitchen tile and into the microwave oven. I take that moment to grab for the gun and pull her across the couch on top of me, holding the gun over our heads. She pulls the trigger again. Blam, gun powder up my nose! A bullet right into the water cooler. Water starts spurting out the hole. Damn, I can't get a break. Her body is firm, lean and bumpy in all the right spots, which is yummy to the touch, but a bitch to wrestle a gun from, while my ears are ringing and my eyes are watering so badly.

25

By the time I'm feeling like a wimp for getting my ass kicked by this chick, my hundred-year-old double front doors come crashing in and J.J. springs into action. He grabs the redhead by the hair, pulling her head back until tears well up in her eyes and she stops cursing at us. At this point she lets go of the gun. So J.J. drags her down to the carpet and puts his hand around her throat and gives her a faint psychotic squeeze.

"You want me to snap it, Jozeph?"

I get off the couch to check the damage in my kitchen and water cooler. "Yeah, sure, go ahead." Stacey Carson's eyeballs max out as J.J. begins to squeeze tighter. I pull the glass water bottle off the cooler and set it down, take a deep pot from one of my slide out shelves under the stove and put it under the spurting water. Her bulging eyes stay with me. I hold a glass under. When I come out of the kitchen drinking from it, Stacey is still staring.

"You feel like talking awhile? Consider your story as farcical dinner theater."

"You two idiots can't intimidate me. And I've seen you on TV, so don't pull that psycho drama babble junk with me, jerk off. I used to be in the biz."

"That explains the body," J.J. says.

"I produced."

"I bet."

"Let the lady up, J.J."

"Do I have to? I feel safe this way."

"She's got some questions she needs to answer. And no more playing stupid with me, all right?"

"Okay, just get this lowlife actor off me."

"Well, excuse me." J.J. lets her up. She sits there for a moment rubbing her throat, before brushing back her electrifying hair, getting up and moving to the oxblood leather couch.

"Where would you like to start?"

"First kick off the shoes."

She does and I take them to the entryway.

"Who is Victor Castro?"

"My ex-husband." She takes a compact mirror out of her pocket. It's cracked. She checks her forehead. "That son of a bitch."

I go get her some paper towels to help stop the bleeding. "What is he looking for?"

"Three blue diamond chips."

She says it so matter-of-factly that both J.J. and I let our mouths drop open.

"You two never heard of blue diamonds?" She dabs her cut.

"Not since the Hope Diamond. And that heart shaped one in the Titanic movie. Do you believe the old lady throws it off the ship? Damn near ruined the whole movie for me."

"It was symbolic, J.J.," I tell him.

"Yeah, that she's senile. And didn't give a darn about her family's financial future."

"These diamond chips may have come from the Hope," she says.

"Come on," J.J. says, playing the skeptic.

"My ex's partner, Essinola, was supposed to bring them across the border and give them to Victor."

"And...."

"He fed them to a dog by accident. That damn cocker spaniel."

"You told this to the cops?" I ask.

"Of course not. Like they'd believe me," she says.

"Do they know?"

"About the diamonds or the dog?"

"About the diamonds, they obviously know about the dog," I answer.

"They know more than they let on."

Bubba comes out of my workout room, apprehensively of course. Hey, we've got guns. And this woman held him hostage. He sits in the doorjamb with wary eyes, looking back and forth.

"Come here, Bubba."

He wags his way over to me. I get down and give him some scrubs. He plops over. All is forgiven. Oh, to have the heart of a dog. "How come you know so much?" I ask.

"Because they all owe me a lot of money."

"So you were funding this covert diamond dog smuggling?"

"No, I am letting my ex-husband, Victor Castro, stay at my place for free. Until he gets back on his feet and out of my life."

"And the reason he is sitting down...is?"J.J. asks.

"We got sued, and put out of business. About three years ago."

"And Essinola is, or was, his business partner?"

"No, they worked for me."

"So, you're Mrs. North American Construction."

"Two husbands ago I was."

This is getting complicated. J.J. and I look at each other. Bubba doesn't understand much more than we do, and cares even less.

"Mr. NAC died, across the border, doing a job. I took over, brought in Castro and Essinola to run the business, and I played secretary and kept an eye on the books. But Essinola screwed up on a safety violation and we got capped on a 3.5 million wrongful death suit. And NAC's license to bid on anything got suspended because we couldn't pay."

"Those all tend to hurt."

"It was all an oversight. But I took the bite when insurance didn't cover it. The company went under. Unfortunately I married Victor, that psycho prick, just before things went south."

"I see. So after awhile he comes back and he's sponging off you. And he's got a get rich quick scam of bringing blue diamonds into the US and selling them."

"Right."

"And you fell for that?" J.J. asks.

"If you mean the story of no one really knowing for sure if they exist, stow it. I saw the show on cable. Believe me, the diamonds exist, and Essinola had them, but wouldn't turn them over to Victor."

"Why not?"

"I don't know. Once he had them, he changed. Became very combative and aggressive with me and Victor. And were you not evicting him?"

"Of course."

"Well, he had some very heavy debts to pay besides your stupid rent. He invested in his sister-in-law's clothing store and they got shut down by the feds. It doesn't matter now, according to the police, you killed them all."

"They told you that?"

"Yes. Well, not in so many words. They said it was your gun. And they owed you money. You did say you'd kill them in the desert...."

"I get mugged out front twice and nobody even notices, yet I get pissed off and yell one time and everyone hears it."

"You were pretty loud," J.J. informs me.

"I was waiting across the street," she added.

"For what?"

"For the dog. The diamonds were supposed to be in the dog."

"So where's the weird dog now?"

"I don't know. He had it in a bag last I saw. I'm just doing what Victor says. But Essinola forced me out of the car around the block. The next day, I was told that the family was dead, the dog gone, and that I should take care of the poodle if I wanted to see any money."

"And Victor told you this?"

"Yes."

"Does any of this make sense to you, J.J.?" I ask.

"Don't look at me. I'm just a lowlife actor. Not even a good one, according to red here."

"I just knew you wouldn't hurt me, okay?"

"So, the dog is still somewhere?" I ask.

"We think. Why do you care?"

"It was a nice dog?"

"No, very weird, evil even, is what it was," she says.

"Yeah and there's still a little kid not accounted for."

"There is? What kid?"

"Essinola's sister had a young boy, Juan, a six or seven year-old, dirty, sticky little monster," J.J. says.

"I didn't know that. I'm not sure if Victor does either."

"So, he could be alive?"

"I guess. Does it matter?"

"He might be with the dog. And the dog could've dumped anywhere by now. So your diamonds could be just a pile in my garden, or a lump of shimmering poo alongside the endless road of America, for all we know."

"Maybe so. Victor thinks it dumped them downstairs in that apartment. Mind if I look?"

"As long as you clean it up."

Her eyes narrow. What choice does she have? "Fine."

"What just happened in the street. How'd you get that gash?"

"Victor tried to run me over. My head hit the hood ornament."

J.J. looks closely at her forehead. "Hey look, you can see the Mercedes emblem thingy. See...?"

"Get away."

"Why would he do that? Aren't you his cash cow?" I ask.

"In more ways than one. I also know he killed the Essinolas."

"So you're my alibi?"

"I guess I am. So, what's for dinner?"

"Why don't I microwave you something? Oh fudge, I can't, you killed it."

"How do you feel about Chinese?"

"Personally? Or politically?"

"I mean their food."

"I'm starving," J.J. puts in.

"Don't you have someplace to go?" Stacey asks him.

"No. Picasso, you want me to stay? Watch your back? She had you pinned when I came in."

True. "Sure. Did you kick in my beautiful doors?"

He nods.

Great, more money!

26

After we come back from not finding the diamonds in 101 and watching Stacy pick up poop, dinner ends with a burp.

"What's the matter with you?"

"What?"

"You looked like you were still digging downstairs."

"It's nothing, just a little pissed," she answers.

"It was a crap shoot you'd find anything, anyway," J.J. says.

"Don't even, unless you like being stabbed with a fork."

"Come on, I still get to deal with the cockroaches in 101."

"Just spray them," Stacey says.

"Boric acid. It's safer. Takes longer, but it's the best," I add.

"You read a lot, don't you?"

"Me? I guess."

"Well, I've had enough. Red, would you like to come spend the night with me down in my man cave?"

"Can I? The name's Stacey unless you want your eyes dug out."

"What do you think, Picasso?"

"Maybe we should punish her and make her spend the night on the foldaway in my workout room."

"Yeah, she put a hole in your wall. I retract the offer."

"Oh darn, and struggling actors are my cheapest fantasy."

"Goodnight, J.J."

"You sure you want to let her stay up here? What if she's lying?"

"Are you lying?"

"About what?"

"About being afraid to go home."

"Victor tried to run me down in the street."

"And he shot at you, J.J., with this gun." Oops, that slipped out. J.J. shoots me a duh look.

"Wait...Victor was here?" Tracey genuinely seemed surprised.

"Downstairs. Looking through the dog piles. I thought you knew."

"Are you sure?"

"He pulled this gun and we clubbed and kicked him. But he just grabbed a gob of poo and jumped out the window, then ran off. About an hour before you ended up in the street."

"Why didn't you tell me that before I cleaned it all up?"

"You didn't ask. So I just assumed you knew."

She actually smiles, knowing we got her good. "Maybe you two dorks aren't so dumb after all. I'll pay you both back, in spades."

Can't wait.

"Is he by any chance on drugs, coke, or crank maybe?" I ask.

"He didn't seem to register any pain whatsoever, and we hit him pretty good," J.J. says.

"Pain is not something Victor pretends to recognize. He's a very dangerous man. I should know I used to have sex with him."

"By the way, the other day when he clubbed me out in the street, there was another person in the car. I pull out the card left at the fabric store and show it to her.

"I haven't seen one of these in years."

"Who is he?"

"My dead husband."

"This is getting weirder by the minute," J.J. says.

"Chances of Hector Estrada leaving this in a fabric store?"

"Very unlikely. My guess is Victor is using them."

"Why would he leave a calling card then murder people?"

"Why would he run me down in the street in broad daylight?"

"So who was in the car with him, the guy always watching?"

"The person wanting to buy the diamonds, most likely. Val Simpkins. And don't ask who he is, because I didn't ask. All I know is he has cash for the chips. End of story."

"For now." I pick up our plates and take them into the kitchen. "You mind if I smoke?"

"Go ahead, but out on the terrace, and pull the door behind you."

Stacey gets up and heads out to the five-by-ten-foot stone and cement terrace that's actually cut back into the living room, giving it an overhang roof. J.J. joins me in the kitchen, wondering the same thing I'm wondering. Can we trust her?

"What do you think?"He asks.

"How far can you throw her?"

"We talkin' off the terrace?"

"Let's keep our little find to ourselves for right now."

"You got them downstairs?"

"Yes, why?"

"The energy, I was thinking, I didn't feel anything yet. You know, like we felt in that room. But I'm down there, sleeping."

"Okay, I'll move them. Just in case."

"Thanks. I'm weird enough as it is."

"Me, too."

"I'd send her packing if I were you."

"You heard her. She's my alibi."

"She could also be pulling your groin muscle."

"This also could be true. And probably is. So, for now, we'll play her game and stay dumb and see where it leads us. As it stands, I'm out three months' rent and have to cover a lot of damage to my building. If these people are responsible for murdering the Essinola family, and these are blue diamonds, or something magical, then maybe I can recoup something from them by returning them to their rightful owner. Or at least clear my name and get my rep out of hock with the cops."

"If they are something more than just diamonds, the rightful owner could be someone you don't want to know. I say give them to the cops and let them figure it out."

"Not yet. Don't worry."

The redhead comes back in from the terrace. I get a large whiff of burnt tobacco and my after meal smoking chimes start to crack like the Liberty Bell on the Fourth of July.

"I'm off to bed." J.J. looks at me. "Don't close your eyes, Picasso."

"If you hear screaming, come running." He closes the door behind him the best that he can, considering he kicked it in. The thought of it sucks all the joy out of the room for me.

"You got a toothbrush I can use?"

"There's a new one in that bathroom, side drawer on the left."

"You got anything to drink? Something hard?"

"Full bar right over there."

"You're weird, but you think a lot. I like that in a man. Actually, these days I like that in a woman even more, but you'll have to do."

"I haven't been writing, and it's starting to get to me. I rant and rave after awhile. Sometimes even foam typos at the mouth."

She cracks a smile. "Where's a towel? I need a shower."

"Hall cabinets just inside the door there. There's medicine behind the mirror if you want to dress the forehead. I have vitamin E if you want."

"You been tested lately?"

"Excuse me?"

"AIDS test. These are still the days of caution."

"They are? I haven't noticed. Why, by chance?"

"When I get drunk, I sometimes get horny."

I am stunned. Aroused, perhaps, but stunned.

"Don't look shocked. How old are you?"

"I'm not saying."

"Good. I'll be out in a minute. Get ready."

"You can forget about having sex with me."

"Why?"

"Because I don't even know you."

"I'm from Minnesota. I'm double divorced, single, bisexual, and clean. I haven't been laid in months. You're weird but cute. I'm getting naked in your apartment. I've been tested lately and I was lying about the bladder infection. What else would you like to know?"

"How about: Are you planning to kill me?"

"Only if you get in my way of finding those diamonds."

She goes in, and I stand perplexed. She's not getting into my bed. I have a bad feeling deep down inside of my survival mechanism. It might be the broccoli, possibly the garlic shrimp. But realistically... it's her.

27

It's about 5:00 a.m., and I suddenly realize I am not alone. I look over and relief spreads upon me like margarine on corn bread, almost a crumbled disappointment, because Bubba is sleeping beside me. He snores, so I don't let him in my bed unless it's his bath night. But something's wrong, I can sense it in the air. My bedroom is at the end of a long hallway that leads to a sliding door that I'm positive I shut. Bubba, as smart as he is, wouldn't open the door because he knows he's not supposed to. He'll scratch at it occasionally when he wants to go out for a pee and I've slept in, but he'll never open it. But here he is, in my bed, still snoring away and the door is open. So why is the door open? And what nonsense will this lead to?

I get out of bed and decide not to turn the lights on. I can hear people in the theater whispering, "How stupid. Why don't they ever turn the lights on in these dumb films?" I just listen for a reason to turn around as I make my way down the hall to the sliding door.

There is a soft light coming from somewhere, just enough to guide me to the opened sliding door. Maybe Stacey couldn't sleep and has gotten up to turn on the TV. Maybe she's still drinking, which is where she was when I left her and Bubba, just this side of being fully drunk, yet sober enough to be articulately foul mouthed.

I make it to the door and peer around only to find my refrigerator door open. The light I'm seeing is from that. There's also a pair of male Doc Martens under the door, and they've got feet and legs in them. Oh no, the shoes aren't moving. I go back to my bed, remembering the gun. I reach for the pillow Bubba uses and find it's not there, but the gun is. Thank goodness for something. Though the missing pillow bothers me. I figure maybe Bubba has pushed it onto the floor. It's not there either. I start to stress. Recently having been framed for multiple murders, I'm nervous it's a happening trend.

Bubba just looks at me like I'm bothering him. He doesn't move, it's 5:00 a.m., and both our lives are full of abandonment. Only thing is, I can smell that the gun has been recently fired. There's a distinct smell of gunpowder emitting from it and I didn't notice it before until I had left the room and come back.

Oh boy, what am I about to find? Who's in my kitchen? And where is my pillow and what was it used for? I have a sick creative mind. And it's calculating several scenarios, none of which end in me being a hero. Is he dead, the guy in front of my refrigerator? And how do I explain this one to Tucker and MacAroy? Okay, I admit, I took the gun from some guy after I beat him with a frying pan. There are two bullet holes through my kitchen wall and appliances from it. The recently fired gun is now in my hand with my sleepy fingerprints all over it. And perhaps another man, a dead man, is in my refrigerator. But I didn't pull the trigger this time, though since I didn't shower, I probably still have traces of spent gunpowder on my hands from wrestling with Stacey when she pulled the trigger and killed my appliances. Did she set me up for this? Is she that devious? Is this part of her grand plan to leave me holding the body bag with the murder weapon and gunpowder residue on my hands? Holy crap, is that why she kept pulling the trigger? I'm sweating, thinking this. What a fool I am if this is her getting back at me. That conniving bitch!

Somehow, I'm having problems believing all this myself as I make my way back to the kitchen again, making sure I'm as alone as I can be. From this end of the kitchen the open refrigerator door is blocking my full view. So I make my way into the living room, passing by the guest bedroom-workout room and find it void of life. Great, my alibi is gone. From the look of my Glenlevit bottle so is my good Scotch. I cat towards the dining room, which I've turned into a pool hall with a purple felt pool table, custom cues, and a very cool hanging stained glass light. As I stick my head around the corner of the kitchen wall I step into wet carpet from the shot cooler. Yikes, wet socks! Worse, a man is face down in a pool of blood dripping into my refrigerator's crisper and is covered in a mixture of waterfowl down and goose feathers. That was a new sixty-dollar pillow, plus covering and pillow case. This will not be a good day. And I won't be eating those vegetables. I'm retiring broker by the body count!

Somehow I will be blamed for this even though I don't pretend to know this dead person. I am hoping it is Castro, but from what's left of his balding head…. Oh Christ! I turn and realize that the parts missing are spread across my oak stained cabinets above the double ovens. "Holy special effects, Dogman, hold the bloody oatmeal!" It's definitely not Castro. Thank goodness it isn't J.J. or any of my other tenants. I can't be absolutely sure, but my guess is it's the other suit in the gray Mercedes, the one always watching. Maybe he raised a hissy-fit and they killed him. Maybe he's the one who tried to kill the redhead and not Castro after all. Maybe I better call the cops because I've run out of plausible maybes. I look at the body in my open fridge. One can never have too many heads of cabbage. Thinking this makes me realize that good old Stacey had a sick sense of humor. Food and dead bodies. I'm forgetting to laugh, but I get the lark. What's worse is that my comely bottle of Dom is missing in all this action. I was saving it for something special. Like a job, or snuggling with a warm body, other than Bubba's. Definitely not a dead head in my fridge!

I check my machine. It's Erin. I deliberately am not able to hear the phone from my bedroom. I don't need demanding tenants waking me up whenever they want. The dark spooky halls seem to be enough to keep them from wandering up here and pounding on my door in the wee hours. However, my dear friend Erin is sincerely concerned about my welfare and was wondering what I was doing for dinner, if I had made it home, and if I would like to hang out with her. She seems a little bratty that I was keeping her at arm's length and hadn't called her. But I know it's just her way of showing me she cares. I haven't been on my computer for any reason, writing or checking on my Detroit Lions. I haven't checked my e-mail messages or Facebook. I don't even know where my cell phone is. I might as well be in a different dimension, in some dark Alien Universe, with all the lack of communication I'm experiencing. Anyway, she's letting me know that I do have e-mail and for me to call her as soon as I get this message. I think 5:00 a.m. would be a tad rude, so I go get Mike Tucker's card from my desk and page him instead.

28

Good old Tucker isn't happy about my page at 5:10. I'm happy to wake him though. I'm starting to think that both Tucker and MacAroy are in on this thing. They show up in ten minutes...fully dressed...if not awake, as though they were sleeping in their car down the block. The Mayor of Los Angeles couldn't get this kind of service from these cads.

"You didn't hear a thing?"Tucker asks.

"I took a hot shower and went straight to sleep. Smell my hair."

"Back off."MacAroy pushes me back.

"Why didn't the dog bark?"Tucker asks.

"He only barks at knocks on the door, or if he doesn't know you."

"Are you saying the dog knows the killer?"MacAroy asks.

"I told you, Stacey Carson was here. She fed him a few times."

"Was she in your bed?"Tucker asks.

"Of course not, she was in the guest room."

"A woman with a body like that and you didn't even try to put the make on her?"MacAroy asks.

"Horrifying, isn't it?"

"I'm just wondering. You're single, she's built, sexy, used your shower, made you an offer maybe. This guy wouldn't be your lover, would he?"MacAroy says.

"Why don't you two clowns get a new act? I don't know who this guy is unless he's the person I saw in a gray Mercedes the other day."

"You just said you've never seen this guy before," Tucker says.

"I can't be sure, is what I'm saying now."

"So, this guy comes into your place. Maybe the redhead lets him in. She shoots him with a gun you have under your pillow. Uses your pillow to silence the single blast to the head, stuffs him in your crisper. Your dog didn't bark, like he did when we came to the door, and you didn't sleep with her. But this gun actually belongs to a guy named Victor Castro, who used to be married to the redhead. He acted as her boss though she owned the whole company, and he clubbed you and took your poodle. Then you took him back," Tucker says.

"We were locked in together. That's where I was. Are you saying you don't know this guy, Victor Castro?"

"We didn't say that," MacAroy says. "We're just clarifying."

"You think this may be the gun that killed Essinola's sister-in-law and shopkeeper, but you took it back from the redhead after she took it from you in the street and shot up your place with it. But first you took it from Castro in apartment 101 after he shot at you downstairs. Is that about right?" Tucker asks, keeping notes.

"That's pretty much it in a nutshell, except Castro was passing out cards that weren't his. Hector Estrada." I go over and pick the card up by the phone. I show it to them. "This is Stacey's dead husband's card. Chances are Victor is using his ID as well."

They look at me funny. "You're just like some rabbit pullin' magicians out of his ass, ain't ya?" MacAroy asks.

"Anything else you'd like to share with us?" Tucker asks.

"There's pictures on the wall of North American Construction that I thought was of him. Now I'm not so sure."

"Why's that?" Tucker asks.

"Sometimes women tend to fall for the same type of man. My ex's ex-husband and I looked so much alike I once saw a picture of him in her father's beauty salon that I thought was me. People who knew him for years called me Jimbo and went to hug me. Some even carried on conversations as though I was him."

"Isn't that endearing? Okay, we'll go over there, get a picture or two and put out an APB on him," Tucker said.

"And you have no idea what they're looking for other than this weird dog?" MacAroy asks.

"I didn't say that."

"No, you didn't. So, what else are they looking for?"

"I have no idea. Now that I have, can I go back to bed?"

"Don't be a smart ass, Picasso. There's way too many 'buts' in your story already." Tucker sighs as he writes this all down.

"It's the truth."

Tucker looks me in the eyes, trying to catch me lying. "The redhead, Stacey, told you nothing?"

"She said Victor Castro tried to run her over."

"But you didn't witness this. You only found her in the street?" Tucker asks.

"This all seems a little cloudy to me." MacAroy scratches his head with his pen.

"Try waking up in a gutter and see how unclear it gets. In fact, have you two even been home yet? Are you staking this place out, or what?"

"We'll ask the questions," Tucker says.

"You seem to be living an exciting life, Picasso."

"This is not a life, it's a nightmare."

"Yeah, that was a nice pillowcase. You get that at Macy's?" MacAroy asks.

"Look, will you call somebody, and get this mess out of here? I'd like to go back to bed."

"Ah, Picasso, Jozeph, you're coming downtown with us, I'm afraid," Tucker says.

He's not the only one afraid! "What for, I didn't do this? I told you, she was here. Look at the holes she put in my walls when I tried taking that gun from her. You think I did this?"

"We're not saying she wasn't here. We're not saying you done this. We're just saying that you seem to know more than you're letting on to, and if you don't spill what that is, you're taking a trip downtown with us. You will sit in a nice holding cell - you remember the place, right - until we get some answers. Are we clear on this matter?" Tucker asks.

I look down at Bubba. It is times like this I wish he were a mean Doberman. But he just looks up at me with sheepish poodle eyes wondering when we are heading back to bed and if that dead body in the refrigerator meant he wasn't getting fed any time soon? My mind is racing. What should I tell these two clods, and can I trust them? I'm dying for a cigarette because I do my best pondering when I'm high on tobacco fumes. What can they do to me for holding back info? Financially, not much, I'm so broke the bank owns me for the next thirty years. But cover up is a big thing now. Damn it. While the truth may set me free, the facts could land me back in jail.

"Did Stacey Carson tell you guys anything when you had her in for questioning?"

"She told us to drop dead, not much else," MacAroy says.

"Just how much do you guys know?" I look them both in the eye.

"That bodies keep showing up killed by guns with your fingerprints on them, is all," Tucker says.

"That is a scant misleading, but there's a good explanation."

"We can't wait to hear it," MacAroy says.

"The guy named Castro, Victor and Stacey, were partners with Mr. Essinola to sell blue diamonds that they believed to be the lost chips from the Hope Diamond. I think this man, whoever he is, wanted to buy them."

"Blue diamonds. Did you say they were from the Hope Diamond?" Tucker asks.

"Maybe. But just chips, you know facets, cuttings that were taken and lost around two hundred years ago."

"And this guy wanted to buy them?" Mike points to the body.

"If that's him. That's what Stacey told me."

"And they smuggled them across the border up the spaniel's ass?"

"Well no, that's where they ended up once over here, and they thought maybe it crapped them out... down in apartment 101."

"Did it?"

"I don't know, maybe it swallowed them somehow. But Victor was here yesterday, and I scared him off. That's how I got his gun. Stacey came and went through the poo, so I made her clean it up."

"Didn't we tell you not to touch the place?"

"It was too poetic watching her dig through it to pass up. I saved all of it in a bag for you two."

"This is one cockamamie story, Picasso," MacAroy says.

"So, what's he doing here?" Tucker asks pointing a thumb at the body again, like maybe he's listening.

"Looking for Stacey maybe, I don't know. Maybe they were concerned she's talking to you guys. They did try to kill her. They owe her money in all this. And she's peeved about everything."

"So she tells you," MacAroy says.

"Yes. Are you guys buying any of this?"

"We'll let you know. I'll wait here. Take him down," Tucker says.

"But I've told you everything."

"It's for your own safety," Tucker tells me.

"Safety? There's murderers, rapists, and some crazy called Mooky in that place."

"And now there's an out of work filmmaker with one messed up, Hollywood imagination," MacAroy adds.

"Speaking of, this is taking too much time. Can't I just stay here? I obviously didn't do this, why would I... and call you guys?"

"It's a strange world. Come on." MacAroy takes my arm.

"Please don't do this."

"One more word and I put you in handcuffs."

"Why not, everyone around here thinks I'm a killer anyway."

MacAroy puts the cuffs on me. By this time it's nearly seven a.m., the coroner has just arrived, cops are swarming the place outside and my tenants are all leaving to work. Just less than half of them watch MacAroy put me handcuffed into his stinky unmarked car. J.J. is standing there under a pine, smoking a cigarette. He's keeping his mouth shut, enjoying the smoke way too much. I just look at him. I need a cig bad. But J.J. doesn't know what to do about me. Making any kind of move with all these cops around could only get him arrested. I'm never sure about J.J. and his past. Some things I don't need to know. Though I know he once lived on the needle, he's an actor now, and he was born in Alaska.

Dang, I didn't move the stones like I told him. I didn't want to take the chance with Stacey around. "Have Erin call my lawyer."

"Okay."

"Feed and walk Bubba. Have someone fix my door."

"Okay. Have a very nice day."

Smart ass. This is turning into a very bad day. Won't the boys be glad to see me back.

29

In my wildest dreams I didn't think I'd end up stuck here all day in the holding tank. But after only tasting two days of freedom, my good buddy Mooky knew I'd be back. He was mentally calling me the whole time I was out on the street. Seeing what I was seeing and feeling my blues. So he says. Once again, I am the crawling, mass murdering landlord. A name bestowed upon me by my fellow inmates. As far as the rest know, I had only been in another part of the jailhouse, being tortured or beaten. From the looks about my head and face, though I had showered, shaved and changed clothes, I am one of them, and still the strangest of all. So the others, some new, some old, stay far away, except of course my good buddy, Mooky. He squats down next to my lotus in the middle of the cell, whispering sweet repulsive things that he will do for me when we get to the big house. He could set me up, cigs, drugs, booze, boys, she-men, pets, all I have to do is let him sell me to the highest bidder and I am in. In what, I'm sure I don't want to know. There is no eclipsing the Mook in his eyes, he controls my mind, lobe to stem. And oddly keeps mentioning relieving me of the blues with a wave of his hand, making sure I live a long healthy extraordinary life as a made man.

I just look onwards until the Mook gets right up inches from my face, ogling me in the eyes, willing me to relieve myself of the blues…asking me if I like to toss the salad with jelly or syrup. Until maybe to protect what I know, I involuntarily poke him across the nose…two fingers, plunk, one in each yellowish eye. He rolls over in gruesome pain, grabbing his face, screaming that he is blind. Maybe he is, but I don't move, and no one saw me poke him. So they just look from me to him and back again, wondering what I had done to the

Mook. Did I out Mook him, out mind control him? Am I the master? Ask Mook who's screaming, "My eyes, my eyes!" while rolling about the floor. Was my will that strong in the eyes of the others? One could only hope.

A big cell guard, the one who had opened and closed the gate when they dragged me out once before, checks in on us. I don't expect anyone to really care what the Mook is screaming about, but believe it or not, the guard opens the gate and moves over to the Mook and rolls him over on his back. "Shut up, you."

"I'm blind."

"Try bein' blind and dumb."

"That guy's crazy...dug my eyes out."

"You do that?"

I wasn't about to answer and break my cover.

"Hey, I'm talkin' to you? Hey, you do this?"

Again, I don't bother answering. Why should I? I'm the mass murderer from the bleak lagoon. Whack, I get an unexpected blow to the side of my head. But it's the second one from the other direction that puts me out.

Why do people feel the need to hit me?

30

Stars jet out like Luke Skywalker switching on hyperbole. And I wake up in a dimly lit room. Definitely not the hot lit room I sat in once before. I'm now in a plush office with drawn curtains. Could be a lawyer's office, city official's lair, prison warden's den, I'm not sure. But the two things sticking out the most, like two sore thumbs, are standing by the door. My good buddies, Tucker and MacAroy. Oddly, they're with a very nice looking woman this time. She smiles as I come around. Tucker and Mac don't. The men aren't shaved. They both still wear the same suits. And the woman's blond hair looks like she rolled out of bed and didn't shower yet. It's hard to say how long they've been waiting.

"Good afternoon, sorry about the metal folding chair, we weren't sure if you'd wet yourself before you came to," she says.

Showered or not, her lips are freshly painted a burnt red.

"How do you feel?" she asks.

I just look at them and blink a few times, testing the waters of movement. No words come to me. I'm not sure how I feel at this point, and probably not until I remember what has happened to me will the full pain of my past experience take its toll. So just in case, I don't even try to remember, or feel.

"This is Mary Devonshire, from the DA's office," Tucker says. "Maybe you've heard of her."

Actually, since Berry brought her up and showed me her business card, I have. Ms. Mary Devonshire looks very butch in her business suit. Why was she at Berry's with lowlife Victor and our now dead diamond broker Simpkins? I'm getting the bad feeling that I've suddenly stumbled into something smelling much worse than all of us.

"Mr. Picasso? Do you understand who I am?"

I lie and nod. Man does that hurt.

"We have ourselves a very sensitive matter here. Something possibly international. Would you be willing to help me?"

Nodding hurt way too much. The guard got me good with his flashlight, so I say: "If you help me first." Speaking feels much better, but my jaw is stiff and bruised on the left side where he struck me broadside and my skull hurts above the right ear where he got me on the knockout blow.

Mary looks at Tucker, who looks at MacAroy, then all three look back at me. "All right," she says, "what can I help you with?"

"The guard who struck me in the holding cell, I want him brought up on charges."

"The guard? I don't understand. A guard did this to you?" She looks at MacAroy and Tucker again.

They shrug, like it's a big mystery to them.

"Do you have proof of what you're saying?"

"Twenty-nine other cell mates, well maybe not the Mook at that point, but the others saw him come in and club me with his flashlight."

"An inmate says you poked him in the eyes."

"His word against mine. You want my help. I want the guard brought up on charges. That's my offer. So unless you have any proof of me doing something illegal, I'd like to go home to my dog now."

"We have your prints on two murder weapons," she says.

"I already explained that. I was sleeping, Stacey Carson, or someone she let in my apartment, perhaps Victor Castro, came into my room and took the gun and pillow and killed whoever that was in my refrigerator."

"Val Simpkins, a very well known art collector that specializes in ancient jewels. And a good friend of many surprisingly powerful people around the world, including mine."

"What was this great internationally guy's head doing dead in my crisper?"

"That's what we want to know."

"Bring in the guard, and then we'll talk."

Mary sets her angry eyes on Tucker again. I don't know if it's the bouncing daylight in here, but her eyes seemed to flash a yellowish hue. Tucker looks at MacAroy, and all three of them shrug. It looks like we'll be sitting here for a while, so I yawn as long and thunderous as I can muster with all the pain. A moment goes by, I can smell my sweat so I check my pits, and yep I stink. Mary looks back at Tucker and Tucker looks at MacAroy and MacAroy says, holding back his own yawn, "I'll go get him."

31

So, this big guard named Liberty is standing in front of me, not far from Mary Devonshire, who lights a cig. "Mind if I smoke?"

"Mind if I vomit blood?"

She puts the lighter away.

"Can we get on with this," MacAroy says.

"What's this all about?"Liberty is playing dumb.

"Mr. Picasso claims you hit him with your flashlight," Mary says. "Did you?"

"That's news to me."

"You satisfied, Picasso?" MacAroy asks.

"No. He hit me twice. I'm in pain. I want to see a doctor, and I want him to pay for my x-rays and compensation for my discomfort. Say, fifty thousand dollars."

"Jesus Christ."

"You can work out the details when my lawyer gets here."

"Don't be ridiculous. Liberty, did you hit Mr. Picasso with your flashlight?"

"I told you I didn't."

"Tell him he's not smart enough to be a good liar."

"Alright, let's stop. Liberty, tell him you're sorry," Mary says.

"For what?"

"For hitting him!"

He looks at Tucker and MacAroy who give him a deadpan, so I know they're in on it, "Okay, I'm sorry."

"Thank you. Now, please drop dead."

"Can I go now?"

"What about my medical bills?"

"We'll have you looked at."

"Sure, at the taxpayers' expense."

"All right, Jozeph. Are you finished?" Mary asks. "Tell us what you know."

"In front of him?"

"Thank you, Liberty. You may go."

"With pleasure." He leaves.

"All right, you want to talk? Talk."

"Tell me what you already know, and I'll try to fill in the blanks. How's that?"

Surprisingly she buys into that. Perhaps she's testing me. Or not planning to let me out of this room alive anyway. Or maybe she's got a storyline with these two cops already.

"In central Chile along the Bio-bio River, clear cutting was done, and a body was discovered."

"That's a long way away from Sherman Oaks, California."

"This happens to be near the home city of Mr. Essinola. You might recall that Talcahuano was devastated by an eight point eight magnitude earthquake, and its subsequent tsunami. Like so many others, it left the Essinola's family homeless."

"Did Essinola happen to kill this body?"

"Not unless he was alive two hundred-years-ago."

"You're losing me."

"On this two hundred-years-old body was a bag of stolen jewels."

"And?"

"These jewels where believed to have been some of the jewels looted from France's royal treasury shortly after the French Revolution began, in September of 1792.

"Yes, I saw the documentary."

"So you know, a blue diamond known as the French Blue also disappeared without a trace at this time and was believed to be re-cut before resurfacing in 1812."

"Yes," I answer.

"Three blue facets were recovered within the recently discovered bag of jewels."

"What does this have to do with me?"

"Come on, Mary knows about the blue diamonds Simpkins was here to buy. They know each other, remember."

"So, they are valuable?"

"Immensely. To the right people, even more so. It is believed that the stone mounted in King George's insignia of the Royal Order, almost exactly the intense dark blue color, is actually the Hope Diamond," Mary says.

"And these facets could be the documentation that would prove that the Hope Diamond is really the French Blue? Which means King George's insignia diamond is...."

"Yes, the stolen French Blue."

I look at the two cops. I've felt the power of these stones, so I'm not fully buying into this Hope Diamond story. But these two guys are doing their best to follow Mary's story. Perhaps they should watch more TV and do fewer stakeouts in their smelly car trying to pin murders on me. "How did Essinola get a hold of them?"

"We think they were separated from the rest of the jewels by someone attempting to keep them from us. Essinola somehow ended up with them and attempted to sell them back to us with the help of Victor Castro."

"And you don't know who that was?"

"We have our suspicions, but it doesn't matter now. The facets are here in LA."

"So Val Simpkins was your guy?"

"He represented the Smithsonian and a faction of the French Government that is interested in the discovery of the stolen French Blue. He was sent to authenticate them."

"So some people want this to be true and others don't?" I ask.

"You see how delicate this is. We need to know the truth."

"I guess."

"Do you have the blues? The diamonds?"

She stands right in front of me. Watching me.

"You mean three little dark blue glassy things that glisten oddly in the light?"

"Picasso...."Tucker starts.

"Never saw them. Other than what I saw on TV."

"We know you have them."

"Search me."

"All right, this has gone far enough. Where are the diamonds, Jozeph?" She asks.

"What makes you think I have them?"

"You talk in your sleep," Mary says.

"I was sleeping alone."

"There's a female voice on Simpkins' voicemail saying that you babbled in your sleep about finding the diamonds."

"That's what you're basing this on? Something this Stacey Carson probably made up?"

"That's all we have. That and the fact Simpkins showed up in the middle of the night to make you an offer for them."

"And I killed him for waking me?"

"Possibly for the money he was carrying," Tucker says.

I look at Tucker. I can't believe he'd try to pin something phony on me, like robbery. "Did he have money on him?"

"We don't know."

"How much did you say they are worth?"

"They're priceless."

"Who do they belong to?"

"At this point..."Mary stops.

Things were looking up. If the diamonds are finder's keeper's, I'm sitting on a hot spot. "I don't have them, so you can tell me."

"At this point, everyone directly involved is dead. But the French and Chilean governments are very interested in making a deal to bring them back to France."

"I see. So Simpkins was about to make a great sum of money by returning these diamonds to the French Government."

"In a manner of speaking."

I yawn again, obnoxiously as I can, reaching way up and smelling my pits again. Yep, I still stink. I wait while everyone in the room but Mary has a turn. Apparently, yawning reflexes are beneath her.

"Notoriety has a lot to do with it. Prestige of returning the diamonds to their rightful owner. And perhaps proving one of history's greatest mysteries. The origins of the Hope Diamond."

"This wouldn't by any chance have anything to do with the original body the diamonds were found on, would it?"

"We can't say."

"This body answers one of the great mysteries and you can't say."

"It's delicate."

"Well, good luck with that."

Mary's eyes narrow.

I'm hitting nerves. I let out a louder yawn. I'm inpatient, at best. This is crazy. All this hocus-pocus. Mary lights up. MacAroy and Tucker just stand there and wait, not knowing fully what to expect.

"You want out of here?"

"First tell me why a dog disappeared and reappeared in my building after having these stones up its butt."

"Did you find a dog?" She asks the two cops.

"Heard there was one. But we never found it."

"The dog isn't important."

"It is to me, and those who took mine to get it back. There was something very weird about that dog. Was it something to do with having contact with those diamonds or not?"

"Don't start this crazy writer stuff here, Picasso," Tucker says.

"Tell us where the diamonds are," MacAroy says.

I put my hand up to block their stares. "So what's with the dog?"

"I don't know anything about this dog acting weird," Mary says.

"Then why don't I believe you?"

"We know you have the diamonds. We just don't know how you're keeping them from us. Is someone helping you?" Have you talked to someone about them?" Mary asks.

"I don't have them. So why would I? I'll call you if I do."

"Take him home."

"What?"Tucker is taken by surprise.

"He's got the diamonds," MacAroy says.

"Let's beat them out of him," Tucker says. "We can't be spending any more time on this. We got...."

"You've got what I tell you've got," Mary tells him.

"I still vote we beat it out of him," MacAroy says.

"What, you think they're gonna just fall out of me if you shake me hard enough? Where'd you find these two goons, Mary? Surely someone with your looks and style can do better than these lug nuts."

MacAroy comes at me, but Mary steps in his way. He's doing his best to glare around her until he catches the look in her eyes and steps back to the door.

"Jozeph, if you come in possession of these diamonds, it would be very wise of you to make sure you contact me through these two gentlemen and give them to me." Mary puts out her cigarette and blows her smoke over my head.

"Or what?"

"Or I'll put you someplace no one will find you for a long time."

"Are you threatening me with bodily harm? Because you're starting to turn me on? Is that what the DA's office does to suspected murdering filmmakers these days? Take them for a ride? When did the DA's office cross to the dark side?"

Mary moves to the door. She looks back at me with eyes now so oddly yellow that I'm almost taken aback by how brilliant they are. And then they seem to readjust to a simmering soft blue as a hard smile comes to her painted lips. I look to see if it could've been a reflection of light off something in the room. It was possibly one of the low lamps on the surrounding tables, but I'm not counting on it.

"The Justice System I'm familiar with is a very tangled place, Mr. Picasso. Deeper and darker than you could ever image. You don't want to go down that path with me."

I'm not stupid. She's telling me there's more here than I want to know. And she's being very candid about the subtext in her words. It's probably more than she intended in front of these goons. I look at Tucker and MacAroy, and they yawn in my face. The dicks.

"Okay, I'll call these two clods if I find the diamonds."

"A very wise decision." She leaves without looking at me again.

"You two are crooked, aren't you?"

"On your feet, Picasso, and keep your mouth shut about this."

32

A little over twenty-four hours after they handcuffed me and took me away, they discharge me back to Mystery Towers Magical Tours. The day has one of those ominous feelings to it like if anything at all bad is to happen in the world, it will surely happen to me. I don't want to think negative thoughts like this, but today I wish to punch out a few people, shoot some others, and tell a few more to screw off. Unfortunately, the two clods driving the car I'm getting out of wear guns and have dangerous friends like Ms. Mary Devonshire.

But I forget them as quickly as a day old headache, when I get a load of the moving van out front of my drive. At first I search my achy mind trying to remember if I had anyone moving in, but I quickly remember that other than apartment 101, I am temporarily filled up. Looking into the van, I immediately surmise that I am about to have my second vacancy. More money lost. Apartment 102 is moving out, and moving expeditiously.

Moments later, Mea Silvers comes out, carrying a lamp and a folding chair, something she probably uses in her photography business. She shoots head-shots for actors. The Silvers Screen it says on her checks. Using the dining room as her studio and the building's exterior for natural light locations. I get the feeling I should've charged her location fees. And knowing rock & roll Phil, he is probably at his recording studio and doesn't plan on lifting a finger to help his wife move him out.

Mea stops when she sees me standing there.

She immediately looks past me to the fleeing unmarked cop cruiser that dropped me off, then back to me, as she comes down the stairs.

"What's up?"

"We're moving."

"Obviously, I think I figured that much. Don't you have two months left on your lease?"

"We consider murder and dead bodies a contract breaker."

"That won't hold up in court."

"You've got our deposit."

"That's for cleaning."

"Talk to Phil about it."

"Where is he?"

"At the studio."

Gee, how did I guess? "Is he coming back here?"

"No, I have his keys and garage genie."

"Don't you think you are, like, way overreacting?" I say imitating her husband. It goes way over her head.

"Phil wants better air conditioning."

"I've got people working on it."

"It's been three months."

"We've ordered the old schematics to make it run right."

"Good luck."

"Will you leave your forwarding address?"

"You plan on coming by for a visit or to send us Christmas cards? Or, like, just kill us?"

"Low blow. I had nothing to do with any of those bodies."

"No, they only rented from you or woke up dead in your kitchen."

"Yeah, I see how it must look."

"There were reporters around today, asking about you. We don't want to be associated with killings, whether you pulled the trigger or not. It's not good for Phil's career."

"Why? It's done wonders for mine. I've gotten all kinds of murder mystery writing offers. As they say, write what you know."

"I bet. The fact is, the bloom is off the rose around this place for us, and we don't feel comfortable living where there's been a murder. And my best client, Phyllis Kaye, is still upset about that damn dog walking through the hallway walls in front her. She won't bring her kids here to shoot ever again. If she tells other parents or their commercial agents, this place could put me out of business."

"Okay, fine, I admit, the dog was a little much. I'll start showing the place today. If I rent it before the month is up we'll call it even. But if it stays empty past a month, I'll make the call then."

"Fine, make that call to Phil's manager."

"I will."

"Bye. Stay away from us."

"Yeah, okay, fine." I use my key to open the garage and watch it close. It is that moment I notice the cover to the garage gate system is off and tossed on the ground. Immediately I turn around and look for my Corvair. "It's gone!"

Someone stole my car, my baby, my red and black Corvair. I search the rest of the garage in hope I might have moved it but I know I hadn't and that it's gone. I've had this dream so many times I keep expecting myself to wake up and find that everything is just as messed up as it was the day before. This time, no, my Corvair is gone. I want my car back!

33

I stand here in my empty parking spot for about three or four minutes listening to the ringing in my ears before I turn to notice that J.J.'s red Toyota pickup is parked in its spot across from me. The light under his studio door is off, but that doesn't necessarily mean he's not in. He could be sleeping. So I pound on his door. I get no response, so I pound louder. This time I can hear faint scratching at the backside of the door, like a dog or cat. I think Bubba may be down here with J.J. Why not, I did ask him to watch after the dog. So, I push at the metal door and it opens. But only a little bit, because it hits something with a soft fleshy thud about ten inches back.

"Ahhh."

"J.J.?"

"Down here."

"You hurt?"

"Give me a sec, I can't see anything, can you turn on the light?"

I reach into the room and hit the bank of switches that are mounted just to the left of the door. The ceiling lights up with a single fluorescent tube. I can see a shoulder, a knee and foot. Then a hand grips the door as though he is using it to help himself up, which is exactly what J.J. is doing. Finally, he is up on his knees and far enough away from the door for me to push it all the way open, uh-oh.

"I think my nose is broken."

"Yeah, I'd say that's a good call. Your ear doesn't look good either."

"What?"

"I said..." I enter the room. The place was already a disastrous pig sty so there is no telling if anyone had disturbed the mess. At one time this was a guardhouse, then later a groundskeeper's apartment. The laundry room attached to it was both the servants' kitchen and laundry, and both were here before the dungeon garage was dug out.

"What happened?"

"I don't remember." He pulls one of his MP3's headphones out of his blood-crusted ear. "Ah, damn."

"Who hit you?"

"Oh, yeah...that chick...that redhead, what was her name?"

"Stacey."

"She clobbered me."

"When?"

"Sometime last night, I think, maybe early this morning. I heard some noise. I'd been up all night just smoking pot and drinking, and listening to music on this. I came out here to smoke a cig and wham, I got it on the side of the head and then she kicked me in the face."

"How'd you get back into the room?"

"I don't know, I might've crawled, oh yeah, I tried to call 911, I thought I was dying. In fact I don't feel so alive right now."

"Was she alone?"

"Alone? I don't know. I barely got a chance to see her. That's why she kicked me, because I rolled over and looked up at her."

"Someone took my car."

"Your Corsa? Why?"

"I don't know. The cover's off the garage gate motor. They must've rolled back the gate."

"Why would she take it?"

"I didn't say she did. Did you notice it gone?"

"Not really, I mean, I think it was there last night. What?"

"I hid the diamonds in there."

"In the car?"

"Yeah, there's that little compartment in the trunk behind the headlights that screws off. Remember where I showed you I keep spare keys?" He nods yes. "I put them in there in a Crown Royal bag full of nuts and bolts. They're inside that tin magnet box I use for keys, but I filled it with silicone caulking to make it look like it was just a setting for the one house key."

"Paranoid, but classy. Do you think they got them?"

"No idea. Where's Bubba?"

"Erin was with him, last I saw. She let a locksmith in to fix your door. She was still up in your place, waiting to hear from you."

"I didn't get a chance to talk to her."

"Man, she must be pissed."

It is then I realized that Erin's Ford Explorer Sport is still in its parking spot. "Oh, no!"

"What?"

"Erin's truck is still here. She didn't go to work."Knowing her, she called in, worried sick about me. I start for the elevator.

"Hey, give me a hand, I'll go with you. I don't want to clean up in my sink."

I go back to help him on his feet.

"Damn, I'm sore."

"She may have had help."

"Feels like it."

34

I help J.J. to the elevator and we take it up to my apartment. The elevator opens onto the third floor and we find my repaired door standing half open, with something very important missing. The doorbell isn't working. Bubba should be in the hall wagging his tail or barking, but he is nowhere in sight. This alarms me greatly. I push the door all the way open to make sure no one is standing behind it waiting to clobber me.

"Bubba? Bubba? Where's my dog? Bubba?" Damn, no Bubba, no dog...just a faint moan coming from one of my bathrooms, I think. I go into the apartment and make a quick right off the foyer into the bedroom hall and another quick right towards the moaning. I flick on the master bathroom light to find Erin lying between the toilet and shower glass wall. She looks up at me with her deep green eyes, her dark auburn hair down around her face, her long legs stacked on top of each other to allow her to squeeze into that cramped position.

"Help me, I'm stuck."

"What happened?"

"They came in looking for keys."

"To my car?"

"Yes. And they took my purse. I think for my credit cards, I don't know, but they took Bubba with them."

"Why?"

"There's a note on the kitchen counter. Help me...."

J.J. painfully helps me lift Erin out from between the toilet and glass shower wall.

"I'm so steamed at you."

"I know..."

"Why didn't you call me?"

"I was in jail again."

"Duh...you get one call."

"It's more complicated than that."

"Did Valerie show up?"

"She didn't have to. They let me go."

"They let you go? Again?"

"Put her down on the couch. Yes, I know it will come to a shock to my good buddies. But I didn't kill Mr. Simpkins, or anyone else."

"No one here said you did," Erin snaps back.

"Then don't seem so surprised."

"I'm not."

"You are too!"

"Why are you yelling?"

"They took my dog, and my car, and they've got the diamonds."

"It's a good thing I put his collar on.... The what?"

"He said diamonds. Blue ones," J.J. clarifies.

"Diamonds?"

"Yeah, we found them downstairs," J.J. tells her.

"Real diamonds?"

"You know the Hope Diamond?" he asks.

"Of course I know the Hope Diamond."

"Will you two stop? Jesus, I've got a headache." I shoot J.J. a look and he goes over and leans on my pool table. I shoot him another look and he moves over to the burgundy chair and flops down.

"That makes two of us." Erin leans her head back.

"I'm with you both on that," J.J. says.

"Does someone want to explain why I was attacked in the bathroom last night and wedged down nearly behind the toilet?"

"What were you doing?" I ask.

"Cleaning your toilet, it needed it, I had used it.... What?"

"What time was that?"

"I don't know, what, about one."

"Do you realize how anal that sounds?"

"So what? I was nervous. It needed cleaning. What're we doing about all this?"

"Finding my dog. And my car."

"And the blue diamonds."

"Come on, you guys, blue diamonds?" She watches us closely to see who'd wink, or do any secret manly handshakes or something.

"Where's that note?" I get up and go into the kitchen and find a note scribbled on the back of the cover page to my new script in progress, *Crazy Kind Of Love*. The lousy no good bastards have even defiled my creative space. I read it over a couple times to make sure I get it straight. English composition obviously isn't this writer's major but he managed to get his point across nonetheless. Steaming, trying to find the words to express myself, I realize my kitchen is spotless. This was a crime scene last I was here. But there's no trace of it anywhere. "Erin?"

"You didn't expect me to stay up here with all that blood, did you?"

"I guess not, but crime scene people do that for a living."

"They were here. Aftermath. There's a card on the bill for fixing the door. They bagged and took everything away. I just added a little polish. I swear."

I look at the bill for the door. Great.

"I had them take one of the doors from storage. It matched up," J.J. says. "They switched out the locks. And repainted."

"Thanks. Looks good." I read the note again.

"What does it say?" J.J. comes into the kitchen, opens the fridge and pulls out the ice tray.

"Give us the diamonds or the dog gets it."

"It does not...."

"In so many words."

"Is it from her?"

"No autograph." I give it to Erin.

"This is a man's writing." Erin knows a world of facts. For her age, twenty-five going on forty, she is very cultivated.

"You can tell?"

"No woman would spell like that. And look at the way he slants this t and h. See? This person's first language is probably Spanish."

"Come on," J.J. says.

"You can tell that by reading it?" I ask.

"Either that, or your dog's been dog napped by a moron."

I'm not so sure he hasn't. "Victor Castro."

"Who?"

"We beat the hell out of him and he didn't even notice," J.J. says.

"I didn't see anyone. I got my head stuck down into the toilet, while they talked and rifled through my purse—a man with a heavy accent, and a bitchy woman. They argued about the note. The light went out and then someone hit me, right here. Look, I've got a lump."

"Yes, you do. I've got three lumps and I was knocked unconscious twice in three days," I say.

"I've got a broken nose, and my ear is half torn off. Good thing I'm not a bleeder."

"Okay, so it's a draw, we're all the biggest losers," Erin says.

"Why don't you go wash, J.J.? There's medical stuff in the cabinet in the master bath. You want to go see a doctor, voodoo man, or kahuna, or your SAG insurance representative?"

"Yeah, if you don't mind. My nose needs resetting and I'd kinda like to keep both ears."

"I don't know, it might make you unique, that certain unusual look directors are looking for."

"Yeah, if they ever recast *van Gogh-away*, *The White Evander Holyfield Story*, or *The Children of My Ear Is Torn*, I'm the one."

"Jozeph, I'm walking in there to help him and when I get back I want a full explanation to what is happening."

"Fine. I'll be right here." I sit down as they go into the bathroom.

35

Blam, the shotgun blast whizzes past my face! I jar awake from the violent reoccurring nightmare from my days as a bartender in Beverly Hills. In it, I watch a little guy get shot down by two cops after he nearly kills me. It's both true and sad and never brightens my day.

It's dark and all the lights are off in my apartment. Chilling. I'm in bed and all my clothes are off, too. I'm not sure how long I've been sleeping. I can't see a clock. It takes me a moment to realize that I'm on the wrong side of the bed, and the ringing in my aching head is actually the phone. I try to move my jaw and it's still very stiff. The sliding door is open again. The machine picks up before I get to it in the kitchen. There are five messages on the machine. I do my best to clear my head. I'm pretty sure I'm suffering from a concussion. My outgoing message takes but a few seconds and then I hear barking coming through my machine. I don't find this funny, because I know the barking is coming from Bubba, who sounds generally scared. Hey, it's Hollywood out here and even dogs have agents. So I listen until the barking stops and a female voice comes on, even more scared than Bubba.

"Picasso? Pick up the phone, he knows you're home."

So I pick up the phone. "That's a neat trick. How'd you get him to bark scared on cue like that?"

"Shut up and listen," she says. "Victor wants the diamonds."

"Could you stop yelling, I'm a wreck. And drop the over acting? I'm recording this and plan to play it on Youtube."

"I'm trying to help you."

"Let me make this clear. You do anything to Bubba or my Corsa and I will hunt you two down to the ends of this earth."

"Look, you want to see your dog again or don't you?"

"Of course I do."

"Then give Victor the diamonds."

"What makes you think I have them?"

"Because we know you do."

"Well, I don't."

"You talk in your sleep."

"I also snore and get erections. What does that tell you?"

"Look, smartass, where are the diamonds?"

"As far as I know, you've got them." This is the truth, so I say it with great conviction.

"I do not."

"How do I know that? Maybe you're just playing Victor against me so he won't kill you before you make a run for it."

"Because, if I had the diamonds, I'd be long gone already."

"So would I."

"All we want are the diamonds."

"All I want is what is owed me. Back rent plus property damages, and legal fees. Not to mention probably some new medical bills."

"So you have the diamonds."

"The answer's still no.

"Do you know where they are?"

"You're getting warmer."

"I knew it. Where are they?"

"Bring back my dog and car and I'll show you."

"Meet me."

"You, not Victor."

"How do I know you won't try to hurt me?"

"Considering the look of my friend J.J., I'd say I should be asking that question."

"Is he okay?"

"According to a note I'm reading, he's at UCLA Emergency Room getting his nose put back in place and his ear re-attached. But that's from awhile ago so he may be dead by now, as far as I know."

"I told him not to turn around."

"Where do you want to meet?"

"You know a place, some place public?"

I turn on the kitchen light to see the wall clock. "It's 1:30 in the morning. There's a coffee shop in Studio City open all night."I still feel groggy, and I'm sure I'm not thinking straight.

"The one just east of Coldwater Canyon on Ventura Boulevard, across from the Sportsmen's Lodge?"

"Bingo."

"I go there all the time."

"So what? You want to meet there or not?"

"You don't have to be a prick."

"You want your diamonds?"

"Do you want your dog, big mouth? Then be there, five minutes." Click, she hangs up.

I honestly want to hurt this woman. She's a turn-on and a turn-off all at the same time. If she doesn't bring my car I can't give her the diamonds. On the other hand, I'm the only human that knows we are meeting other than maybe Victor. Bubba knows, but as smart as he is, he might not be any good on the witness stand.

I have five minutes to drive from Sherman Oaks to Studio City. Even in midday I can make it, so I take a moment to jot a note to Erin and J.J., seeing they are the only friendly people on earth who suspect I'm not a murderer. Maybe I should call MacAroy and Tucker and let them know where the diamonds are.

Where had the day gone? At the last minute I decide to see who called. The first message is from Erin, letting me know that UCLA has decided to keep J.J. in for observation. They're checking to see if he has a fractured skull. Great! This should be cheap. As far as Erin is concerned, she came back with Janet and helped me into bed. I was on the living room floor. But isn't sure if I would remember because I hadn't fully waken up. She is right about that. She had Janet and her boyfriend come back to check on me a couple of times and get my driver's license and social security number for the hospital billing and make sure I was still alive. They didn't want to stay because they were afraid. I don't recall any of this. I need to see someone about my head. I feel dazed and confused, as I think this all out.

The next message is from J.J. wanting me to call the hospital to okay some billing because the doctors were giving him a hard time about me picking up the tab without signing anything. He must have called while Erin was on her way back to UCLA.

The third message is from my friendly Detective Tucker, who said he had come by to ask me some questions and wanted to know if I had skipped town already. He wishes that I ain't dead, and hangs up. I'm almost touched by his concern. Heaven forbid I should screw up their case by becoming a victim while they still need me as a witness, perpetrator, or schlemiel fall guy.

The last message is me talking to Stacey. I decide to save all the messages and listen to them again. Stacey's message may be helpful in keeping me out of the holding pin and away from Mooky. Mooky? Why am I thinking of Mooky? I suddenly realize I don't have a car. There is no way I can get to Studio City in five minutes without a car. I use *69 and get Stacey's voicemail.

"Stacey, it's Jozeph...I can't...."At this juncture of the game I suddenly know I'm not alone, and why I'm thinking of Mooky. He is mind controlling me, and standing in the light of my opening refrigerator.

36

"Stacey, please don't hurt my dog. I can't make it to the coffee shop...."Mooky holds his finger up to his lips.

"Tell her you're heading there. I got a car."

"Never mind, Stacey, I'm on my way." I hang up.

"How's your head?"

"Hurts. How's the eyes?"

"Blurry. Do that again, I will wad you up into a ball."

"Stay out of my face."

"You talk in your sleep."

"I've been told."

"And you snore."

"You were in here watching me? That's creepy."

"What's this about the blues?"

The blues again. Mary called them that. "Mooky, look...."

"You can't hide anything from me, Jozeph."

"Okay, what do you want?"

"The blues, of course. Isn't that what we all want?"

"Who are you?"

"No one knows for sure," he says.

"You wouldn't by any chance speak French?"

"You are a smart one." He rattles something off in fluent French. Then Italian, Portuguese, Spanish, some kind of Arabic, and Russian, when he starts on Chinese or Japanese, I put my hands over my ears.

"Look, Mooky, or whoever you are, all I want is my dog and car back and some back rent, plus expenses if possible."

"Then we better move out.

37

We take Moorpark up to Coldwater Canyon, and hang a quick right. Mooky has a nice black Cadillac. It looks new. I don't bother to ask where or how he got it.

"You want to tell me what I'm mixed up in?"

"Not really. Where are the blues?"

"When I get my dog and car back, I'll tell you."

"I looked in your car, I didn't find them. So where are they?"

"Ahhh…."

"You mess with me, I will kill you, Picasso."

"Anyone hurts my dog, you'll have to."

"What's with you and this dog?"

His mind control doesn't understand about a man and his dog?

"Okay, so he's your best friend, so what. He's a mutt."

"He's a French poodle, and an innocent bystander to all this. I'd just as soon kill you all than let anything happen to him."

"All dogs are a blend of something down from wolves. They're mutts, believe me. Just like you humans."

"Who are you and how did you get in and out of that cell?"

"You don't want to know who I am, Picasso. You just want to give me those blues."

"Then tell me this. Are you a good guy or a bad guy?"

"You've been writin' for Hollywood too long. In the real universe there is no difference."

"I prefer the uncolorized view of life."

"Then let it rest that I'm neither."

"So you don't work for or against any governments? You freelance."

"How much do you know about the Hope Diamond?"

"I know a French merchant traveler, Jean Boptiste Tavernier, supposedly bought the diamond in India."

"Supposedly is right."

"You saying he stole it?"

"I wasn't there, now was I? It came from the Kollur mine in Golconda, India. They think."

"Originally about 112 carats, plus."

"Plus 3/16. Now about 45.52 carats. Let me guess, you saw this on the Discovery Channel."

"It so happens."

"There were several cuts made over the years."

"Which cuts do I have?"

"No one knows yet. You get a good look at them in the light?"

"Yes."

"D'un beau violet or a dark grayish blue?"

"Whatever."

"Did you ever see it glow in the dark?

"Yeah, right."

"The facets that some of us are looking for would exhibit an unusually intense and strongly colored type of luminescence after exposure to short wave ultraviolet light. See anything like that?"

"There was something unusual about them. It was more of a empowering feeling than a look."

"Good. Do you know who was found with the diamonds?"

"Somebody is all I know."

"Then maybe I won't have to kill you after all."

"Is this what it's all about, what cut was found, and the body?"

"It could create an international incident. We don't want that."

"Who are we?"

"You and me right now."

"Did these have weird effects on that dog in my building?"

"What did you see?"

"Appearing and disappearing, and it walked through walls."

"So you really think you saw any of that?"

"No, I'm starting to think I imagined it. If that's what you want to hear and it will keep you from killing me or Bubba. But the dog was very strange, evil looking when it first turned his eyes on me."

"I wouldn't go around repeating that."

"Why not?"

"Because you sound like one of those nerds who pay to attend all those science fiction conventions, just so they can dress in stupid costumes outside their basements."

"So, this is all sci-fi? And none of it real."

"We hope so."

"You don't want them to be Hope chips with some magical bad luck powers?"

"Some mysteries are better left unsolved. I get paid either way."

"To bring the diamonds back to which government?"

"That's where you get it all wrong, Picasso. So just sit back and do as I tell you. Where should we park?"

"Hang a right here. Can they see in these windows?"

"No."

"Then pull up and park on this side. We'll wait for them."

"My guess is they are waiting for us."

"You want to expose yourself?"

"Only when I have to. You into that?"

"Shut up."We sit at the corner across from the coffee shop, watching traffic for a short while. I hear myself talking just to make sure Mooky is alive. "We've got people wanting to expose these chips and those who don't, am I right?"

"Well, you're not wrong."

"Which side does Victor, Stacey or Mary fall on?"

"Does it matter?"

"Not to me, as long as I get my dog and car."

"Your dog doesn't look unhappy."

"Where? Look at him. Tell me you wouldn't kill for that dog."

"Don't go squirrelly on me, Picasso. Okay, here's the deal. You go in and get your dog. Tell her where the blues are, and take your car home. I'll deal with it from there."

"Will you kill her?"

"Only if I need to."

"Who killed Simpkins and the Essinola family? You or Castro?"

"You want the dog or not?"

"Is the diamond in the Smithsonian really the same diamond Tavernier sold to King Louis XIV in 1669 for nobility? Is that what this is all about?"

"You ask too many questions for your own good."

"Are you working with or against Mary Devonshire?"

"Neither."

"Whose body were the diamonds found on?"

"Get out of my car. You got two seconds. One, two...."

"Okay, okay...just tell me one thing. What are these diamonds worth to you?"

"Your last breath."

"Okay, I get your point." I reached out my hand to shake his. He hesitates, setting his now simmering, otherworldly yellowish eyes on my extended hand before sticking his out to shake. Yellow eyes? Mary had those same alien looking yellowish eyes while threatening to kill me. So, I poke them!

Humanly good.

38

I'm not sure why or why not. It just comes over me. But I get him point blank. He lets out a very strange painful scream mixed with who knows what kind of language and pounds on the steering wheel before pointing his gun in my direction. Only I am already out the door. A window in a Corvette parked behind me burst into action as it shatters into the front seat setting off the alarm. There's no way his silencer can muffle that. I am behind his car and halfway across the street by the time Stacey sees me coming. She looks from the honking car to me running towards her. There is only one way out of the coffee shop, the front door, so I wave for her to come out. She has Bubba in her arms. She runs out, jumps the white metal railing, and sprints to catch me. We make it around the corner but we still have no coverage as the windows from the coffee shop tumble down behind us.

Whoever or whatever Mooky is, I'm sure shooting at me out in the open isn't part of his underworld agenda, but I pissed him off. Maybe I did poke Mooky to keep him from killing Stacey. He denied it, but he and his yellow eyed friend, Mary, can screw off.

The two people smoking in the outside chairs scream and dive for cover, pulling a table over top of them. Behind us I hear the screeching of wheels, then wham! Metal on metal. I think Mooky made a u-turn and hit someone's car.

I don't bother turning around to see if Stacey is keeping up with me because Bubba passes me running like a poodle out of food. "Holy chest pains, Dogman, the sky is falling!" One thing Bubba doesn't like, and that's acorns or alien tiles crashing and smashing from up above. Near the next corner, I see my car is parked in the red zone out front of a two story office building.

I yell back at Stacey to see if she's got my keys, and she does, so when I get to my car I start yelling for Bubba to stop. He doubles back and wants in my car real bad. So do I. So I dive in behind the wheel. Bubba jumps in and Stacey tosses the keys and flops into the passenger side.

I start the car but don't pull away. Cigarette smoke? I look in the rearview mirror to find Victor sitting up in the backseat with a cig stabbing out of his half moon grin with his mean penetrating yellow eyes faintly lit from the street. Yellow eyes again.

"Surprise, surprise," he says.

39

What do I do in this situation? Someone who I know will kill us all is right behind me. But someone else who will kill just me is even closer. Who do I worry about the most? Victor is not a happy man. His face is badly beaten. I don't have time to ask him why.

"Move the car!"

"I think we should wait for Mooky."

"Move the car, or I'll shoot your stupid dog!"

Bubba seems to know his life is in danger. He looks at me, "Holy gas guzzler, Dogman, what are you waiting for?"

"Throw the cigarette out." I'm insane from the blows to my head. No other explanation. But my last breath won't be of second hand tobacco from this creep.

"What? Move this car!"

"What's the matter with you, Picasso, he'll kill you."

"Fine, and Mooky, who by the way, is right behind us, will kill the two of you." I hit a button on the dash and my top starts to electronically fold back. It cost me a fortune to get it fixed but at the moment, it seems worth it. "There, I made it easy for you."

"I've got a gun."

"You also stink. When was the last time you brushed your teeth?" He sticks the gun in my face as I turn to him. "Here, give me the damn cigarette." He looks to Stacey for moral support, as I reach for the cig. When he locks eyes with her, I poke them! And grab the gun. It goes off, blasting a hole in my windshield and Bubba upchucks right there on the carpet. My ears are already ringing but I yank the gun forward as he pulls the trigger again. This time taking out my rearview mirror.

I'm going deaf and broke by the bullet here. But I get the gun away and I whack him with it. Stacey lashes at me in protest with her broken nails and I whack her with it too. I don't care. I'll whack just about anyone at this given moment. Bubba's looking at me as though he's lost every inch of civilized notion about me. He's scared and not so sure he likes me. I suppose he has no idea I'm doing this as much for his safety as mine. All he can tell is I'm making a lot of noise and whacking people. My top finishes folding down into the boot. I look into the side mirror and I can see Mooky running up the street. His eyes are barely open. He reaches about three and a half car lengths behind us when, "Duck!" Zip! Crack! Another slug kicks through what's left of my windshield.

Stacey and Castro are hugging the carpet as I scrunch down into the seat, throwing the Corvair into gear. Only, I don't see the car, because I'm not looking and it slams into my rear end, doing Buddha knows what to my taillights. Man, when this is over I'll beat some collective butts. The car screeches to a stop and a teenage princess yells for me to stop, adding high pitched screams, as Mooky throws her out and jacks her bashed in car. A hit and run for my life.

I'm speeding down Ventura, all four carburetors breathing wide open, and my broken exhaust howling. I zoom past a famous deli, an office supply and the smell of a yellow hotdog train, trying to make the next green light at Whitsett doing sixty in third.

My saving grace is that I'm now armed, still breathing, driving my car away with my dog, and hoping I have the diamonds everyone wants still hidden in my trunk. The thought that Mooky couldn't find them perplexes me in thinking that Victor and Stacey don't have them either. That only leaves Mork and Mindy of the LAPD and their fishy eyed friend, the assistant DA.

Shifting into fourth and hitting eighty then eighty-five, I'm across Whitsett Avenue under the yellow light and making Laurel Canyon's light in a blink of an eye. I'm actually hoping someone pulls me over.

In front of an all night restaurant, Victor sits up in the backseat and stupidly tells me to head to the airport. Like, which one: Santa Monica, Van Nuys, Burbank, John Wayne, LAX?

I slam on the breaks, swerving around a Jeep pulling out. "Shut up. We're calling those cops and let you work it out with the DA."

"Don't be stupid, Picasso, those two cops and that woman are as crooked as they come. Head to the Van Nuys Airport. We've got a plane waiting for us," she says.

"That may be so, but I've got a jail cell waiting for me unless you cruds come up with a magical explanation to keep me out of it."

"Just hand over the blues and I'll deal with them," Victor says.

A wash of yellow fluid, thick as molasses, comes flooding from the back seat. I don't have to look to know that part of whatever Victor was, is now in my front seat. Bubba is completely crazed. The only thing holding him in the car is Stacey, who is so far down in the seat that I'm wondering if maybe she's a contortionist. Whatever this sticky stuff is that's all over us isn't human blood. The look on her face is so mortified that I'm sure she had no idea her ex-husband wasn't from this planet. I make a drastic left onto Radford Avenue, forcing a gray convertible Mustang to make a screeching turn into a fast food, while what's left of us head towards CBS Studio Center.

I figure the first cops I'll see will be the security at the booth there. When I make the turn Victor slumps against my seat and slides down in between them. There's so much alien yuck all over my car I don't think it's ever coming out.

I make another drastic right into the lot, clipping the mailbox, and blast past the guard gate on the exit side and keep on moving. The guard comes out to watch us speed by. I weave through the office buildings and parking spaces then pull to a stop in the parking lot facing the stages. Not much is happening, a few transportation, grips, and electricians working the grave shift.

I bound out, and get behind the car. I'm waiting for Mooky. The CBS Studio Center employees are waiting for someone to yell CUT! But no one does. And Mooky doesn't show. So Stacey, Bubba, and I wait on the farthest edge of our lives for whatever happens next.

40

Within thirty seconds that seems like an hour, about ten LAPD squad cars fill the void between the buildings. All of a sudden I'm the bad guy with a guest role on "This is Your Last Breath."It takes about ten seconds and I have twenty young muscular men and women armed to the teeth pointing their arsenal at me, and a helicopter's searchlight pointing me out. I'm outgunned. I'm so key lit by cop lights I'm ready for my close up. We're like shooting night for day, and the scene about to be shot is me. It takes me a split second to realize that video camera lights are everywhere. I'll be damned if I'm not on COPS or Dumbest Criminals or something. At the moment, I'm despondent. Then I suddenly realize that this is a good thing, not a bad thing, if I want to stay alive long enough to explain any of this weird stuff to the media and beyond. And I do, even if I don't know how.

I also don't want to move too fast. No need for anyone to make wrong assumptions as to what I'm doing holding a gun pointing in their direction with a shivering redhead in my front seat and most of her yellow blooded ex-husband's forehead on my dash. Especially since she spent the night at my place and a dead guy already ended up in my refrigerator.

Next thing I know, Bubba jumps up onto the backseat, jumps down, then takes off running through the jungle of blue pant legs. I want to go after him but I can't move. I'm petrified at best.

"What'd you let him go for?"

"He bit me!"

"Come on, Bubba?"

"Well, he did."

"You, behind the car, drop the gun and move to the back of the vehicle. On the ground, face down. NOW! You, in the vehicle, drop whatever you have and come out of the vehicle and lay face down in front of the car. RIGHT NOW."

I can barely hear anything but ringing. I drop the gun and move to the back of the car. I get down on all fours and gently stretch out. I'm very deliberate with my movements and as gentle to myself as I can be because I'm getting the feeling that for the next few hours this is the last of the mercy I will experience. I can't see, but Stacey must be on the ground in front of my car. Within seconds of me resting my face on the asphalt, I get a good sucker jab from a knee against my spine. My hands are grabbed nearly simultaneously, twisting my arms out of my shoulder sockets, and I get cuffed, as someone else kicks my gun away and picks it up with a pencil.

"I can explain this."

"You have the right to remain silent...."

I'm starting to think these words will end up as my epithet so I stop listening. My mind is on Bubba and what is about to happen to him out here in the wild of Studio City. Bubba has no idea where he is. He has no idea that these men and women in blue, though they might not seem like it to him, are actually the civilized guys and that they are ultimately here to help us. I can't imagine that these nice kind folks want to hear, no less believe, my tale of the "Un beau Violet" that was once owned by King Louis XIV. Particularly the part on how I happened to find what is believed to be cuttings from it stuck in dog droppings in one of my apartments. And that they may or may not disprove the authenticity of the Hope Diamond in the Smithsonian, because I think aliens are looking for them.

The cops are talking to Stacey, and she's telling them something through a fist full of tears. About what I don't know, but no one is talking politely to me, yet. I don't suppose, by any fat chance, she's telling them good things about me.

"Would you like to know more about the alien body in my car?"

"Shut up," said the she-cop with her knee in my back.

"The body is Victor Castro who may have killed four of my tenants, he's a yellow..." Stars flashed inside my head. I'm really getting tired of this whole thing. I know if she just takes the time to listen to me, she'll understand that I'm not alone in this deal. I'm not too thrilled that everyone seems so concerned about Miss Red over there who is putting all her acting talents to the test. And no one is even paying attention to the dead body in my car. I can imagine the twisted tale of how I've managed to kill her beloved husband. Who's to say the gun I have my fingerprints on didn't split his head wide open? Other than the fact that I was driving at the time like an insane person, and the bullet was coming from behind him. And what came out of him is all over me and my dash is yellow and not red. But who is to say? It is Stacey's word against mine. Not that I can tell from the hubbub if she's given them an earful about me or not. Though every once in awhile, the cops listening to her woes, crane back to look at the lowlife face down on the asphalt.

I look up to catch a good view of my tender face in the chrome cup of my right rear wheel. Wait a minute, the nasty yellowish yuck that I was covered in is gone. What? I don't have a trace of it on me from what I can see of my refection in both the chrome wheel cup and bent exhaust pipe. This can't be good.

If I could just get this person on top of me to listen, I know she could see that the guy in the car is dissipating quickly or something like that. If she sees it in time I could explain about this Mooky character shooting him and convince them all that I'm not the slime bag murderer the media has made me out to be. But every time I even look like I'm about to say something, I get an enormous pressure on my spine that all but makes me black out. To make matters worse, lying on my bruised face like this is killing me. And my nose is starting to itch from the valley dust on the asphalt.

Finally a cop with shinny shoes comes over to stands above me. He turns to look across my seats at another cop on the other side. "Didn't she say there was a guy still in the car?" I hear the cop ask.

"Nothing I see," the other cop answers, "some clothes is all and that dog that took off. His registration says he's Jozeph Picasso."

"That Jozeph Picasso?"

"Yeah. It's him alright."

"Put cuffs on her. Don't tell her anything. Get her in the car."

"What about this one."

"Take Picasso downtown. Someone wants to see him ASAP."

"Roger that. On your feet," the she cop holding me down says.

I get pulled to my feet and yanked about. I would begin to regret ever buying my building, only it's too late, I've already gone beyond regretting that halfway through remodeling the damn thing.

Somehow I have to convince this woman that my dog needs me. That I'm really just a civilized writer who has recently quit smoking. That I'm desperately in need of sitting in front of my computer and getting work done. After having a stimulating cup of coffee and a nice quite newspaper read. I know she will never understand. I fight to look into my car as I go by. Nothing. Not a trace of Victor other than his clothes and shoes. I try to hesitate enough to lean in and get a better look but I get yanked nearly out of my own shoes.

"Move it."

Do you believe in aliens?"I ask the she-cop.

"Do you believe in tasers?"

I guess she doesn't. Dissipating yellow eyed aliens, this is getting really out there. Mook and Mary are likely more of the same of whatever Victor was. And they all want those stones. The blues. Well until someone else claims having them, I've got them, and in more ways than stones. How I barter my way out of this is any human's game. Because somehow keeping them away from Mook and Mary is probably the only thing keeping me alive. How that is happening, is beyond my imagination. So if I'm about to see Ms. Devonshire again, it will be a very interesting reunion, if not deadly.

41

There are other moments in my past life where hitting rock bottom wasn't quite as retched on my psyche as being dragged along its muddy underbelly until the vision of ever rising up to the surface again vanishes from sight. The thought of moving nowhere fast sets in, as my past, present and future realities collide. I'd say that bedrock bottom is just about where my lifeline's been trolling for about three hours. After they stripped me of my civilian clothing, they took several blood tests. And scanned me with something I've never seen before. Then they shackled both my hands and feet. I'm now wearing starchy prison blues. I'm connected to a shiny metal chair in a sterile looking grayish room with light coming from somewhere that I can't tell. There's also a shiny metal table. No one's come to speak to me since. I haven't talked to my lawyer. Technically, I'm not under arrest. If this isn't parallel to being a houseguest in a psych ward, then I am dead. And right now dead doesn't seem so bad.

Another half hour passes, and I'm just sitting here, calmly shackled, when the door I didn't see slides open behind me. It's Mary Devonshire supposedly from the DA's office. She's now in a doctors jacket and an expensive turtleneck sweater, but the three-inch heals are a nice touch. Very odd and un-district-attorney-like.

"Where am I?"

"Someplace quiet. Don't worry, you're in no danger."

"And I thought you came in to slap me around again."

"I just might."

"Now we're getting somewhere."

"Where are you from?"

"Can we cut through the nonsense? You've taken my blood. You've scanned my insides. I'm guessing you know everything you need to know about me. So let's move on to what you really want."

"The question is, what do you really want from all this?"

"I want to scratch my nose, and beat my head on that wall over there until I croak for getting myself into this mess."

"Are you that uncomfortable?"

"Can I call you Mary?"

"If it makes you feel better."

"Mary, I'd like to punch you right in the chops. That's how uncomfortable I feel. No gender bender, just whack you in the kisser, because you're the only one here."

"That's why we have you shackled."

"Fine. Now what do you want?"

"I want the blues."

"The blues. I want my car fixed, my building repaired and the money the Essinolas stole from me. I want to be examined by my doctor to see if I have a concussion or if my jaw is broken."

"I see. You're not making friends here. You have no idea what you're into, do you?"

"I know my car is trashed, my poodle is gone, my apartment building is quickly emptying, my good name is smeared, and people are acting very strange around me. And some guy named Mooky is trying to kill me."

"Mooky?"

"Why don't we all stop pretending we don't know Mooky."

"What does he look like?"

"He's the guy I poked the other night in the holding cell. He's the guy who miraculously showed up in my kitchen. He's the guy in the stolen SUV shooting at me. Mook's also the guy who killed the whack job who exploded into a yellowish mass of mush on my dashboard. Which by the way, somehow dissipate before the cops could get a chance to ID him. He's the guy who also calls those diamonds the blues. And has weird yellowish eyes when he gets angry. Just like you. So come on, admit it, you know him. You sent him to kill me."

"I see."

"Look, I've really got to go...you know...."

42

When the door slides open, they've left the chains on but have taken the chair off me and let me enter by myself carrying it. Mary is waiting for me, still in the pumps and still in the jeans and white coat, legs dangling from the table. I'm not sure what to expect. Except now she's armed.

"Sit down."

I put the chair down but don't sit.

"You know we had to take care of some very revealing footage of your stupid little escapade?"

"Who are you really?"

"Mary Devon...."

"Cut the bull, Mary. Or whatever you are. This isn't a jail. What are you? CIA, FBI, MOB? ET?"

"You don't need to know about me. You're here so I can help you, is all that's important."

"Is all? What have you done with my clothing? Who's listening? What is Mooky? Who put you up to this? What are the blues? And who's singing them besides you, Mook, and the dead bodies piling up around me?"

"Knowing will not set you free, trust me."

"Why take my blood? What are you looking for?"

"Routine checks that we do on all visitors here."

"MacAroy and Tucker, they singing along with us?"

"They are cooperating, under orders."

"With whom, from whom?"

"Jozeph...."

"I want out of here, right now."

"Then give us what we want."

"So you can kill me afterwards? Is that it, take me someplace no one will find me for a very long time? You're working with him. That's how he got in my cell. You, Tucker, and MacAroy, scheming to get me killed. I want my lawyer right now. I want to talk to the media." I pick up the chair. She points her gun at me.

"This is crazy."

"We don't want to hurt you, Jozeph."

I start to yell, "You and the yellow eyed Mook on the same side? Maybe from the same planet? You want your blues? You better come clean with me because otherwise you can forget about getting them before I sing to the LA Times or TMZ and the rest of those blood rags. We're not alone here in Hollywood. They'll have a field day with the sad lyrics I've already written down. I...."

"You've written things down?"

"I write every damn thing down, make copies, take photos and send them to myself. With what I have, this will go viral in seconds."

"You mind not yelling and using foul language? I find it annoying and vulgar."

I raise my voice even louder. "Too bad, bitch. You can take your spaceship and shove it!"

She pulls the trigger. The gun makes no sound. Not even a flash of light, but my arm stings. "Ah, crap....." She zaps me again, just below the spot of the first time. "Damn...what is that thing?"

"The next yell or foul language out of you, you'll find out."

"Okay, I get it. Am I bleeding badly?"

"Hardly...this time."

"You can tell that from way over there?"

"Flesh wounds."

"Okay, you've got my attention."

"Where are the blues?"

"Where's my car?"

"We've gone through the car?"

Surely if everyone's searched the car they looked in the spot where I left them, in the hidden compartment behind the headlights in a silicone filled spare magnetic key box. They'd sense the energy as much as J.J. and I did. And know what it meant more than us. Does someone else already have them? Who else is involved here? The cops, Tucker and MacAroy, could they have figured it all out first?

"I just want to know if my car's safe."

She studies my face. "Your car's in a safe place."

"What about my dog, Bubba?"

"I have no idea."

"Okay, here's the deal. The same deal I made with Stacey. I want my dog and my car back. Only I want my car fixed this time. Along with my apartment building, all losses, and I'll tell you where the chips are."

"But we don't have your dog."

"Then you better hope I find him."

"He's only a poodle."

"He's only my best friend."

"If you don't have the diamonds. You are of no value to us."

"Just take me to my car. I'll call you when I find Bubba."

"And if you don't?"

"No deal."

"It's not working out that way."

I open my mouth to yell and she shoots me again. Without the opportunity to flinch this time I get a better picture that she's using what appears to be a perfectly normal nine millimeter, but somehow isn't. I see not a flash, it's more of a quivering vapor bolt. Definitely an advanced laser, yet the effect is very much the same as a human made gun. Whatever, I'm bleeding badly this time. I plop down on my ass, my head swirling not from seeing so much of my own blood but from getting a distinct whiff of my own skin curdling. I'm not in immediate pain. More like an itch. But if the sadistic, deadly yellow gleam in Mary's eyes is any indication of what fate has in store for me, I'm about to encounter Mr. Pain.

43

So, that's how I got here. Patched up and blindfolded. Shackled hands to feet. I'm on my knees, about to greet death. No one will be framed for killing the likes of me, because no one will find me for a very-very long time. Just like Mary promised. I'll be hidden deep down, feeding whatever crawls at the depth of the hole dug before me. How poetically pathetic.

"You believe me now, Picasso?"

"The Mook?"

"The one."

"Where am I?"

"God's country."

"This doesn't feel like Bel Air to me."

"You got a smart mouth for a man in a whole lot of trouble."

"Am I about to die?"

"Of course you are."

"Even though you don't have the blues yet?"

"If you're dead, they stay lost, so we done our job."

"But they're not lost. Just hid real well."

"Same thing."

"They'll turn up again."

"If they do, I'll be back."

"If they do, you might be dead."

"It doesn't work that way."

"According to Mary, or whatever her name is, it does. She thinks something is helping me hide them. She thinks it's you."

Mooky stays silent for a while. I know he's thinking because he's mind controlling me. Right?

"You still there?"

"What'd she say to you?"

"Asked me what I want. I told her. Now I'm here with you."

"But what'd she say? About me?"

"To me, nothin'. Pretended not to know you, actually. To the guy driving that car, now he's the one."

"The one what?"

"Hey, you're the mind reader, right. You're supposed to know all, be all, the Mook, the man, in your face, in your mind, you tell me."

"What'd she say, Picasso? I'm gettin' pissed."

"I didn't get the whole thing. Something about the guy in my car you shot. And something that's keeping her from sensing the blues."

"Yeah, so? What about it?"

"Just that the trail ends with you now."

"What'd she mean by that?"

"What does it sound like? She thinks you're helping me."

"Sounds like bull to me."

"It sounds like she doesn't trust you, Mook. You playing both sides and all. You the Mook, the mystery salad bar man, the fall guy."

"Nobody crosses me."

"Like to see you tell her that in that exact tone."

"You talkin' crazy now or what?"

"Inside joke. Why are we here?"

"You're to tell me where the chips are or I kill you. When you tell me, I kill you anyway."

"Is there a hole in front of me?"

"Yeah, there's a deep hole."

"You dig it?"

"I fill 'em, not dig 'em."

"Well, you're filling this one, personally."

"With your body."

"Our bodies."

"You got it wrong."

"I got three laser wounds from a very unearthly weapon that says I'm very right."

"I see them, so."

"This Mary chick, she's an alien like you, isn't she?"

146

"Crazy talk again." Mooky racks a shell into a gun's chamber.

"Are there satellites that can pinpoint us right now?"

Mooky goes quiet again.

"You are an informed being, Mook. So you know if what we're doing right now matters so much, then you know someone's watching and something's listening. If I tell you where those chips are, someone will beat you to them. And that someone will put you in this hole with me. Because that someone won't want to share with you. And that someone is Mary whatever she is. You'll be singing harmony blues with me. This hole will be our closing night. If you believe she put these holes in me in such an orderly manner, you know she's capable of standing hundreds of yards from here and still drop us both like bucks at a salt lick."

"Shut up."

"Think about it."

"I'm thinkin'."

"There any hills around here?"

"Shut up."

A sudden energy zips by my head so fast I can feel it through my blindfold! Next thing I know I am falling into the world of pain.

44

A lot of it. My already sore face kisses the bottom of the grave, a deep one, with a dank smell. No one is expected to dig me up until one hundred years from now when our so-called civilization finally creeps out to wherever we are. And some backhoe digs down and splits my skull. I'll end up in a morbid murder museum as a display of twenty-first century patsy, sucker, fall guy, and Hollywood punching stunt dummy. A dark reminder of what becomes of an unwanted filmmaker in that town. All I need to prove the point is a dozen or two shovels of sand and a permanent laser wound or two.

I try rolling over and I find that Mooky is straddling me.

"Take this blindfold off."

"Not yet."

"Help me find my dog. I'll give you the chips."

"Someone's firing some very sophisticated weapons at us."

"I can't tell... am I hit?

"You're alive for now."

"They missed their chance. Now you'll have to cover your ass and get to the chips first."

"Where are they?"

"Come on, Mook...do I seem so stupid?"

"Picasso. You piss me off with this game of yours."

"Really? You make me happy to be alive, Mook."

"Get up. We're not sure why we can't find them, or what's helping you hide them. But it ain't me. So get up and give me those blues before we find out. Or this could end up bad news for all of us."

"I would, but the bridge of my nose is jammed to this gravel wall." He pulls me up and takes off the blindfold. At first I'm not sure what to think. I am making it up, I thought, this conspiracy theory of mine, but sometimes truth is sadder than reality. Mook's trench coat is covered by dark yellowish, matted yuck that I assume is whatever his blood is supposed to be because his left shoulder droops as though it's been severed from his spine. "Jesus."

"You hear anything?"

"Just your gasping."

"Good. When you stop hearin' me you're on your own. Can you run fast?"

"Not like this."

"Stand over there. Hold your hands out."

"Wait a minute. This is eye level to my balls here."

"You got to get to my car. It's about thirty yards, that way, and you can't do it like that. So close your eyes, you puss."

I hold my eyes tighter than humanly possible; my hands out as far as the chains to my ankles will allow me. With one shot my hands are free from my feet. With another I can separate my feet and a third gives me back my reach. I grab Mooky's gun, and push him down in the hole.

"You gonna leave me here?"

"I should."

"Yeah, I suppose you should. Only you're not a killer, Picasso, you're just a filmmaker. Fantasizing about killing ain't as real as pulling the trigger on a live target."

I point the gun at him. I want to pull the trigger. I want to split his eyebrows really, really bad, but I can't. I can't get myself to pull the trigger. I am a puss. If he'd been trying to kill me at that moment, maybe, most likely yeah, I'd pull the trigger. But watching him sit there in pain makes me feel for the Mook. Even if he's not human and some kind of alien mobster. I'll never make a good landlord. I lack the killer instinct.

"What should we do?"

"Wait for them to make a move."

"You could bleed to death by then."

"If I do, the keys are under the seat. Just kick dirt on me so the birds don't feast on my brains. I'll be all right if they find me in time."

"You in pain?"

"Payne is my middle name."

"How original. Look who's writing for Hollyworld now."

"William Payne Washington the Tenth. Mooky the Mook."

"What should I do with you if help comes?"

"UCLA Emergency. Check me in as William Payne Washington. They'll know what to do with me."

"You got a phone in the Cadillac, don't you?"

"Yeah. All that interactive computer junk. But don't use it. Use the cell on the seat. Dial 911*7."

"What're my chances of making it to the car?"

"Slim to you're out of your white boy head. But they'll be down here soon. If they ain't on their way now."

"Can they hear us?"

"Maybe not. They're up in the hill, where the sun sets."

"I'm not waiting for them down here. I'd rather die out there."

"Whatever. Just dial that number if you make it."

"What blood type are you?"

"They'll know."

"Are you really an alien, Mook?"

"Hey, you get me out of this, and some wildly important people will owe you big time. You'll be made for life."

"By whom or should I say what?"

"By me. By some of my friends."

"I believe some of your friends want us dead."

"Those aren't friends. Remember that, not mine and not yours. This is just business, freelance stuff. The car's plated to withstand anything including lasers. Get behind it, and stay there."

My arms are not at their full strength and I'm standing below eye level. Getting out of our grave isn't the easiest thing to do. "You got any suggestions on my getting out of here?"

Mook crawls onto his working hand and knees and looks up at me. "If you aren't able to walk over the dead to stay alive you'll never make it out of here. I heard King Louis the XVI say that to Marie Antoinette just before we cut off their heads."

"So you were there."

"In more ways than one."

Mooky has a way with words. He's also full of it.

45

A swan dive into desert growth is always fun under starlight. I can't hear the laser shots or where they are coming from but I don't need that incentive to pick me up and make me dash for the Cadillac. Once behind it I start counting body orifices. I have my own, plus the three Mary gave me, and a new one just above my ear that took about a quarter inch of hair off my scalp. Great, now I have a permanent bald spot. But I'm breathing. I force open the smashed in driver's door and get hit with the entails of whatever the Mook had been smoking. Great, he's stoned. I'm thinking of taking a hit myself but I already think governments and aliens are after me. So why bother?

Mooky's cell is on the seat. He yells for me to turn on the stereo so he can die to a beat. I turn the ignition on and a dead man's rap music blares. It's better than the sound of the lasers zipping off the other side of his Caddy. I grab his phone and sit inside the car hanging my head out the broken window with the phone, so I can hear. I dial 911*7 and a Ms. Blair comes on the line even before it rings. Now that's service.

I can hear clicking and then she comes back on to tell me that Mook and I are just west of Interstate Five overlooking a gravel pit, some scant twenty-five miles south of Bakersfield near the 99 Junction at Arvin. We turned left onto the first gravel road heading south into the mountains. We're at the end of it.

Man, I've got to get me one of these. I tell Ms. Blair what is taking place and that she should send a helicopter loaded with the Mook's blood type. She says no problem, Mr. Picasso, someone will be right there.

I look up into the sky and smile, mouthing the words thank you. And she says you're welcome and clicks off. 911*7? I got to remember that next time I get a flat. Big brother is watching and his name is Ms. Blair. Mook yells for the music to be turned up. So I do until the whole car is vibrating with dead man's music. Something about doin' it, killin' them and dyin' too young, a modern day, inner city love song. Something catchy I'm sure parents everywhere can't wait for their kids to hum around the house.

46

Within four minutes a normal sounding helicopter touches down, followed by five state trooper cars, lights flashing and sirens blaring, and dirt swirling everywhere. They huddle down behind their cars as I wave for them to take cover. I'm yelling what they need to hear but it's so noisy with the music, helicopter, and orders being yelled back and forth that they can't tell anything except there's a bleeding madman waving a gun at them and pointing to a hole. Just in case, they point their guns at me, yelling for me to get down in the dirt. I'm getting pretty good at this.

They move over and take the Mook's gun away from me. One of them gets up the nerve to investigate the hole and jumps down inside. He yells for the others and two of them jump out of the helicopter and head to the hole and the one inside lifts out the Mook, who for all practical reasons seems to be dead.

I tell them he is William Payne Washington, and that he wants to go to UCLA. This isn't a problem and within minutes, the Mook and I are airlifted out of there with one of the officers tagging along for the ride. He's got a note pad and starts asking me questions. The medical crew is attending to the Mook by hooking him up to a clear color IV and oxygen, making sure they stay between me and Mooky.

Mooky still appears out cold. But I glance around the guy hooking up the IV to see Mook when asked who he is, and he smiles at me. I don't know why, I don't owe the Mook anything, but I lie. I get the feeling they already know what he is and maybe this is a test to see if I'll keep my mouth shut. So I tell him that William and I were abducted at the Mobil Station while in route to LA and robbed, tortured and shot. I don't say anything about the people up in the hills. I don't know who or why they were doing this to us. The gun? I tell him William had wrestled it away from one of them and that is how we got away. The shackles and the prison blues? I tell him they were put on me while I was unconscious from the blows I took to the head, so I'm not so sure why.

The cop looks closely at my bruised face and smiles at me like he knows I'm making it all up. He obviously doesn't care as he takes off what's left of my shackles and handcuffs. As for what they looked like, I could only tell them that there was a man and a woman. She had jeans and high heels but the man I never got a good look at. The fact that Mook still has his wallet is a blank to me, and that I am getting tired and my head hurts. Not to mention I think I'm about to be sick from the air ride, so if he doesn't mind I'd like to sit quietly and suffer. He sits back, satisfied, writing in his little book. I look at the Mook, who is under from whatever they had given him.

"Will he live?"

"Mr. Washington will be just fine, Jozeph. You saved his life."

"Yeah, I'm a heck of a guy."

"He owes you big time."

"You have no idea."

The young medical guy looks at me blankly, so does the cop. Oddly, they are identical twins. I just smile and close my eyes. The only thing I'm not truly lying about is being sick. I fight back this urge as they move their attention to my wounds and dab at my scalp.

No mention of the Mook not having red blood, or that his is yellow. And now that we are up in the air, and I'm sitting back I suddenly realize that we are no longer in a normal sounding helicopter. I sit up with the thought of that helicopter hovering when I was looking for Bubba! We're in some kind of alien flying ship.

"It's okay, Jozeph," the officer assures me.

I look at the cop. "Are we...?"

"Just sit back and enjoy the ride," he says. "Few humans ever experience one of these, and live to tell about it."

Comforting.

47

At UCLA we land in what once again sounds like a real helicopter. We are inside within seconds of touchdown. The emergency room is waiting for us. It must be a slow night for them. I am taken to a small room where first a chubby young blond nurse who smells delicious because I'm so hungry comes in and takes vital information. A heart attack and the flu are not my problem. She makes note of my face bruises before leaving me there while I assume all the important surgeons are dealing with the Mook. Oddly, no one mentions my dirty prison blues again. I mean, I look like I dug my way out of death row.

I start to dose off when a sad faced surgeon with a long unpronounceable French name and matching nose comes in. He introduces himself in such a thick French accent tinged with something from northern Africa that I can't quite understand what he's telling me. He looks at me, standing close enough for me to smell the sour coffee on his breath. He rests his hand on my shoulder to draw me closer as he touches my face and scalp wounds with a sterile wet pad to remove any dirt. So I look past him into the hall for help and whom do I see, but my friends Tucker and MacAroy. They don't come in until the doctor is done fussing with me. I won't have nasty scarring is what I could grasp from him. Fine, I don't want any. I just want out so I can find my dog. After he leaves, Tucker and MacAroy come in like a couple of kids retrieving their ball from inside an old lady's house, hang dogging their heads, shoes shuffling, hoping I don't call their mothers.

"How ya feelin'?"

"I feel like calling Channel Seven."

"Don't blame you."

"You want to tell me what just happened?"

"We...that is, the two of us, made a mistake, is all."

"Is all?"

"Yeah, we were holdin' the assumption that we were under orders from city hall to go along with what Mary...."

"Or whatever her name is...."

"Yeah, there's that...."

"Who is she?"

"You don't know?"

"Of course not."

"We don't either."

"She said she was Mary Devonshire and we thought she was."

"Sure looked like her. And had all the right credentials."

"She tried to kill me."

"Yeah..."

"And the guy in the other room."

"What guy?"

"The Mook, William Payne Washington."

"Who?"

"Come on. The guy I was flown in with."

"You came in alone is what we heard."

"Bull. There were copter pilots, a cop and emergency guys."

"Picasso, you came in alone in an ambulance, no copter, no cop, just you and the two man crew. It's in your chart. There's no one else here but an overdose and some Mexican kid complaining about a bad crotch rash."

"Don't start this with me."

"Look for yourself."

I hop out of the bed they have me in and walk out into the hall. I look down into the room that I watched them take Mooky into and it is empty. I stop a young doctor and ask him where they took Mr. Washington and he looks at me like I've escaped from the mental ward.

I move over to a room full of people in blue pullovers, the night crew, and I look up on the surgery board and no Mr. Washington is written above my name. I turn to the people watching me and none of them seem to be the people that were there just ten minutes ago.

Tucker and MacAroy come up behind me. Maybe they'll take me back to the mental ward.

"Doc said you could go. You want a lift?" Tucker asks.

"I want some answers fist!"

"Well, we ain't got any of those. But if you want a lift we got one waiting out in the garage. Want it?" He asks.

"Yes, I want it. And I want to know where my car is."

"It's where you left it. In the studio parking lot," MacAroy says. "And they want you to remove it."

"What about my dog?"

"What about your dog?"Tucker asks.

"We don't know nothin' about your dog," MacAroy says.

"Is my life still in danger?"

"You tell us," Tucker says.

"You're the cops."

"You're the victim."

"You guys kill me."

"Better us than someone you don't know," MacAroy says.

"So where do we stand?"

"Right now, in the garage." Tucker's doesn't even smile.

"Boy, you guys need a new gag writer. I'm not available."

"We don't know much more than you," MacAroy says.

"Unless you want to tell us where the blues are," Tucker says.

"When I get my life back."

"Come on, Mac."

"What about my ride home?"

"Call a cab."

"What about all these yellow eyed aliens? Mary, Mooky and that Victor Castor guy? Don't you want to hear about any of that?"

"Why would we want to listen to your crazy-ass Hollywood imagination, Picasso?" MacAroy says.

"Because it's true? I came here in a spaceship. Mook had his shoulder severed by a laser and was bleeding yellow yuck all over the place. Look closely at my wounds. They're from some kind of an electromagnetic energy gun."

I pull off a gauze wrap on my arm and there's nothing there, just hair and undamaged skin. Not a scar or a scratch, nothing. I feel for my temple where I was grazed and the hair is back to where it was. I move my jaw, and feel the sore spots on my face and head. Nothing. I feel good. "What the heck?" I look at my reflection in a truck's side mirror and I've got a full head of hair. Not that I'm complaining, but damn it, I was hit just above the ear by an alien laser. "They must have healed me. Look, I don't have a scratch on me anymore. I feel great."

"Give me your agent's number."

"What for?"

"So I can tell them to drop your dumbass and send you packin'" MacAroy says.

"Hey, you both know damn well there's something weird about Mary Devonshire and who or what she really is. So don't try to demean LA's finest by pretending she's not something other than human. And don't pretend that there's not stuff happening right here in LA that we don't understand yet, because that's bull and you both know it."

"You're right, it is bull. And you're full of it, Picasso. So don't share your paranoid crazy imagination with us. We've got upstanding careers to consider. You got some proof of any of that stuff then hand it over to someone who cares. If you don't want to help us find those diamonds, then you and your imaginary alien friends are on your own, driftwood," Tucker says.

"See ya around," MacAroy says.

"I got your driftwood. You two guys are a couple of pricks."

"Maybe you'd like a ride back downtown with us?"

"People are dying and disappearing all around me. Don't I warrant some protection?"

"When you deserve a warrant, we'll be glad to serve it to you."

I can't believe this. The two prods get in their smelly car and leave me standing at the emergency door sucking in ambulance fumes. I'm more confused now than I ever was. I arrived in an alien spacecraft, damn it! What happened to Mooky and who or what is he? And who are his friends I'm supposed to be made by? Worse, do I really want to know? What just happened to me? I think a moment. Damn, despite everything, I feel great. I mean, no pain anywhere in my body. Not a single twinge. My mind is clearer than it's been in days. Not that I want to, but I should feel like crud. That doctor. What did he do to me?

Everyone's playing dumb around me and I'm looking even dumber. I don't like this. I'm not much at being on the outside looking in and seeing my own demise with no doors to get out. I'm still the man I was last night. Why leave me out here? Has someone found the blues? If not these guys, who's hiding them now? And where? Are there no records of the dead bodies falling around me? What's really happening to me? Why am I not under arrest still? I'm in prison blues. I want to feel shitty about this, but damn, I feel great.

"Are there really aliens fighting over those blue diamonds?"

In hind thought, I don't want to know any of this strange unearthly stuff. I just want it to all quietly go away so I can go back to being a nice, crazy unemployed filmmaker polishing his next first draft. In fact, I'm starting to feel rather fortunate I'm not still in jail and or at the bottom of some nameless pit. So that's my mantra as I try to figure out how to get back home. The only real important thing right now is that I find my dog.

Bubba is probably wandering around the wilds of Studio City, licking and playing with every stranger he meets. Luckily, Erin put his collar on him, so if anyone finds him they can call me. But a dog like Bubba is quite a bonanza and who knows maybe the person who finds him will keep him. My ex would never let me hear the end of it, if I ever hear from her again. Leaving me with her dog, she deserves it, but not Bubba. I'll never date an actress again after her. Self-centered little...ah crud...I gotta get home. And I don't have a dime on me. I look back into the hall I came out of to catch a glimpse of a clock on the wall. What? How did it get to be 5:30 in the morning? J.J. won't want to drive with his broken nose. And Erin will kill me if I call her, and kill me if I don't call her first. Well, she'll have to stand in line.

48

By 6:45 I'm home checking my answering machine for calls about Bubba, or if anyone wants to hire a suspected mass murderer to write their obituary. No calls from tenants or perspective dead people. And I still don't know where or who has my cell phone. So I call it. Nothing. I call my cell messages. Not even a friend, other than Erin, checking in to see if I'm okay. Well, despite how great I feel, I'm not okay. I feel my head where I've taken a couple blows and there's no sign of any tender spots or lumps. So I get naked and study my face and body in the mirror above my wet bar. There should be scrapes on my forehead from falling into my grave face first. But my mug, other than looking like it belonged to a street wizened bowery boy, is completely unscathed. Did the doctor with the weird French accent do this? Is he an alien, too? If they can remove the physical scaring and pain, why not mental anguish as well? I'm tormented at best.

I had to use the hospitals phone to call Erin. She came to pick me up before work so traffic wasn't that bad for her, but sucked on my way back from Woodland Hills. She agreed to let me use her plum Explorer for the day that has an old car phone in it. So on our way back over Beverly Glen she gave me an ear full on what J.J. went through with his nose, ear and skull. Apparently he didn't see the same doctor I did.

As far as she knows, they decided to perform a little magical cosmetic work while they were there, so J.J. is a little more black and blue than expected. He has health insurance through his acting union, Screen Actors Guild, but there would be a balance due because of the extra work done and J.J. expects me to pick up the bill. Fine, bend me over a chair and give it to me good. Why not? The rest of the cosmos is at the moment. I'll call my insurance guy and see if my property insurance covers beatings from crazy people and yellow blooded alien ex-husbands.

Erin said she let herself into my apartment late last night to see if I was slouching about dead. The phone rang twice while she was there, but each time no one was on the line. Since no one else bothered to call, there's still a chance I can star sixty-nine whoever did call in case they have Bubba. So I do just that, forgetting the time, and I get a recording from a young lady at CBS studios saying that Miss Davis isn't in at the moment, but leave a name and a number and she'd get back to me. Miss Davis at CBS. Most likely it's about Bubba but it could be about my Corvair rotting with the stench of disappearing alien blood and brain bits in their parking lot. So I leave only my home number and name. Since it's so early I decide to lie down and try to sleep, but chances are I'll just think of Bubba and toss and turn. Still feeling great all over, I stink, so I take a long hot shower doubling up on the body wash. I'm amazed at how much dirt rinses off me. I tromp back to my room smelling peachy. But I'm probably asleep before my feet leave the gray carpet because I don't remember passing my closets, pulling back the sheets, or closing my eyes. At least all what's happening to me is good for something. I'm actually sleeping better than I can ever remember. Amazing what the body will let you do when Alien's free it of all pain.

49

Sleeping naked is one thing. Waking up naked is another. I get cold, even in the dead of summer, which it is in LA. Even though I don't have a phone in my room I can still hear the faint beep of my machine if I leave the sliding door at the end of the hall open. I must have done just that because the beep opens my eyes in the middle of that same violent nightmare I get when stressed. It involved the little guy I watched get shot down before me and did nothing about it back at the end of my Beverly Hills bartending days. I'm not sure why it's back, it just is. Oddly, for the first time it doesn't leave me with a queasy dooming spirit. I actually still feel good, rested and energized.

But this sultry voice comes over the machine's speaker moments later, cerebral yet smoky, and resonating with genuine, homespun sex appeal. I know the voice, but haven't a clue to where. Wow, my worries promptly scatter with her sound waves until they are no longer with me. The voice says she's returning my call and that her name is Claire and if I get this message before noon I should call her at her dressing room because she'll be there until lunch. Otherwise, she'll be on stage twelve at the CBS Studio Center all day and I can find her there for the next twenty-two weeks.

I'm standing at the phone by the time she gets around to mentioning Bubba. Her voice is so appealing I can't get myself to pick up the receiver. I'm half asleep and tend to sound like a babbling fool around women anyway. So why set myself up for embarrassments that I can avoid? I look at the clock; nine-thirty. Not bad, a couple hours sleep. A Claire Davis at CBS Studios wants to talk to me. Interesting.

50

I shower again because I'm somehow still feeling dirty but oddly viperous considering the erratic sleep I've been getting. In drying off naked in front of the mirror I can't help but notice this time that my muscle tone looks as though I've pumped iron for two months straight on steroids. I stand there looking at my abs knowing I didn't have six-packs when I went to bed. I'm amazed because being a sedimentary filmmaker I haven't worked out in probably a year. Instead, I've been slowly getting fatter since quitting smoking. In fact, I never had noticeable abs in my life, even when playing ball. The only ripple I ever had was my belly button. Yet there before me in the mirror and attached to me, are real manly abs. Not that I'm complaining. But where and how did I get them and is someone coming back to claim them when they realize I've stolen them? And wow, look at my hair, at least an inch longer. What did this doctor do to me?

After flexing, fluffing my hair, and admiring myself until I can't take it any longer, I drive Erin's truck down to the half outdoor, eclectic coffee shop in Studio City on Tujunga just south of Moorpark. It's owned and operated by a tall stylish man who is often there behind the counter. I arrive with a spring in my step I wasn't born with. I almost feel like I'll get discovered or even fall in love.

This coffee and tea shop is a cool neighborhood showbiz hangout. There's an independent bookstore in back. It's also a good place to pump a few writer friends about certain TV shows and actresses, so I don't sound stupid when I call Claire. True to form my friend Jimmy is inside at his usual perch reading the paper and talking to another comedy writer by the name of Dan. These guys have been around forever and have written for the Carson Show and all the early sitcoms. They now struggle to stay afloat because the same youth movement that affords me work, in my scant carrier, is designed to strangle these guys out of the business and kick their talents to the curb. I'm on my second Joe before I venture any further than good morning to these guys. I want to be fully awake to chat with this caliber of wise guys or they'll chew me up with their mid-morning repartee. There's not much that catches my eye in the LA Times news sections so I browse the sports, not planning to stay.

The shop's owner comes in, waving as he goes, making sure the drawer has proper change and checks the morning's totals. I'm lying low, so I just smile and wave back. Jimmy and Dan digest the day's input from the paper, watching the young ladies entering and exiting the building. Always a nice array of showbiz types, about one third lesbians. Some stop to say hello on any given day, but for some reason not today. After joining in with my tidbits of the daily news, I come to the point about Claire Davis.

"Who is she?" Is basically what I want to know.

"Don't you watch TV, read the Calendar Section?" Jim asks. His face has that wizened look from years of fast living. Only it's not from that, because he's really a comedy writing wise guy who lives his life in arm's reach of a genuine old fashioned clacking Underwood typewriter. He doesn't even own a computer.

"Not much in the last couple of days."

Dan gets up and moves to the counter for a refill. Jimmy opens the LA Times Calendar Section and points to a picture of a lean, strikingly blond starlet standing on stage in front of a microphone. "That's her right there. You don't recognize her from here?"

"No, I don't...wait, she comes in with all the dogs."

"She walked them for, you know...."

"Lazy fat cats," Dan finishes for him.

"Yeah. She'd come in, double-park, grab a cap to go, and drive off with a carload of mutts. Now she does only on the weekends, but without the dogs," Jimmy expounds.

Dan comes back and looks the page over. "The one with the short shorts."

"He means the one with the hot butt." Jimmy is always more direct than Dan, but I know what Dan means. Claire Davis has the sweetest bottom and legs I've seen outside Hollywood Park Horse Race Track. Not much on top, which is okay by me, though some women can fool you with the way they dress. She has an angelic face and natural, light blond shoulder length wavy hair. She is probably closer to thirty, but plays single, in her early twenties.

"What's the show she's on?"

"On? It's her show."

"You don't just get a show. What else has she done?"

"She's been on all the shows, guest starring, you know. All last year. Does stand-up. She's hot, man, hot."

"What's the show?"

"Claire."

"They named the show after her?"

"Yeah, that's what they do now. Look, guaranteed twenty-two episodes. Why, you got a pitch meeting for the show?"

"Me? No. I haven't written half hour."

"Maybe you should, if you know her," Dan suggests.

"Obvious he doesn't. What's up?" Jimmy inquires. I get a flash from the gleam in his eyes of what it must have been like in the old days when TV writers gathered around Musso and Franks, The Derby, and Copper Penny, trading tidbits of inside info, smoking cigars, talking horses, baseball, and broads.

Jimmy and Dan sit waiting, watching me. "Nothing," I finally answer, "I just have to call her today. Something unrelated to showbiz. I just don't want to sound stupid."

"This something to do about the bodies?" Jim asks.

"What bodies?"

"Like you don't notice people staring at you," Dan says.

I look around and, yes, people are looking at me, but I thought I was just having a good hair day. Instead I'm Jack the Knife.

"What's this?" Jim opens the paper to a picture of Simpkins, Castro, and the Essinola family superimposed over a spooky black and white shot of Mystery Towers, with "PAY THE RENT OR ELSE. Landlord—filmmaker, Jozeph Picasso—arrested for mass murders."

I nearly have a stroke right there. "Give me a break."

"Says something about brutal murders at Mystery Towers. A notorious haunted inn built in the late 1800s, but left vacant on and off for fifty years, until recently remodeled by various owners into spooky Sherman Oaks apartments. That must have cost a bundle," Jim says.

"Most of the work was done before I bought it. Is that it?"

"No. It mentions that you are the primary suspect out on bail after a high-speed car chase and subsequent shooting at CBS Studio Center."

"I'm not out on bail! I wasn't arrested. They just questioned me."

"You escape?" Dan asks real loud, knowing damn well I hadn't.

People are staring at me now. The little girl, Cinder, behind the counter, looking very cute today, freshly back from her dance tour, goes for the phone. "Wait. This is a mistake. I didn't kill anyone."

"No one said you did, Picasso. Did you?"

"Of course not, Dan. Put down the phone, Cinder."

"I'm calling my mother."

"In Ohio?"

"She's visiting. She wants to meet famous people."

"I'm not famous."

"You are now. So, Picasso, you have any of them two bedrooms available? Preferably something without a ghost, maybe?" Jim asks.

"Yeah, soon as I get done cleaning stains...."

"Bloodstains?" Dan asks.

"Dog urine. Look, I'll see you jokers later."

"Hey, is a mandatory autopsy covered in the deposit?" Jim asks.

"You guys should write for TV. I almost forgot how to laugh." I get up, grab my paper clippings and head for the door.

"Hey, Picasso, you listing the vacancy in the obits?" Jim calls after me.

"Yeah, in The Alien Chronicles." I hit the sidewalk. What did I expect? A hug and a howdy-do? They're gagmen on a roll at my expense. Lucky me. Being the butt of their jocularity deflates my day.

51

I'm inside Erin's truck before I see the ticket on the window. Damn it! Son-of-a... forget it, it's one of those lifetimes, I can tell. Thirty bucks down the drain. I look at the meter and there's still ten minutes left. I get out and take the ticket and look at it. It's from nearly a month ago, at another location and another plate number. I turn it over, there's nothing written on it, so I open it, and inside is a note written on blue stationary. I pull it out and it says: "Call me, killer." And a local phone number.

I'm starting to sweat so I turn on the truck's air, and remember that Erin has an old car phone. I open her center compartment and take it out. I look at the number on the note. I dial the number.

On the third ring Stacey answers the phone.

"Where are you?"

"Sitting in a friend's truck."

"Come get me."

"Do I know you?"

"You know damn well who this is."

"What do you want?"

"You know damn well what I want."

"I was hoping you dissipated with that freak of an ex-husband of yours last night."

"What did you do to him?"

"Me? I had nothing to do with it. He's on your team."

"Well, don't look at me. I was trying to pin his body on you. The next thing I knew he was gone."

"Where are you?"

"Are you coming to get me?"

"Later, I got to be somewhere soon."

"Come right now. I want to know what you're doing."

"I can't." If I did, I wouldn't be responsible for my actions. There's a sudden beep on the line. "You've got another call coming in."

"I'm on a pay phone."

It beeps again.

"Hold on." I look the phone over and manage to click it over to the other line. "Hello?"

"You don't really care, do ya, Picasso?"It's Mooky.

"Mom?"

"You don't send the wounded flowers?"

"Nor the disappearing. What happened to you? What happened to me?"

"You don't need to know."

"Why does everyone keep telling me that? My life is at stake. I need to know why."

"Don't be so dramatic. I'm gonna cry."

"Can you hold a moment?"

"Tell her to kiss off."

"Where are you?"

"It doesn't matter."

I click over to Stacey. "Stacey, I'll call you back in about three hours."

"I need to see you now."

"I can't, I've got things to do."

"Listen, you prick. I want those chips. I'm being threatened by crazy people over them. If you try to give or sell them to anyone else without me involved, I will kill your dog."

"You don't have my dog."

"I didn't say I did. I just said I'd kill him."

"You're sick, Stacey. I'll call you in three or four hours."

"I'm waiting at a pay phone!"

"In that case, maybe in five or seven hours, or sometime next week. You better hope it doesn't rain."

"You prick!"

I hang up on her. "You still there?"

"You gonna see the actress?"

"Jesus."

"I told you. Don't worry, you're in good hands. Like I said, my friends and I owe you big time. I may be who you think I am, but I'm not unappreciative."

"That's swell. I need good alien friends like you."

"Don't be sarcastic with me, chump."

"Do black aliens still use that word?"

"Who said I'm black?"

"I, you, you're...look, are you gonna tell me what I'm into?"

"What I'm gonna do for you is safely take those blues off your hands and make sure you are taken care of, all charges are dropped, and all expenses covered. What kind of car do you want?"

"Look...."

"I got a real nice white Grand Cherokee Limited waitin' for you when you meet me with the stones. It's not new but looks it. Paid for, even. Thirteen hundred miles, only. The person who owned it won't need it anymore."

"I don't know what's right or wrong."

"Livin's right, dyin's wrong. Remember that. Keeps things real simple."

"But you owe me."

"Yeah, so what? Don't mean I won't kill you if I have to. I'd still appreciate what you done for me as I watch you bleed out. It's the kind of lovin' being I am."

"Look, William, you do lousy LA turkey, so let's...."

"Mooky. The Mook...drop the William Payne Washington stuff, he ain't no more, never was and never will be to you again. He gone from this life for good. And if you ever meet him again, you best hope you don't remember any of this."

"What...? That's not your real name?"

"Of course not."

"Okay, how can I get a hold of you, Mooky?"

"You speak French?"

"No."

"You speak Spanish?"

"No."

"You do Portuguese?"

"No."

"German, Russian, Japanese, Middle Eastern, or African?"

"Why would I?"

"Well, then, bro, we keep it simple and I just keep talkin' LA turkey to your ass. Oh, if anyone lookin' like me comes to your door, kill him. Unless I call you first."

"What?!"

"You heard me. It ain't me at the door. You got to trust me on that. Feel under your friend's front seat, you think I'm not serious."

I feel, damn there's a gun. "This is getting too weird for me."

"Hand the blues over and it's over. We're done and your troubles are yesterday. Have fun with your little starlet. Just remember, nothing is what it seems. Nothing." Mooky hangs up.

If anyone looking like me comes to your door, kill him? What's that about? There can't be two Mookys, can there? Twins maybe? The air is on full blast and I'm still sweating up a storm. I call the number that Claire Davis gave me and she picks up on the first ring. That voice.

"Hello."

"Claire Davis, please."

"Who's calling?"

"This is Jozeph Picasso. She called me about my dog Bubba."

"Oh, are you the writer that's in the LA Times Valley section?"

"Yes, the murderous slash sometimes filmmaker, that's me."

"You sit with the paper and cut out articles?"

"That's me, but...."

"I have your dog."

"Thank God. Is he okay?"

"He's fine. Can I keep him if they put you away?"

"They're not putting me away."

"Darn, he's so cute. I guess you better come get him. I'm already in love. Much longer and I'll cry when you take him away."

"I know what you mean."

"He's the best behaved dog I've ever seen."

"Yeah, that's my Bubba."

"Bubba?"

"His mother named him." I'm sounding idiotic. "He's from a small town in Texas. I, ah...."

"What are you doing for lunch?"

"Eating crow, so far."

"Come over to the studio. I'll leave your name at the gate. Oh, do you like mahi? I'm having mahi salad sent up. You want some?"

"Sure. That would...."

"Better hurry, it's on its way. Just ask for me at the gate. They know what to do."

"I'm moments away."

"Bubba, your daddy's coming. Bubba wants to know if you murdered anyone yet today."

"Tell him I said very funny."

"I will. See you in a few." She hangs up.

That voice. My heart is in a flutter as I put the truck into gear and check for any oncoming traffic. The coast is clear so I pull out. She remembers me. Maybe I could talk her into coming to visit Bubba once in a while. Wait a minute. She's an actress, and actresses of any shape, size. sound, fame, or success, are off my menu forever. Damn and I'm starving for positive attention and overwhelmed with a willingness to share this new found body, too. I'll just take Bubba and get out of there. I've got enough troubles right now. I don't need some self-centered actress driving me crazier than I already am. Then fine, it's settled, no matter what. Take the poodle and skedaddle. Holy heartbreak, Dogman, she's a thespian. I seriously need help. But damn I feel good about it.

52

In ten minutes I'm at the gate, armed and dashingly dangerous. They know who I am. I'm the guy in all the papers. The Killer Filmmaker. It's the first time a studio guard called me "Mr. Picasso." Usually I get "What do you want?" But now I'm "Mr. Picasso."

"Yes, Mr. Picasso. Right over there, Mr. Picasso. Park your truck anywhere you'd like, Mr. Picasso, Miss Davis is waiting for you, Mr. Picasso."

Finally, I have to tell someone that I didn't kill anyone. And most likely won't kill anyone today. So they can dispense with the politeness and continue to treat me like a wannabe. Instead, I get a "Yes, Mr. Picasso."

So this is what it's like to be famous, or at least notorious. And I'm about to meet a beautiful woman. A woman whose behind I've been staring at on and off for six to eight months by now and wondering what it would be like just to talk with her. "Decaf mocha to go," and "Thank you," is all I've ever heard her say in person before speaking with her on the phone. And now I've got her voice on my machine. Damn, I forgot to save it. The beautiful Claire Davis.

A scrappy young production assistant, PA, meets me at the stage door. She is as butch as she could get without sideburns. She leads me through the studio to the back where a row of doors are facing a bank of mirrors surrounded with high-voltage light bulbs. No one yells action and the red light is off above the studio door. So I am assuming lunch is being served to below the line types.

Still, as I cross the studio, I feel hidden eyeballs off in the crevices of the dimly lit stage following me. I'm the murderer, the killer landlord slash sometimes writer/director, who is about to have lunch with the star of their show, the butter on their bread, and the cash cow from which all their dream homes are being milked. If I kill her they're out of work. I feel like a bad Neilson rating, a two percenter. I stop in the middle of the studio. The PA stops when she realizes I'm not following her. She turns back and finds me staring back at all the workers. "Mr. Picasso?"

"She doesn't rent from me," I say to the room in general. "So I'm not likely to harm Claire. You can all rest assured that your jobs are secure, your SUV payments will be mailed, and all private school bills paid. Are we clear on that?" The room just collectively blinks like nothing had happened. I guess once you've been in showbiz for so long, nothing seems out of the ordinary, as long as the show goes on.

The PA, who hadn't bothered to introduce herself to me, is looking a little more peeved than polite at this point and probably thinks I'm nuts. "Try to keep up, Mr. Picasso. They just want to know what a real killer looks like."

"I just said...."

"It doesn't matter what you say. Your rep is screwed on this lot. We don't like you. And we want you to go away."

"Oh, to live in nowhere land."

"You're here."

"Looks the same to me."

"Miss Davis' dressing room."

"Oh."

"She doesn't like shoes in the room."

"I should remove them?"

"Yes. There's a rack you can put them on just inside."

"I'm feeling right at home."

"You want I should knock?"

"No, I can handle it." I take off my shoes and Bubba starts barking just inside the door. The walking doorbell barketh.

"She's got a dog."

"I know. It's mine."

"You have a poodle?"

"Even killers have mothers."

"True."

True, like she meets them all the time. Hollywood, home of the blasé attitude, man. Like there's so much extraordinary make believe violence in their workplace that a possible real life killer without makeup pales in comparison. I go to knock on the door and it opens. Claire stands there in all white terry cloth sweats. Her hair combed back into a bun, no makeup, eyes bright blue, right out of Victoria's Secret. Holding Bubba, who's squirming up a storm. Maybe he'll let me trade places. Let him stand here like a sap with his mouth dry, holding his shoes. She hands him to me without a word and steps aside for me to enter. There's a shoe rack as promised so I dispense the shoes.

Bubba is ecstatic to see me. He licks me wildly. I'm hoping Claire is taking notes on how lovably fit I am, but she's not. The PA stands at the door waiting for a tip maybe, I don't know. I look back at her, "Just leave my luggage by the door." She doesn't get it and a puzzled cold front washes upon her face like a northern shore. Claire smiles warmly, thanking her, and closes the door. She turns to face us, watching quietly, as I set Bubba down. He shows off running to his new squeaky hotdog and starts gnawing on it, spreading out, his back legs parted, tail wagging, looking up at us, eyes shifting back and forth like he's expecting us to come together so he can see us all at once. "Hurry up, Dogman. Kiss her. Or I will."

"He's so cute."

"He's a character."

"You sure I can't keep him?"

"I'll loan him to you once in a while."

"Hum...I might take you up on that. So, you're Jozeph Picasso."

"And you're Claire Davis."

"Sit down. Would you like something to drink? Beer, wine, soda, water...anything?"

"Soda would be fine."

"Diet okay?"

"Please, no. Regular." She moves over to a small wet bar and pours us both a soda. She comes back and I have to look away because I haven't taken my eyes off her for a second and I'm staring.

"So, lunch is ready. I ordered rice and vegetables. I forgot to ask."

"This is fine. So, where'd you find Bubba?"

"He was sitting in a convertible in the parking lot. An old red one I think they used for stunts, it was pretty beat up. He was a mess. I think he had skunk all over him. I had him cleaned and deodorized. I hope you don't mind."

"No, I...shoot, I didn't notice. I'm sorry. Can I write you a check?"

"No. Please, it was a pleasure just having him around. I had to stop my dog sitting job when I took this gig and I'm so lonely around people without them. Bubba is the sweetest. He's good, no matter where you go."

"His mother, my ex-girlfriend, is an actress. She traveled a lot with him, Summer Stock and stuff like that. He knows his way around the biz. He's been in a movie or two, I think. And once on Broadway. Watch this. Bubba, stand up. Sit down. Roll over." Bubba does all this without thinking. "Good boy."I give him a chunk of mahi. He looks at me, "Now you do it, Dogman."

"That was.... What shows?"

"I don't actually know offhand. Bubba, where's your resume?" Bubba jumps up on my lap and licks my chin.

"So, you both write and direct."

"Yes, allegedly."

"I read the article on you. They weren't nice at all."

"The old mass murderer treatment, you know."

"You have scripts?"

"Yes one needing polished. I sold the other."

"This new one, anything I might be interested in?"

"To act in? Well, I think so. It's a dark romantic comedy, with a foiled murder plot. *Crazy Kind Of Love*, a first draft at this point."

"Like to read it. When I'm done here I'll need something to do."

"You'll get plenty of offers."

"I want to be in charge. Find my own projects."

"Sure, why not? So, why don't you get a dog?"

"I will. Traveling as much as I have I didn't have time for my own. And puppies are so hard to train when you're working like I am. I'll probably go to the pound and pick up a trained older dog. You sure I can't adopt Bubba?"

"He's my best friend. I've nearly died trying to get him back."

"Back? From where?"

"It's a long story, but strange people have taken him from me."

"Really?"

"Trying to make me give them something else."

"What?"

"The less you know the better."

"Am I in danger?"

"There's no telling at this point."

"Will they try to take him again?"

"They might. There's a woman who's threatening to kill Bubba."

"What? Who is she, give me her number. I know people."

"Look, Claire, things aren't what they seem. I'm in no position to waste your time with details. But if I could ask a favor of you, you'd be doing me and Bubba a great service."

Her eyes get wider, if that is possible, and she looks at me with great intensity like I am about to tell her the secret behind the Hope Diamond or something. Come to think of it...but I have no plans of reliving all the details, so I keep things brief and just touch upon what I'm into by reiterating that the less she knows the better it would be for her and Bubba. I don't tell her about blue stones, Mooky, aliens, the shootings, the cops, or any of the gritty yellow blood stuff. I just tell her about Stacey and her crazy threat to kill Bubba if I don't give her something. I would give it to her, if I thought it belonged to her, and if I had any idea whether giving it to her would keep Bubba and me safe. She seems to be grasping what I'm telling her even though she knows I'm not telling her the details. She just nods her head in agreement, picking up Bubba and holding him at the table, giving him scraps off her plate.

"So, you want me to watch him for awhile?"

"If you would. He seems safe here."

"What about this woman? Will she bother me?"

"I don't think she knows anything about you. She's dangerous... look never mind, it was a dumb idea."

"No, no, no...the studio made me move to a very high security place, and Bubba is no bother. Believe me on this. I want him to stay with me."

"Should anything happen to me...."

"So you're still in danger?"

"Yes, and if you don't hear from me every couple of days...."

"Whatever you want."

"Then I want you to give Bubba a good home."

Tears well up in her eyes. "I'm so sorry."

"It's okay."

"I'm sorry, it's just that...the thought of leaving this poor dog...."

"Claire, please.... I...."

"No, I...please forgive me. You do whatever you need to do and when you're ready, Bubba will be here, safe and sound. Just promise me I can come visit him or you'll bring him by once in awhile. He was so lost. Weren't you, Bubba?" Bubba rolls over in her arms licking at her angelic face. The little bugger. She holds out her luscious chin to give him a clear shot of the baby white skin of her upper neck. Some dogs have all the licks. I continue to eat. I have to go but I don't want to. Leaving Bubba here isn't just a ploy to see her again, though it is a damn good one. I've got the feeling I'm gonna be on the run soon.

"I have to go."

"Already?"

"This whole thing...."

"When will I hear back from you?"

More than anything I want to take her with me. She just looks at me so clear-eyed, the tears having come and gone - actresses - and smiles just enough to let me know she is aware that I am a man. We sit there for a moment looking into each other's eyes like they do in acting classes examining the other's face. I feel so manly inside.

"You have a nice strong nose."

"Thank you. My mother's and a plastic surgeon's."

"Would you like to attend a screening tomorrow night?"

"You mean us?"

"Well, you and me. Bubba, I think they might say something."

"Well...."

"It's at Warner Brothers. A friend of mine's in it. I forget what, something funny and romantic. I hear it's really good."

"I...I would, normally, but honestly, I have no idea where I'll be. This thing, it's not over."

"I see...but if it were over, you'd want to...I'll leave the info on your machine just in case...just show up. I'll save a seat."

"Sure, I mean, it'd be fun, hanging out with you and your friends...I don't get out much."

"Just get shot at and find dead bodies all around you."

"Yeah, well, sometimes I write and direct."

She just looks at me with those clear pools again, a smile peeking on her lips. We sit there for a moment longer, watching. She isn't on my diet, being an actress, a cherry pie behind frosted glass.

Sadly, meaningful moments like this are probably the ones I'll someday sit in a nursing home smelling badly, wishing I could recall.

53

By the time the glow of the moment wears off I am pulling into my driveway. Tucker and MacAroy are waiting for me out front of the building under the pine trees. What a smack in the face. I'm fretting the feeling that these two bums would stoop to anything after the other night of bull at UCLA Emergency. I don't have to use my garage opener because the garage door is rolled open and apparently turned off.

This kind of stuff really sends me. Everyone wants security unless it's too inconvenient, at which point, forget everyone else. True LA. So I pull to a stop and get out of Erin's SUV and give the two dicks a fixed stare. In the past they couldn't have cared any less about what I think of them, but at the moment they seem too glad to see me.

"What do you want?"

"We're just checking to see if you made it home."

"Have I?"

"Apparently, yeah."

"Good. So long. Drop dead."I get back into the SUV and drive down into the garage. I get to Erin's parking spot in 5-A, grab up my paper and head toward the mailboxes to check the garbage dumpster area. The dumpster is fine and I don't get any threatening mail, so maybe the rest of the day won't be detrimental to my sanity.

I'm still wondering what the deal with the garage door is when I look out to the street and notice that a TCI cable truck is parked across the way. Involuntarily I check the cable box above the mailboxes and then turn, hearing a snipping noise, to check the one near the laundry room.

Sure enough there's a middle-aged guy in a TCI shirt with a beard standing there, working on the box. I walk back to him and ask him what's up. He says he's doing a disconnect for 102. This makes sense. So I don't think much of it. Only I ask him if he had anything to do with the garage gate being open and he says: "No it was opened already." Damn neighbors. He doesn't need anything from me so I turn the gate switch back on, move to the elevator and press the button as the gate closes with a clang. The button still doesn't light up, even though I know the bulb is new. It's the little things. I can hear the elevator motor kick into gear and start coming down, so I'll just deal with it later. I'll probably get a note from the wicked witch living in 105 and if I do, I'll let it remain like this forever.

The door opens and I get in. As I turn around the first floor button lights up, and the door closes behind me. At the first floor the elevator stops and the door reopens, and Tucker and MacAroy are there to greet me with big smiles. I'm starting to feel like some long lost cousin.

"What?"

"What's with you, what'd you do, go to the gym?"

"So, who wants to know, you or your district attorney friend?"

"We were just doing what we were told."

"Okay, then go screw yourselves."

"We didn't say we liked it."

"Look, you two are so full of it you're a fly's best friend."

Tucker puts his heavy hand on the door and pushes it back open. "Do you mind?"

"Yeah. There are things goin' on that we don't understand."

"That makes three of us. Me and you two lapdogs."

"Shut up and listen. Your only value is those chips. You give them to the wrong people and you could end up a squashed bug."

"You call this livin'?"

"Don't be a wise guy. Think smart. Hand them over to us, and live a little longer."

"You guys end up big heroes if I turn them over to you, don't you. Great big raise, maybe a promotion and finder's fee?"

"We didn't ask to be involved in this," MacAroy says.

"So be a nice murder suspect and hand them over," Tucker says.

I just look at them with contempt. They know they're jerks. I don't need to tell them.

"It's just our job," MacAroy says.

"And part of your job is to waste my time?"

"Excuse us?"

"You're both too fat for that." I let the elevator shut in their faces. I don't generally dislike cops. They're hardworking, mostly honest, and underpaid, but these two cow pies are on my stinky finger list.

I get upstairs and I almost expect to hear Bubba coming around the corner when I open the door. But instantly remember I left him at the studio, which saddens me slightly. Until my mind clicks onto a stored vision of those baby blues. The lucky dog.

I move to the phone to check my messages. There's a message from young smoking Serina and her mother in apartment 106 about her bug spraying that's scheduled for today. This could be my chance to show them the blues. If I still have them.

I've got a few minutes, so I return her phone call and Serina answers. I ask her if they're ready and she says they will be. I call J.J. next and get no reply. Probably showing off the new nose I bought him. I call Erin at work and she tells me she's getting a ride back with her roommate so I won't have to pick her up. I thank her because I want to have my car towed over before I spray. Just then my phone clicks.

54

"Did you hear that?"

"Yes, I did. What was it?"

"It's probably nothing. Can I talk to you later?"

"What's the matter?"

"Nothing, I've got to spray in 106 and I want to eat before I do." I pick up my phone and look at it. I don't see anything.

"Jozeph?"

"I'm here. I'm just jotting something down."

"Are you alone?"

"I don't know."

"What?"

"Erin, I'll talk to you later okay, I'm starving."

"Fine."

"Look...."She hangs up on me. Okay, so I'm acting a little strange but I heard a click on my phone line and there's a man downstairs standing next to the phone lines claiming to be with the cable company. And two dirty cops came along to distract me and tell me next to nothing. Surely they have better things to do. I go out to the terrace and look for the truck. I get the license number and write it down. If they don't have a call for this building today then I'm not crazy. If they do I'm paranoid, and should be.

I make a quick trip to the restroom to brush my teeth and wash my hands and pits while I wait for the tow truck to bring home my pride and joy, my Corvair. I'm nervous, or wired, so I go through my mail. It'll take about an hour before my car arrives. The crime scene crew dusted and cleaned it. Even though the blood, body, and brains were gone before anyone else but Stacey and I knew they were there.

Evaporated, disappeared, dissipated, transported, or all of the above into thin air.

In the meantime, I also call the cable company and ask if an order for disconnect is scheduled for my building today. Sue Anne said yes. I ask her for the truck's license plate number and she says that a Tonja Deed would have to call me back. I ask if she could put Tonja on the line for me and I find out good old Tonja isn't in this week. How frustratingly convenient.

I hang up to the sound of the towing dropping the '66 out front. He's early. I meet him there, checking him out closely, making him think I'm a little weird by writing down his operator's license number on the visor. But I want to make sure he is who he says he is. And not someone Mooky or Mary sent to spy on or kill me. I'm overboard with this, I know, but once you've nearly been planted in dead sand out in Bakersfield, you begin to question which way the water flows.

The cable truck is gone. I'm not expecting a call from Tonja Deed. So I drive my Corvair into the garage and to its resting spot. I get out, looking around, and move over to the trunk, built in the front, and open it. I find that my secret hiding spot behind the headlight is wide-open and nothing is left inside it. They're gone! Everything is gone. Including my spare tire. I look over toward a large fifty gallon drum I keep by the cement pillar for rakes and shovels and see that smatterings of nuts and bolts were tossed at it. Could it? I move and look into the drum and there in a pile at the bottom are the things from my trunk. Including the spare tire. How did I not see this? I reach in nonchalantly and grab up the open tin key hideaway box. Noting with deep regret that the car key is missing, but gently pull away the white silicone to find the stones snuggled up together nice and warm. It worked! My guess, Stacey did this. Mooky, Mary or Victor wouldn't have missed the energy these things put out. Unless.... What did they mean by something is helping me hide them? What is it? And why would it?

A sudden impact of paranoia hits me right between the shoulder blades and I find myself stumbling forward and in need to hold onto the garage support column. What is watching me? Is something about to take these from me? "I am not alone down here?" But I have the stones. They're mine again. Mine.

With great effort to mask my reprieve, and not to spin gleeful cartwheels, I put the three blue stones into my pocket, pinching them with my fingers, almost disbelieving the level of joy that I found them again. Until it hits me, the fear that I could lose them to something I'm unaware of. An inner power starts inside me, a self confidence to my bones. Almost evil. These are mine. And I'm keeping them.

If anyone saw me, and suspects that I have the blues, I won't make it out of the dungeon. But just knowing I have the stones in my possession makes me feel good, strong, and somewhat invincible. Not that I plan on taking any bullets or lasers anytime soon to prove how manly I feel, but there's definitely something about these stones that give me more human stones, boulders even.

I move to my trunk and wait ten seconds and no alarms go off, no one shoots at me, yells, or anything. I close the hood and the trucking guy is standing right there! I almost faint.

"You want to sign?"

"What?"

"I need you to sign."

"I thought I did." My eyes must be as wide and crazy as ever. The raw energy rushing through my veins, bubbling to the surface and oozing out of my pores, because he steps back from me.

"I made a mistake. I forgot I'm driving the flat bed."

"That's not you on the visor?"

"No. That's my cousin."

"Back away. Back away, right now!"

"What the heck, man. I just need...."

"Just back away right now. Look at this car. People are shooting at me. Now back away." I grab up a crowbar out of the drum.

"Look, you fruitcake, just sign my ledger before I call the cops."

"Okay, I am sorry. Put it on the back fender. Stand over there."

He sets the book down. I don't care what he thinks. There's way more to this than I understand. I'm not taking any chances with these chips in my pocket. He moves away and I make it to the book. I sign it and set it back down. He comes back over as I move away.

"You're a freak, man."

"I'm a live freak, man. And I'm staying that way."

He backs away and leaves me feeling stupid, but freakishly alive.

55

After messing around with my car for a few more minutes, taking in the real damage that had been done to it, actually choking back a heartfelt sob, I move over to where I keep the Boric Acid Powder. I keep it hidden behind the door leading to the air conditioning compressor. A huge unit about the size of Erin's SUV, built behind the elevator shaft. I have full intentions of taking my pain and sorrow out on something, even if only the lowly bugs living in apartment 106. I cross back the length of the dungeon, past J.J.'s studio and over to the phone line to take a look, without really looking.

I'm doing this as I check the cable box and make sure it's locked, the whole time looking over the phone lines planted on the wall right next to the cable box. The light from the laundry room makes this all possible.

I have no proof but if someone has bugged me then maybe they are watching me as well. It's not hard to figure out whose line is whose and see if anyone has tapped into any of them. I look at every wire coming in and going out and I don't see anything different with any of the wires, particularly mine marked 308. Honestly, I can't think of anyone but humans needing to touch these wires, which means, Mooky and his marry cohorts could be listening and watching every movement I make from far above the blue skies.

I go through the laundry room checking to see if it's clean and oddly enough no one has stormed it. So I go out the back, up the stone stairs to the small fenced in garden.

I'm just getting started with this, but come spring I plan to do a whole rock garden, forest floor thing. Anyway, I notice it's not time to water so I move on around and through the pool gate and see that someone has once again moved all the chairs askew. Surprise, surprise. I put them back, because that's what I'd do if I didn't have blue diamonds in my pocket. I make it up the stairs to the first landing where I open the door with my key and move past Erin's apartment 104. She's not home, though sometimes she comes home for lunch. I remember I have her truck and find myself disappointed I won't be able to show her my new found muscles.

I go through the next fire door and stand in front of 106. I'm not really there to kill bugs. Though, I am. I've got other killer things in mind. It's her mother oddly enough that I'm interested in talking with. I knock and Serina's mother comes to the door. As usual, she's dressed to go out. She's a good looking single woman in her forties maybe, despite her dyed blond hair, but not nearly as attractive as her daughter Serina. She smiles warmly and is impelled to step very close to me.

I stand back, the Pest Control Man, looking at her, wondering how I can bring up this conversation about the diamond chips without making her and Serina think I'm completely out of my mind. I know telling them anything would only endanger them. Especially if someone is listening, so I'm reluctant to bring it up. Paying for one nose job is enough for one week. But I get the feeling if I leave this building with these stones someone will follow me. And that someone will kill me for them. I might as well meet them on my own turf right here in Mystery Towers. So I ask Shoul, "Could you appraise three small diamonds for me without actually touching them?"

"I'm Persian. I could appraise them from across the street."

Just like that. Like that was enough explanation. "Could you appraise something here if I hold them out?"

"You mean like a ring? Sure." She looks to my fingers.

I'm not wearing the ring my father gave me with a single diamond and two rubies. Though, when I get back upstairs, I better check to make sure it's still there.

"No, I mean, diamond chips. Something I found."

"You found diamonds?"

"Really?" Serina suddenly becomes interested. She stops when she sees me. I can see she's checking me out as though she's never seen me before. And she hasn't, not this me, the all and mighty buffed me. I smile at her, and she smiles back. Reel it in, Picasso, it ain't you. It's the stones.

I turn back to Shoul, "Well, yeah. Can you look at them?"

"Come in." She steps back as I enter. "You've been working out?"

"Yes, a little."

"Damn. Are you on steroids?" Shoul asks.

"No, of course not, I went to the gym to work off some stress."

"I need to go to that gym, look at his ass," Shoul tells Serina.

"I am," Serina says.

"Look, eyes back to these, ladies. I'd like to know their value or even if they're diamonds."

"Sure, my friends ask me all the time." She goes to her purse. Maybe her girlfriends get engaged a lot and want to know if they're being stiffed with zirconium. I don't know, but she pulls out these glasses that have this magnifying loupe kind of thing attached and she puts them on.

"So where are they?" I open my hand to reveal the three chips. She looks at them with her naked eye first.

"They're blue?"

"Yeah. Or violet," I proudly admit.

"They could be valuable," she tells me.

"Like the Hope Diamond?" Serina asks.

"These are just chips." Trying to play it down.

"But still...where'd you get these?"

"I found them."

"Where?"

"What's the matter?"

"Is this anything illegal? Something to do with the Essinolas?"

"Come on."

"Like, you're already a Norman Bates suspect."

"Thank you, Serina."

"Where did you find these? Are they stolen?"

"Can you just tell me about them, and leave it at that? It's for your own good. I swear I didn't steal them. But knowing what I have here could keep me alive."

"What about us?" Serina asks.

"The less you know the better."

The two women look from one to another then back at me. "Bring them into the bathroom."

I follow her into the bathroom and she turns on the heat lamps. I hold out the diamonds, noticing that she's used the double sinks as ashtrays again. If I bring it up now she'll just deny it, so I don't bother. She maneuvers herself over the largest one first and holds my hand up to the light and examines the chip. She backs away and tells Serina to fetch the tweezers. Serina is gone for ten, maybe twelve seconds and comes back with a six inch stainless steel pair. Shoul picks up the largest chip again. She hums and haws a few times, picks up the second largest chip, goes through the same process and then repeats it with the third.

"So?"

"They're not diamonds."

"What?"

"I don't know what they are. But they're not diamonds."

All of a sudden I feel betrayed. Hoodwinked. The Hunchback of Mystery Towers. They had to be. People were killing each other over these damn things. "Are they glass?"

"No, they are definitely not glass. They're not diamonds either."

"I don't understand."

"You can get a second opinion, but I know they're not diamonds. They're too clear. No diamond, especially a blue diamond, is ever that clear and flawless. My guess it's manmade. If they're not, then they're not from here. Maybe from an asteroid. If it's a true mineral though, it's off the charts."

"Are you serious?"

She leans in close, smiles up at me. "Yes."

I put the chips back in my pocket. Stepping back again.

"I've heard of such stones, but never seen them. They're very rare, very expensive and very powerful in healing human tissue. There are myths from generations back in my family, too, about ancient aliens living and controlling us with blue stones."

"Come on." So I am having an out of this world experience. Why not, I want to keep these stones already. I feel so powerful with them.

"My father was a jeweler, my grandfather was a jeweler, my brother is a jeweler, and I've been selling diamonds since I was

Serina's age. I know diamonds. There are still rumors of these kinds of things within our diamond community. But no one I've ever met has ever seen one or lived to tell about it."

"We have now, mom."

"But you can't tell anyone." I open my Boric Acid container.

"A promise is a promise. I wouldn't be able to prove it so what's the point in telling anyone? Making clients think I'm nuts isn't good for business."

"So, now what?" Serina asks.

I start sprinkling the white power under the bathroom sink. "Tell you what. I'll give you a month's free rent for helping me and keeping this between us. And freeze your rent for three years."

The women look at each other again. $1,600. "For real?"

"You won't tell anyone about this?"

"We don't believe in aliens."

"Exactly. Neither do I. I just want to quietly find out what they are. And give them back to who they belong." I sprinkle the same in the second bathroom.

"Sure. They could still be manmade. But I don't think so."

"It will be better for all of us if you never saw these stones."

"If people are bothering you, I'll tell them they're not real."

"No, that won't...I'm sure they already know." My mind starts to spin a few choice words I want to say to my good buddies Mooky, Mary, Tucker, and MacAroy...but first things first. Time to murder some cockroaches. After that...who knows, maybe I'll foam at the mouth.

I turn to leave and Shoul reopens the door. "Serina will be out tonight if you want me to look at anything...else."

"Shoul."

"Just in case you need more of my expert advice."

"Mom, I can hear you." Serina says dying in the background.

I turn from Shoul at the door and head back to my apartment. A big Sméagol/Gollum smile on my face, "Yeth, I muth keep the stones."

"What?"

"Nothing."

"You're getting weird, Jozeph."

"I know."

56

If these stones are not from Earth, I don't have to worry about screwing over the Smithsonian any longer. I didn't want to in the first place. I just want my apartment put back in place and the money the pig family owes me, plus my car fixed. I want people to leave my friends, dog, and me alone. With how I'm feeling inside right now, this sense of power I have, neither good nor evil, I just might make them do as I please with my bare hands around their alien throats until they tell the truth of how to end all this unearthliness.

Like this, I close my eyes and, Blip, I'm back upstairs at my door. What the...? These stones. I run to the mirror to check if my body is inside out, or if I left a leg behind. I transported! Nothing. I'm fine. I'm all here. That was so cool. How did I do that? I close my eyes. I'm still here in front of my wet bar. Shoot.

I don't want to use my phone, but if I don't, no one will come looking for me tonight when it's dark. I have no idea how to look for them. And I want to get whatever my butt is stuck in over with right now. So I call MacAroy and Tucker. Why not torment them while I wait to see who shows up first?

The Mook says shoot anyone who shows up looking like him unless he calls first. Hope they don't call me on my lost cell phone. Did he say exactly that? I don't remember. I should've written it down. Three minutes after hanging up with MacAroy, who's on his way with Tucker, the phone rings, with my cell phone's caller ID. Apparently, I'm calling myself.

"Yes?"

"Open the door."

"Who's there?"

"Me."

"You said to kill you if you showed up at my door."

"Unless I call first."

"You're at my door right now, Mook. Or are you mind controlling me again?"

"A little of both. I'm standing here, though."

"How do I know it's you? How do I know you're not a killer clone, some digital dropout identical twin of the Mook here to kill me?"

"Look out your peephole and you'll see me standing here talking to you on your cell phone."

"And it's you?"

"It's me. The real deal."

"How many yous are there?"

"You're starting to catch on, aren't you?"

"I don't want to catch on. I want what is mine and to get back to looking for a better life of screwing off and forgetting all of yous."

"Yes, that will be for the best."

"So, how do I do that?"

"You can start by opening this door."

"Not good enough. Who are you?"

"Genetic engineering. Okay? It's how we survive long enough to travel the universe. I was cloned ten times before I got from my planet to yours. There's dark matter and energy, black holes and dimensions involved, but you don't need to know any of this. Consider it much like your multiple births here on earth but with fully grown much superior beings and at different places and times. Now open the door."

"What are the chips, really? Why do they make me feel like this?"

"Let's not talk about this over your unsecure line. You want to open up?"

"Who was found with these chips? Who is the body in the cloud forest? Somebody famous, was he human?"

"Does it matter? You said you didn't want to know."

"I changed my mind. I'll forget later."

"It doesn't work that way. We're no men in black."

"Then I'm not letting you in."

"We've got about two minutes to finish. After that everyone dies."

"Who is Mary?"

"Bad, very bad."

"Who are you?"

"The good guy. Is that what you want to hear?"

"Yes."

"There ain't a good guy, bad guy thing here, Picasso. If there is a good guy, you're him. The rest of us would just as soon see you dead over this."

"MacAroy and Tucker."

"They have no idea. If you give me the stones, all your troubles are over. And they'll go away."

"That sounds a lot like being dead. You can guarantee that won't happen?"

"There are no guarantees in this universe. Life is just a random series of violent acts. One big bang."

"These chips aren't from the Hope Diamond?"

"Yes and no."

"But they're not Earth bound diamonds."

"Yes and no."

"So they are not a natural mineral."

"You're a smart man."

"Though, they're possibly still from the Hope Diamond."

"Not if they are what we think they are."

"And they are...."

"If I tell you that I'll have to kill you regardless."

"Then you can't come in."

Mook kicks in my door. Instead of freaking out, I flush all over with a soothing sensation. And I think I involuntarily shoot him.

57

These stones! He falls back out the door and lies there in the hall bleeding that something other than red blood stuff. The hairdresser's mother visiting from Guatemala across the hall sticks her head out to find me standing over Mook with the smoking gun. Her two yappy little dogs are nowhere to be found. I didn't shoot for any vital spots but Mook flinches and I think I got him good in the chest. He lies there, oozing his yellowish yuck.

"You just messed up, Picasso."

"I don't feel like it."

"It's the stones talkin'."

"You were killing me anyway."

"Maybe not."

"Maybe I should shoot you again."

"It don't matter."

Just then the rising elevator stops and MacAroy and Tucker fill its opening door. They look down at the Mook giving no clue as to recognizing him. Mook just closes his eyes.

"Drop the gun, Picasso." Tucker reaches for his gun.

"I don't think so." I point mine at him and MacAroy stops Tucker from drawing on me.

"This will go down a lot smoother if you just drop the gun and let us take care of everything," Tucker adds.

"I'm tired of this craziness. Mook, if you're dissipating, hurry up. In the meantime, I want you two bullshit artists to grab his feet and pull him inside. Just keep him on the entry rug and off the carpet."

"This is dumb, Picasso."

"Just shut up and grab feet. I've seen his act. Grab them!"

Tucker and MacAroy grab up Mooky by his feet and drag him into the foyer and drop him there. I motion for Tucker to close the door and use the chain to lock it this time. Tucker does, but doesn't want to. I tell them to throw their guns onto the floor by my feet. While they do this, I start wishing I'd done this a long time ago.

"Come in and sit. Now." Tucker and MacAroy come in the living room admiring my sixty inch TV and surround system.

"Here's the deal." I look over, Blip, and find myself looking out my terrace door and up to a light growing in the eastward sky and coming this way. "Mook, I don't care how this is happening, or how many bullets it takes to kill you, and I will kill you, if you and these cops don't start telling."

"There's nothing to tell," Tucker tells me, apparently not noticing that I just reappeared across the room.

"Go sit on the couch and think that dumb remark over." There's no sound coming from an approaching helicopter that should be filling the air at about Coldwater Canyon by now. Could be the same one I saw when rescuing Bubba. Two small to be the one I traveled in with Mooky. Blip, I move back to the front door.

I grab the entryway rug and drag Mook in front of the wet bar.

"Now, who wants to start talking first?"

I turn to find Tucker and MacAroy with their mouths open.

"What the heck was that? You Blipped," MacAroy says.

"And who the heck is that?" Tucker asks.

"No more hocus pocus, guys. Something is happening to me because of these stones."

"They don't know me, Picasso. I told you they don't have a clue."

"You were in the cell with me, both times."

"So. These guys are patsies. Mary was using them."

"Hey, watch what you say, or we'll shoot you."

"Then you tell him what's happening."Mooky closes his eyes.

"In five seconds someone will be here, so somebody tell me."

"How do you know someone's coming?" MacAroy asks as he and Tucker look up to the growing energy hovering above us and coming right through the ceiling.

"What is that?"Tucker asks.

I look up. "They're here."

58

The sound of two sets of heavy boots and something else thump down onto the gated rooftop terrace. "High heels." Great. They walk above my bedroom and living room, heading to the access stairs tower.

"Who's here?"MacAroy genuinely looks concerned.

"Picasso." Tucker says gritting his teeth.

"We're about to meet the real Mary. Aren't we, Mook?"

"And a couple of me."

"So there were three of you on earth?"

"Four. The two hundred-year-old body was also one of me."

"What is he talkin' about?"

I hold out the stones. "Tucker, Mac, these stones are not from this planet. And neither is he."

"The heck he's not."

"Watch." I Blip next to them. They don't dare move.

"You better give them their guns back. Picasso. Give them their guns back! Gentlemen, don't let them take you alive."

I hold out my hand. Blip, their guns are back in their hands. They look at each other. Tucker gets up and moves to Mooky and looks down at him. Mooky winks. Tucker steps over him and goes into the darken hall leading into my bathrooms and bedroom.

"These people are aliens, not human?"MacAroy asks Mook.

"They'll put you in a jar and live off your fluids. Or clone you, and have one of them take your place, if you provoke them. Just give me the stones and I'll take care of this."

I grip them tighter. I don't want to let them go. I don't want to die either but I do not fear that as much as losing this power. The blues. I want these stones. I look at Mook. He's mind messing with me. I know, willing me to give him the stones. I know he's helping me but I fight him. "I can't, Mook."

"You have to," he says. "Or we all die."

With all my will I hold them out and Mook reaches up and calmly takes them from my opening hand. He holds them above his chest where I shot him and he sits up like nothing ever happened to him.

I nearly collapse to the floor, weeping. I feel so suddenly hollow. I stagger up. Shaken inside and out. My stones!

"Don't shoot me again, Picasso. Or you'll live the rest of your life in a test tube feeding alien babies through your balls."

"What do we do now?" MacAroy honestly looks childlike.

"We're having a close encounter," I tell him.

"Just shoot them in the heads." Mook goes over and unchains the door and backs into the living room.

MacAroy is about to wet himself when the door comes crashing in a third time.

Mary fills the door in heals and jeans. "Don't listen to him, MacAroy. You know damn well this is official government business and those stones are classified objects. Hand them over to me and we'll be on our way."

"You said you were from the DA's office. Now you're some kind of Agent Scully?"

"The universe is more complicated than you can ever imagine, Mac. Now, who's got the stones?"

Mary enters my foyer standing across from the hall door where Tucker hides in the dark. A gun like object hangs down at her side in her right hand. It isn't any gun that they've seen before but I unfortunately have. In what little light is coming from outside my apartment Mary looks the picture of a lady in control, except her eyes glow brighter as she scans the room. Maybe it's my imagination, but I don't think so.

"Picasso, we don't want to hurt anyone here. We just want the blues. They don't belong with you. You see what they can do to you if you touch them with your skin. They need to come with us. We know how to deal with them."

Mooky steps into foyer from the living room and faces Mary. He holds out the stones.

"Picasso, you fool. You helped this thing live."

"Here's the stones. As promised."

"Mooky, don't," I say.

Mary raises her gun to kill MacAroy and Tucker shoots her from the hall. Her neck and lower skull blasts out across the entryway and sprays all over my new watercolor and the wall. Her body crumples limp to the ground. Mook rolls out of the way and I dive with lightening speed for the carpet as another Mook fills the door brandishing a weapon resembling the one Mary has and starts to laser the room with that same weird wavy energy I was shot with.

My sixty inch takes a direct hit! The sound of four grand exploding deafens the air as it turns to a box full of flames

Mook tosses the stones out onto the throw rug and the second Mook involuntarily moves quickly to pick them up. Tucker blasts him from the hall and the top of his head zips off and a yellowish, glowing substance bubbles out from the cavity. He plops down on my carpet and on top of Mary whose goo is already fading away like Victor's.

Mook makes a move for the blues and I give him a kick in the backside and he sails beyond his lookalike, giving me time to roll the body over and grab up the facets. I also grab up the second Mook's gun, or whatever it is, as well and point it at Mooky. "Just sit there. Come on out, Tucker." My blues. Mine, mine, mine!

"Jesus." Mike Tucker's fat face is drawn and ashy, his eyes soppy.

"Nice shooting."

"Jesus H. Christ," he says.

The pulsating of the helicopter returns and the second set of boots retreats across the roof followed by the helicopter quickly fading.

"We're alone," Mook tells us. "For now."

"You've got some explaining to do," I tell him.

"In a minute we all will if you don't help get these bodies out."

"Who's coming now?" I ask. "I'll make popcorn."

"The lady across the way just dialed 911 and we're about to have visitors of the LAPD kind."

"Jesus, I don't want my career to end this way," Tucker says.

"No one will believe this," MacAroy tells us.

197

"Within minutes these bodies and all that's them will decompose, dissipate, into thin air. If their brains were intact, these stones would heal them, even if they stopped breathing."

"What about real people like us?"

"If you carried them around your person for about a year, no living thing on earth could harm you, short of dismemberment. You're feeling the power already, aren't you, Picasso."

"I think I'm even hung better, this is amazing. I feel like I've snorted ten hits of Viagra. So, I'd be immortal? Like a Highlander."

"Closer to a vampire, except for a bad headshot, of course."

"Hey, this is Hollywood. A bad headshot will kill you in this town." I couldn't resist.

"Jesus."

"Will you stop saying that?"MacAroy tells Tucker.

"What about the Hope Diamond?"

Mooky starts speaking with a heavy French accent. Don't ask me why. Hey, he's the Mook. "These were the chips from the original stone first brought back from an alien crash site in India and acquired by Jean Baptiste Tavernier. They were not from a Kollur mine in Golconda as he claimed. As Picasso knows, they are not diamonds."

"Was there some kind of curse on the stone?"MacAroy asks.

"A curse? No. Just us trying to keep control of the stones. Bad things did happen to those humans and aliens who got in our way."

"So the Hope is the Hope. It's just not the original stone, the one stolen from France after the French Revolution in 1791."

"Actually, I took part in a week long looting of the crown jewels in September of 1792, searching for them. The other jewels were to be returned, minus these last facets. But my bastard clone could not let them go, and ran off to the new world. He broke his friggin' neck, smashing his skull open in a mudslide."

"Am I the only one confused here?" Tucker asks.

"No," MacAroy adds. "Not really."

"But he had the blues."

"In a protective container to keep us from finding him."

"Where's the rest of this diamond?" I ask.

"Where it should be."

"Is it on earth?"

"Sometimes. In part. They were cut and divided among many. To balance the power in the Alien Council. And keep them away from something no human or alien in the Universe can trust with them."

"Jesus."

"Will you stop? MacAroy, take Tucker out in the hall," I tell him.

"But…"

"Please. I need to think this out."

"We better wrap up these bodies. You don't want to be found with them. You'll be covered up so deep by your government only I will know what happened to you. Do you have another rug?" Mooky asks.

"By the terrace door."

Mook picks up the rug, "My car is parked out front."

"You'll get ticketed after six."

He looks at me. "I have intergalactic diplomatic immunity."

"Jesus."

"Shut up and help me," MacAroy tells him. "I ain't havin' no one find us with aliens. I don't care what anyone says, this ain't gonna make you captain." They wrap the bodies up in the rugs and drag them out into the hall, pushing the button as the lady across the hall opens her door to watch. "We're cops, go back inside."

Sirens can be heard coming down Graystone. "You guys better hurry."

"Forget the elevator, take the stairs. Go out the south door and gate to my car." Mook tells them. No sign of the French accent.

"I ain't carrying these things," Tucker says.

"Get your ass over here. You want to explain how you shot two aliens from the back?" MacAroy is raising his voice now.

"They were about to zap you," Tucker defended himself.

"Are you hearing yourself?"

"Okay, down the stairs it is. You guys gonna help?"

"We got other business to take care of," I tell them.

"It's the dented black Caddy out front. I just unlocked it," Mook adds. "Keys are in it. Park it somewhere, it will find its way back."

"Jesus."

"Would you look at this slimy yellow yuck?"They go down the stairs, the bodies and alien juices already dissipating as they go.

59

Mooky comes back into the living room and sits on my couch.

I look at my painting and wall and find the slime already beginning to fade. This is really happening. "What about these?" I hold out the gun like objects.

"You want them for souvenirs?"

"Ray guns? Yes, well, why not? Maybe I'll reverse engineer them and put some alien zap into drive by shooting."

"You're a funny guy, Picasso. I'm gonna miss your whining."

"So I can sell them?"

"Sorry, can't do that. Let me put the safety on them." He reaches out and hits buttons I have no idea are there and the guns just disappear.

"They invisible?"

"Gone. Up there. Call it laser control. And by the way, you were right, those weren't lasers as you would think. They were advanced sound wave technology. Mary is developing them with the help of human manufacturing against strict Alien Council ruling.

"Some kind of electromagnetic energy gun?"

"Very perceptive. It's why she's after the stones. To keep the Council from stopping her from making a killing. Literally."

"So all this was an alien power grab to make weapons? Wait, you said she's after them in present tense. There's more of her?"

"Of course. Very dangerous, and won't take it lightly that we killed off one of her precious clones. You've met the real Mary."

"I have?"

"The one that shot you. Nasty woman."

"Was I in a spaceship?"

"Yes and no."

"I wasn't up there. So I was down somewhere?"

"It's better that you don't know any more than you suspect. Controlling the stones is the only thing that got you back out."

"I knew it."

"They were checking your blood for signs of touching the stones. To verify that you had them."

The handgun he gave me rises off the floor and hovers before me.

"Want it?" He asks.

"Yes, but I better not."

The gun moves to him and he puts it away.

"Was that a spaceship landing on my roof?"

"As far as anyone else could tell it was a helicopter hovering."

"Aliens ride around in advanced helicopters? Come on, Mooky. Tell me this is all crazy talk. That this woman won't come back looking for me."

"You know it's true, Picasso. You were in one, and there's no telling what Mary will do to get even with us. My guess she'll leave you alone as long as you don't pose a threat to what she wants."

I sit down. This isn't good. "You're starting to freak me out. Why would she trust you?"

"She didn't. The deal was that she'd clean up this mess. I'd get the stones from you for her."

"The deal was for her to kill us?"

"And replace you with clones. Her group is very good at it."

"But she shot you."

"Yes. You see how dangerous she is. And why the council wants her taken out. She can't be trusted, by anyone."

"All this because of that dog."

"It's all around you, Picasso. Let it go. Just live your life, and do your best to forget all this."

"How can I?"

"What do you want more than anything else in the world?"

"Love."

"Done."

"What?"

"I love you, man."

"From someone, a female, who's from here."

"Oh, well, what about that blond, the actress?"

"Stay away from her."

"She's single, likes your dog, you should go to the screening."

"I'm getting love advice from an alien? What next?"

"I'm the Mook. I am your intergalactic love connection. Do you think it's easy trying to get you humans to crossbreed?"

"Give me a break."

"Without help, you people would still be swinging in trees and humping your sisters in caves, like we found you. You think I'm quackery, think twice about how you so called civilized humans bred wolves to look like your poodle and that cocker spaniel. You people were ugly."

"That's it, get out of my home. I don't want to know anymore."

"You still have my chips. Do you want to live forever, or should I kill you now and get it over with?"

"But I have the chips...."

"Yes, the chips. They will bring you back to life by repairing your vital body functions if your brain is still intact. If, of course, they're in contact with your person for about a year, like I said, you'd be something like a vampire."

"Feeding on human blood?"

"Not necessarily, but the craving could develop, and has."

"Wait, there are aliens *and* vampires on Earth?"

"Picasso, where do you think all these horror themes come from?"

"Fiction, I hoped. From minds of imaginative men and women."

"Just be careful of who you rent to from now on. I mean it."

"What about the guy in the cloud forest? He was your clone?"

"He wasn't a good clone. Consider it in your low minded showbiz terms as an organic digital processing during birth, and you'll begin to follow. Only we're not actually dividing single cells, we're dividing completed forms. It's painless, but defects can transpire sometimes freely during intercellular travel. Not in a Petri dish like earthlings do now, but while what you sci-fi freaks consider teleporting, or downloading, sharing mentalities. When our brain cells freeform, it can cause minute drags in the cloning process. Sometimes it'll take a hundred years for the malady to surface. Take riding llamas for example. I be the Dalai of llamas but my thieving clone fell off one and broke his head open in a mudslide. He died instantly, the stones buried inches from his grasp. He vaporized only after they dug him up. Causing one big religious stench that took a great deal of effort on our part to clean up. We came as soon as we realized the chips were found again. But Mary and those fools downstairs beat us to them amidst all the chaos. They are important for our survival here and our cloning processes. We can also create whole humans from single body parts, or combine multiple human DNA into one being, as long as they don't start to decay."

Like Frankenstein?

"Who? Kidding. But, yes."

"So these stones are like a Lord of the Ring kind of thing? Everyone wants the stones?"

"If it makes you feel better. They can do many things, depending on who has them. This Essinola dude got mixed up with Mary and Victor. He stepped in our way, killing our alien courier. So here we are trying to fix it."

"So Victor Castro worked for...?

"Mary. There's more of him about. If you see one, don't freak out, he may not know you.

"Yeah, right."

"Look, we believe there was something much more powerful involved in this that took control of Castro and Essinola. Something that none of us know up close and personal. It's the only way they could've gotten those stones away from us. It has something to do with this building."

"Who? What?"

"Not who or what, It. I've had the displeasure of dealing with It more than once. Never goes as planned. And we're not exactly on speaking terms for flashing one of my good clones to dust. It has been lying low in Europe for many years in one of its human clones. With these diamonds being rediscovered we fear It made a move on them to bring them here to this building. We have no way of knowing for sure how because It never shows itself. Only that It let you keep them from Mary and me long enough to bring us all here to Mystery

Towers for reasons we don't know yet. That in itself should concern you as much as us."

"Why here, I mean, am I in danger of It? Is there something wrong with this building? Are the stories about this place true?"

"We don't know yet. Mystery Towers appears to be a vortex that It can hide things from us when it wants. Like the stones. You felt them. But we couldn't. We all knew they were here, but didn't know where. Something blocked us. We don't know how. But It shifts. Jumps to human to human, clone to clone or even us. Freaky stuff you don't want to know about. Seriously, forget I told you that part."

"What? How?"

"Don't think about it."

"You're killing me. So, you don't want It to have them?"

"It created the stones. Just fear you never have to find out how."

"Fine. Where's the dog? The cocker spaniel?"

"I don't know."

"The redhead, Stacey?"

"They are both out of the picture is all I know for sure."

"Jesus."

"Not him...."

"No, I mean...."

"Alien humor."

"I'm not dreaming this? It sure seems like a nightmare."

"No. Give me the stones and I'll give you back what you've lost."

"My life, my car, my apartment building, my TV, my microwave, my reputation, my sanity, and everything else in between?"

"Doctor bills, everything, and more. Your reputation, maybe."

"What more?"

"I'll let you live."

"You're too kind. Will I remember any of this?"

"Of course. Write a book or a screenplay even. Science fiction is in these days."

"Maybe I will."

"Just don't try standing on street corners or gathering in deserts insisting that it's true. I've put enough humans in asylums as it is."

"I see. Everything the way it was?"

"I ain't doin' the work. I'll give you the cash, just pay the bills."

"All right. What about the Jeep?"

"It's yours. White, tan interior, brush guards, Grand Cherokee Limited. Very plush. You be styling while you be milin', my man."

"Who'd you say it was registered to?"

"Nobody anybody will ever miss."

"Are there a lot of you...whatevers...around? Here on Earth?"

He just looks at me. I get the feeling he's starting to mind control me because I hold out the chips against my will and he takes them again. It almost hurts letting them go this time. Kind of a heartbreak feeling, a letdown, a broken guarantee that I would live forever. Only to find out I'm still mortal and this arrow in my heart, this loss of the stones, is the end of me; living up to their name, because I actually already feel that blue.

"Cheer up, you'll be back to normal in a few days, though there have been some linger depression side effects in some humans. But I'll talk you down if you try jumping."

"Thanks."

"Kidding. Don't go on the roof for a few days or play with guns, though."

"Shut up."

"Expect a package soon." He heads for the door as the cop cars pull up outside.

"How do I explain all this? Look at my TV."

"Let Tucker and MacAroy handle it. Believe me, they'll keep the rest of them off your back once they have time to realize what I've told them is true. They're trapped if they don't."

"Wait. Are you and Mary from the same planet?"

"Not even close. There be good and evil in all races, and as vast as the universe is, how can you even begin to imagine that you and I are all there is? Think of where you have been and you'll start to realize where you will end up. As small as your world seems to you today, our universe appears to Beings like me. You, me, a rock, that chair, we are of the same things, evolving mass forces, it's just a matter of mathematics. One plus one equals three, not two. You, I and we together make a third concept. Just remember, you are not alone. You are a made human. From us above, below and all around you. I've got my eye on you, Picasso. You're a messed up Hollywood filmmaker, but you got real heart."

"Yeah, just don't be mind controlling me. I'm too close to being insane as it is."

"You never know. Break a leg."

"I mean it."

Mooky goes to the elevator and pushes the button. The door opens. Of course, for Mook it lights up. He goes in and turns to me, smiling. "Thanks, Picasso. Remember, if I come to your door without calling first, shoot me again."

"Yeah, yeah…in the head next time…wait, this isn't over?"

"Probably not. You're not normal anymore. You've been touched by the stones. There's value in that to us. And to It."

"Leave me alone. I mean that. What about my phone?"

"I'll get you a secure one."

"I don't want anything more to do with this, the blues or It." The door begins to close. I yell. "You hear me, Mooky, I'm finished! Done! Forgotten! You tell It and the rest of you yellow eyed freaks to stay the hell away from me!"I grab the door and push it back open. Blip. The Mook is gone. "You blipping alien!"

The hall staircase door opens and two cops come through it with guns. "Don't move!"

"Two cops downstairs will explain everything."

"Put your hands on the wall, Mr. Picasso."

"Come on…."

"Now!" The shorter one pushes me against the wall and roughly frisks me. "Clean." It is at this time I realize she is the same female cop who kneed me in the parking lot. She begins to read me my rights as she fits me for a new pair of handcuffs.

"You know, I didn't get your name last time."

"Officer."

"Nice to see you again, Officer. Welcome to Earth."

60

I'm sitting here wondering what karma I'm paying for this trip down poky lane. Despite being summer, it's cold in the holding cell. Even with the twenty-seven other men's putrid aroma whaffing over me.

"At least you ain't in here on your own this time, my man."

I don't move a muscle.

"So, you want out of here?"

"Mooky?" I don't even bother to look.

"You seem surprised."

"Yeah, a little. What gives?"

"They sent me to whack you."

"But...."

"They decided we can't have you blabbing all over the place."

"About what exactly? That there's glowing yellow eyed aliens running around our planet cloning us and stuffing the real us and our dogs into test tubes to feed their alien babies?"

"There's that. We can't have people knowing what they really are. Could cause mass hysteria and we'd have whole nations beaching themselves like dolphins."

"Why, because the food chain doesn't end with us?"

"Ain't we penned up in here like pork rinds to the slaughter? Look how fast these prison numbers are growing. There's a reason."

"You're mind controlling me aren't you?"

"You want out of this feeding frenzy?"

"Do I have to poke you?"

"No, you just need to talk to Tucker and MacAroy."

"Those two cruds haven't lifted a finger to get me out of here."

"They owe you, my dumb, red blooded friend. So they be here."

"Sure they will."

"They killed two of us yellow brained aliens on your carpet and dragged their bodies away and left you to explain the holes in the wall and door."

"It's my word against theirs."

"No, it's your word against the bullet lodged into your hallway wall. The one that went through the base of Mary's skull."

"Tucker's gun?"

"See how it works."

"I'm starting to."

"If they ain't here in five minutes, tell the guard you want to confess but you want to confess in front of Tucker, MacAroy, and their bosses because they were the first to arrest you."

"This will work?"

"Either that or Tucker and MacAroy will have you dragged to someplace dark. But they won't."

"I'm not so sure about that."

"MacAroy is due for a promotion. Tucker is bucking to retire as captain in seven years. Both of them already have marital problems. You think they want some crazed killer claiming he watched them gun down two aliens in his apartment, and can prove it?"

"Wouldn't someone have taken the bullet out of the wall already?"

"Sure."

"So won't ballistics see that there were two guns involved and ask me questions about the gun I shot you with anyways?"

"Yes. But you have a choice."

"Tell the truth or lie."

"No, be locked up forever or lie."

"Like how I was being robbed or something?"

"Yes, now you're catching on."

"And I can tie Tucker and MacAroy in how?"

"You called them, remember?"

"And there would be some record?"

"How about a taped conversation?" Mook hands over a tape.

"How...you bugged me?"

"Of course not. I just listened in. Only a copy."

"Then Mary sent the cable guy?"

"Ask yourself. Who was waiting for you?"

"Mork and Mindy? Isn't that illegal?"

"Something about a court order they thought they had. In four minutes the guard's coming to get you. Do you think they want to explain that an alien posing as the DA gave it to them? There are people gathering who want to speak with you. Tell only Tucker and MacAroy you have access to this tape. And you'll be free."

"White blooded people or yellow gooey brained people?"

"Special people. It's all here, shooting, the whole enchilada."

"What do I tell these special people?"

"That you were robbed at gunpoint. They took the diamonds."

"What about the part with Tucker and MacAroy?"

Mooky holds out his hand. In it are two crushed gun slugs. "My guess is they will be here before anyone else. Don't tell about the tape unless you have to. When you need it, you'll have it. It's your ace, my friend."

"I can walk out of here?"

"Just let them do the talkin'. Our legal will do the rest."

61

"On your feet, Picasso."

I never thought I'd be glad to hear that voice, but at this moment Tucker sounds as close to freedom as I'll ever get. I look at the Mook. He seems vacant. Is this almost over? Who do I trust?

"Unlock the door."Liberty, the hunk who clubbed me with his flashlight, unlocks the door as I get up. Mooky slides along the floor and blends in with the crowd of tattoos and bad hair days. I turn to smile at him but he isn't looking my way. He is off into another world, another place, maybe even another Mook. So I get up and move to the heavy iron door as it slides open.

"Leave the cuffs off," Tucker says.

"But…," Liberty protests.

"Leave them off, Liberty. It's okay. We got the wrong guy here," Tucker insists.

"Wrong guy? Ain't this Picasso? The guy you had me clobber."

MacAroy and Tucker gives him a look.

"You still got to sign for him," Liberty says.

"Don't give a…. Sign it, Tucker." Tucker signs the papers and the guard closes the gate behind me. I want to give all these creeps the finger or make a face. But when I look back, Mooky is gone. All I can see are the sad eyes of misguided grown children. Under better circumstances they could've matured into white collar thieves, movie execs, oil barons and investment bankers.

"Where are you taking me?"

"Shut up. Move it." MacAroy pushes me through another opening gate and it clangs behind me in that ominous echo that reverberates with finality, as though my life is measured on the sound waves driving up the hall. At the end of this hall, Tucker stops and takes out a key and opens a solid metal door that is unnoticeable except that it has an inset handle you twist to open. So, Tucker pulls it open and inside is nothing but eerie pitch black. The hair on the back of my neck jumps again, and I suddenly begin to sweat.

"If you think I'm stepping in there, you're both crazy."

MacAroy looks up and down the corridor, then pulls a blade out of his pocket and puts it to my chicken wing and presses. "How much blood you willin' to spray before you wise up?"

None. I enter the stale room. The burnt nicotine stench is overwhelming. They step inside with me, and the door heavily clicks shut, sealing us in with my pending cries for help. We stand there endlessly as one of their hands slides up and down the chalky flat paint trying to find a switch. After about three of my pathetic past lives flash before my eyes, all concluding in torture and murder by the hands of brutish men, a small dim light jumps to life under a desk lamp revealing that we are in some kind of guard break room. A cot lies up against the far wall with an oil stained pillow and a dark gray wool blanket. Nothing is on the desk but the lamp, a butt crammed ashtray, and dust. No one's cleaned in here for a while. A beat-up wood chair sits behind it. A matching chair is pushed backwards in the corner. "Okay, I bite, what's up?"

"We got a message," MacAroy says.

"From?"

"You know," Tucker says.

"Your wife?"

"Jesus, let me whack him," MacAroy says.

"Okay, so you heard from him."

"Things are bad, you know, there's not much we can do for you. But he wanted us to come and talk, make a few suggestions."

"What am I looking at?"

"According to your neighbors' accounting of the evening, there were many guns used in your apartment. Men claiming to be police, a female involved, thumping on the roof. Lots of yelling and slamming of doors. Somehow your TV got set on fire, nearly melted to the carpet. It's all very confusing, though, because no slugs or guns turned up during your arrest. So, we don't know what to make of it," Tucker says.

"What now?"

"You know who says he took the bullets. So we're here with you."

"Tucker, you shot two aliens, remember?"

"Whatever you say along those lines, you say on your own. My gun has been missing for twenty-four hours."

"Amazing how those papers got filed just in time."

"We're not interested in your sci-fi stories. We're making you one offer. Keep your mouth shut and live a nice long sane life in prison for the murder of the Essinola family or die tonight back in a cold cell."

"I could get gassed for that. At least ten people I know heard me threaten to drive them out there and kill them. I wouldn't stand a chance in court. In case you clods don't get it, premeditated murder could get me the death penalty or a life sentence without the possibility of parole."

Tucker sits on the desk. "Yeah, special circumstances could come into play. But we would be there for you if it does."

"Do I have loser written on my forehead? Do you honestly think I'm sitting still and letting you two blood clots railroad me into prison for the rest of my life or be killed for something I didn't do just to cover your pensions? What the matter with you two?"

"There's a room full of people wanting to talk," MacAroy says.

"Who are they? Let's have at it."

"Now hold on. We got a problem with that." Tucker makes a fist and pounds it into the palm of his other hand. "We can't let you run your mouth talkin' alien nonsense to a bunch of people who might want to ask us a few embarrassing questions."

"Then you better think of something quick, because unless you get me out of here I'm telling everyone all about you and Mary."

"We were afraid of that." Tucker looks at MacAroy and both men move toward me.

"Are we not forgetting something?" I ask.

"We don't think so."

"I called you, remember, MacAroy?"

"Yeah, thanks a lot. But we don't plan on tellin' nobody that."

"You won't have to."

"Come again."

"I have a recording of our conversation…Mary arriving, Mooky taking a slug from me, you blowing Mary and her friend away, dragging their bodies out… destroying evidence, all the high points of your little alien murder for healing stones cover up."

"You're bluffing."

"Well, that's partially true, but it's realistically possible since you had my phone tapped. Now someone wants to talk to me, and I've got a choice to make on how to handle this. Personally, I don't want to meet these people. And I'm sure you don't want me to because I have no intentions of spending my life with anyone named Bubba other than my poodle. Got me?"

They look at me with pained, practiced, wrongly accused faces. I just keep looking at them, from one to the other, until we all tire of the charade and start to figure whoever talks first, loses. I'm already in jail and a marked man, so what else do I have at stake?

"How do we know that's true?"Tucker asks.

"Ask the Mook."

"You talked to him?"MacAroy asks.

"Talked, seen, and smelt. He was in the cell, you didn't see him?"

"We just talked to him five minutes ago. He ain't in the cell," Tucker says.

"Didn't you boys learn anything? The Mook is everywhere you want to be."

MacAroy and Tucker look at each other, neither wanting to admit I'm right. My guess is the Mook Blipped in on them, too.

"Now, how do we play this? All of us with aliens? Or someone breaking into my apartment, taking the blues, and me rightfully defending myself. And all charges against me with the Essinola pigs shot in the desert, plus Simpkins in my crisper, dropped. Which is it? Because at this point, the thought of you two sleeping on park benches is starting to appeal to me."

"Or we could just kill you now."

"You'd have to wait until after you find the tape and have one of your friends on the inside, say a guard or two handle the dirty work. But of course, I'd probably end up rooming with the Mook and you know how he likes to play mind control."

"He what?"

"Who's to say you ain't messin' with us right now?"Tucker asks.

"Oh, believe me, I'm not messing around. No more cops and robbers. It will be dishonest cops and cannibal aliens. Think of the late night network possibilities. The Flunky Files."

"Jesus," Tucker says.

"Take me back to my cell, or butterfly me."

"We can't just let you fly out of here without talking to these people first," MacAroy tells me.

"Make some calls. I got nothing but time. Come get me when you want me to talk to them."

"Jesus. Maybe we should kill him," Tucker says.

"We've killed enough whackos. All right, say we don't pin none of this on you, then what?" MacAroy asks.

"We part like the Red Sea. No proof it happened."

"Knowing but not saying."

"If they let me walk. I'm as dim on the matter as you two bulbs."

"Knock off with the wise stuff, I'm in no mood."

"Look, the dissipated alien in my car, Victor Castro, he's the one who killed the Essinolas. You know it and I know it. If you want to pin their bodies on someone, pin it on a dissipated someone. Just go into that room and tell those people that whatever they're looking for, I ain't got, and whatever they think I did, I didn't do."

"Yeah, but we ain't got proof or even a body on him, on you at least we got fingerprints on guns."

"There's the little kid who walked around eating sandwiches in my halls with a soda can on his foot. Find him, and maybe you got an eyewitness."

"What kid?"

"The mother and worker in the clothing store, Essinola's sister? There was a third person in that situation. The sister had a young kid. And there's Stacey, if you can find what test tube she's in, she's my alibi."

"You got a name? Wait a minute. What test tube?"

"Ask the Mook."

"Never mind. We want nothin' doin' with him."

"Okay, I got a tenant's kid who played with this other kid, he'd know. Apartment, wait…. You get me out and I'll get you the info."

"We might need it to spring you."

"I don't want you sniffin' around my apartment building while I'm gone. And by the way, I'm spending the night in here unless you can get me out sooner. It looks comfy and just lonely enough." I move over to the cot and sit on it. "Ahhhh, man, what a rotten life."

"And it ain't half over."

"You got that right. Kill the light on the way out."

They look at me a moment. A punk con telling them what to do. "Yeah, but we're lockin' your butt in. And there ain't no head in here, so you just got to hold it."

"I'll live."

"We'll let you know," Tucker says.

They hit the switch on the way out and lock me in.

I lie back on the cot wondering if this will ever end. Damn it stinks in here. Man, it's a dog's life. Only in my uncivilized world does the dog get the pretty girl. And I end up locked up in a smelly cage.

62

By the time the key clicks in the door I'm wide awake needing Joe and my newspaper. The door opens and Tucker and MacAroy are both there, unsmiling.

"You want out?"

"Of course."

"Let's go."

We make our way down the hall. Guards and cons alike pass us by. The visage doesn't vary much from guard to criminal. At the last gate a skeleton of a woman waits with my belongings. She looks at me through her thick glasses. Her deep black eyes read nothing but contempt. I like her, too. She appears as though maybe she stopped eating at age twelve. She gives my street stuff to MacAroy.

"Get out of here."

"What? No hug?

"How about a punch in the mouth?"

"Had plenty, thanks." I walk out the door a free man, with my hands full of belongings, wallet, keys, about eight-five cents in change. Life is grand.

To verify the point, parked across the street with its emergency lights on, is a white LTD Grand Cherokee. Not new, but it's in like new condition. And It's parked in the red zone. Without a ticket.

I look around and I find Tucker's car parked further down the street. I saunter over to it. Lo and behold the window's stuck half slanted open on the driver's side like the tracking gave way or something. I look inside and there's two half full supersize sodas. I grab them up and empty them onto the front seats, ice and all. Then replace the empty cups in their holders. The why doesn't matter because I can't resist the irony of given them both a wet sticky seat for a change. Why not show a little unconditional love for my good buddies, Tucker and MacAroy. They did spring me, after all. So let them prove I expressed myself so artfully. From this moment on, I'm taking the presidential oath of innocence. I'm clean of all charges unless someone can prove it and in that case I can't recall a thing. I am not, nor have I ever been a member of any sticky party.

I turn away, feeling so cool, I be superfly steppin' to Curtis Mayfield up the street, moving past the Jeep, when I hear my name. I look around but no one's there. "Mook?" I scan east and west and no Mook, no anyone. I scrutinize the Jeep. Am I not Superfly? I take one step toward it and the door unlocks. I nearly have a super coronary. At a closer glance, the keys are in it. Could this be my ride home?

Just then Tucker and MacAroy come out of the building. They don't look happy. I'm wondering how hard their butts were chewed for clamming up. Or if they had some help from Mook. They move up the street to their car. I don't want them to see me, so I jump into the Jeep and lock the door in case whoever really owns it comes back and wants to rip my head off.

I turn to watch Tucker and MacAroy get in their car and drive off fast, and then slam on their breaks, springing out of the car. Tucker is jumping up and down, screaming about his wet bottom, and MacAroy is spinning trying to see what got his butt ice cold wet. It's time they change those stale suits anyway. So I probably did them both a favor. I can't hear them but watching them through the tinted window is a big release of all this alien nonsense. It could very well be the beginning of finding a new life without them. Who knows?

They know it was me. They look around. I turn away and watch in the side mirror. Tears of laughter are rolling down my face.

Damn, they start coming my way. I panic, time to superfly and take wing. I put the Jeep in gear and drive away. Tucker starts chasing me down the street. After a dozen steps he stops and starts yelling at MacAroy about bringing the car, but MacAroy screams back even louder about the seats, until Tucker goes back and begins pounding on his hood.

My day is complete as Curtis and I superfly around the corner and out of sight. I look forward just in time to slam on the brakes!

63

The Mook stands there on the crosswalk carrying a wrapped birthday gift. I skid to a stop inches from pulverizing his kneecaps with the black brush guard on the front of the Jeep. I thumb the electric window and it silently slithers open. After five years of cranking the window of a '66 ragtop this sound and feeling means more than gold to me.

"You like?"

"This is mine?"

"I said so, right?"

"Yeah, but...."

"But nothing. Here, happy birthday."

"My birthday isn't until July."

"Take the package."

"What is it?"

"Our deal."

"Is it ticking?"

"It's money. Take it before I change my mind." Mook goes off in a strand of some dog sounding language that I'm sure isn't from here, but sounds oddly enough like insane Middle Eastern tainted with an elitist French accent.

"Screw you, whatever you said, and all your clones. Is this money legal?"

"It's as legal as you and I are ever gonna get. It's a gift, from my people to you. You'll find a complete estimate of damages to your being, things, and friends, plus twenty grand for your troubles.

"Twenty grand? What about taxes?"

"Done."

"They're paid?"

"Taken care of, is all you need to know."

"So I can deposit this money and start writing checks."

"Give it back and get out of the truck."

"I don't want the IRS wondering and investigating me and all that other nice stuff over this. What would I tell them? The nice Mr. Alien gave it to me?"

"You've got friends in high places, Picasso. Don't ever worry about things. Things may get tough, and things may seem to get out of hand with no end in sight. But don't ever worry, you're a made human, from me to you. It will all work out before it's over."

"That's what I'm worried about. No offense, Mook, but this is bye-bye time. I'm driving into the Sunset and I don't want to look back and see any Mooks in my rearview mirror again. Okay? Please?"

"Whatever. But if you need me, I know where to find you."

"Don't. I'm perfectly capable of trashing my own life. And you better not have put any kind of tracking probe on me."

"I got your probe right here. Your papers for the truck are in the center console and a nice secure phone. Text, internet, everything. With those security items I told you about. No bill will be in the mail so don't look for one. You try the stereo yet?"

"No."

"Phat man, phat." Mook starts walking up the block. "Hey, the sodas in their seats. A jewel. A real jewel."

"Mook?"

"Yeah, white boy?"

"Thanks. I mean it. You're a man of your word."

"Or something." I reach down and put the Jeep back in gear. Blip.

"Yeah, or something. So...."

The Mook is gone. Just like that. Gone. Deported, transported or something. I only hope I'll never need to see him again.

I drive off wondering how much more than twenty is in the package. I can't begin to estimate the damage I've had to me, my friends, my car, and building. One thing for sure, the Jeep is one nice ride. And mine, all mine. Damn. Thank you, Mook, whatever you are.

I have a lot of explaining to do. How will people in the biz trust me after all this? How will they treat me, thinking I got away with murder of my tenants? There's nothing I can do about it now. The world is aware of what's happened. Erin is probably beside herself, worrying about me splashed all over the network news: "The Apartment Manager - slash - Sometimes Filmmaker Who Got Away With Murder."Just where do I put that on my resume? What should I do about Mystery Towers being a vortex? Is that for real? Like living there isn't a weird enough magical-ride without mentioning free alien adventures included. And what is this It being thing? What does an It want from me? Why did it include me? Was Mooky messing with me? How do I word any of this in the vacancy ads?

Bubba has likely forgotten who I am, lost in the arms of his TV starlet. The dog. But really, I don't feel like talking to anyone, not even Claire, though maybe I will show up at the screening. Who knows, maybe I'll even let her keep Bubba for a few days here and there if she gets him on her show, just so we can stay in touch. Wouldn't that be perfect? Bubba getting the girl and the studio job out of all this killing and alien espionage.

I turn on the stereo and drive down the 101 ramp, planning to see where my newfound life takes me. I'll deal with the details later, call Erin from the road, and collect up Bubba from Claire when the time is right. And even though I've sworn off actresses...she's a.... Man, how fitting, The Moody Blues' *Voices in the Sky*.

I point the Jeep north and blend in with mass civilization and their dogs, on the move to endless unknowns. I adjust the electric plush tan leather seats. Nice.

We are not alone. The man really isn't a man or a woman after all. And could be something much worse, something known as an It. And me...I'm now... Alien Made.

The End
Jozeph Picasso - Alien Trilogy Act One

ALIEN BIZ

Jozeph Picasso Alien Trilogy
(Act Two)
Filmmaking Adventures

PROLOGUE

My twelve seconds of Riley are officially up. At Tujunga Wash I, Jozeph Picasso, hang an involuntary stage right, when all bazooka hits me. I'm awash in roaring rapids. Rolling head over heels like a turkey pinwheel. Things I can't see, tossed ocean bound junk are bouncing off me. In between these twirls of doom, I'm sucking sewer enhanced stench while fighting off the San Fernando Valley grit trying to ooze between my teeth. It's not working. So I'm forcing down the gag reflex and moving excessively fast. The Colfax Bridge is coming up quick. I'm still breathing but I'm bobbing, claiming what life I can savor between mouthfuls of gutter runoff.

At the top of the converging waters, I end up facing skyward heading headfirst. I'm rudderless though, much like my life, a metaphor I'll die reflecting, because the torrent trying to suck me under is so much like my past it's almost funny

What a floater I am. Claire Davis will give my dog, Bubba, a good home and a showbiz career and before long, another man will come into her life, getting the opportunity of a lifetime. Even Bubba will forget all about this waterlogged Dogman.

One thing is for sure; I'm not looking forward to pounding my noggin on the Colfax Bridge. So with all my strength I use my arms to rudder me blindly around so that I'm moving boots first.

Big mistake! Immediately, the backwash of water on the bridge support drags my boots under -- and TWANG! My right oil resistant Elk Wood boot is stuck in something I can't see. I don't have to, I'm stuck in a frigging submerged shopping cart's upper kid carrying rack and this isn't good, not by a long shot.

I'm flung momentarily skyward and out of the water and quickly face down into the murk. The river is now streaming over me with its entire worth, and I have no recourse to right myself. I'm without vote on the matter. I'm just another aquatic reed in the stream of brown yuck. I'm a moronic yesterday's goner.

Then it happens. I can actually feel my hip socket shatter with a sharp lightening blast of pain, and I roll over knowing that I've just snapped my upper leg in two if not at the socket itself. There's no bone holding me to the cart now, just butt muscle and other gooey human fibrous tissue.

This really doesn't do me any good either. Now I'll just drown in even more pain. Much, much more! As if, three or four broken ribs weren't bad enough, and a lung full of city backwash. However, after one or two good twirls of upper leg tissue, I'm facing the boisterous sky again. Damn, I'm a half arm's length under water and in so much pain my eyes rivet shut.

"Mooky!"

Where is the Mook man when I need him?

"Mooky!"

Didn't he say he'd be around if I needed him? Well, I got a news bulletin. I'm bound to a shopping cart, and I ain't hungry on dying. Yet, here I am, drowning like a human cockroach flushed down the toilet of humanity. I have maybe twenty seconds of bubbles left, and from there it's just a matter of letting the river run its course. By the time it recedes to its normal trickle of greenish-black, oily yuck, I'll be nothing more than an unrecognizable lump of human protoplasm sporting a bad hair day. Damn. Why does it all have to end this way?

Karl J. Niemiec

About the author

After journalism school at University of Detroit, hitchhiking around North America writing journals, then screenwriting classes at UCLA, Karl J. Niemiec spent 30 years surviving Hollywood, and turned those filmmaking adventures into Jozeph Picasso - Alien Trilogy.

Karl now lives with his wife Erin, and four children in Carmel, Indiana.

www.ingramcontent.com/pod-product-compliance
Lightning Source LLC
Chambersburg PA
CBHW060915180626
46817CB00004B/1263